A PATH THROUGH THE STARS

BOOK 3 IN THE STARPATH SERIES

KEVIN J SIMINGTON

TABLE OF CONTENTS

1

———

Zac Perryman was standing outside the door to a small reception room on Gateway Station. The space station guarded the entrance to the subspace portal at the L1 Lagrange point in the Altarian system. Not that there had been much guarding to do lately. The portal had been mysteriously and permanently locked onto an open wormhole for 141 years, with the Altarians unable to either use it or close it down.

But now, two stunning developments had occurred. A void jumper had emerged from the wormhole and, seconds later, the wormhole had closed down. The two events had sent shockwaves throughout the Federation. The six occupants of the spaceship identified themselves as coming from Nova, a planet in the Icarus-R421 system, the same system that Zac and his three friends had travelled from 22 years earlier. The Altarians had rushed Zac to Gateway Station to conduct the first meeting, so that the new arrivals would not be distressed by the Altarians' modified physical features.

Starla Bree, commander of Gateway Station, had personally

escorted Zac here, and she now stood beside him, towering over him, outside the reception room.

"They haven't had contact with anyone yet," she said, "so they'll probably be a bit anxious."

"I'm anxious as well," Zac admitted. "There's a chance I might know some of these people. Until today, I thought everyone we knew had died over a century ago."

"We all did. The time dilation you experienced in the wormhole seemed to preclude any possibility of you encountering people from your own time. But it's apparent now that this spacecraft entered the wormhole only 22 years after you. There is a very real possibility that you may know some of them."

Zac took a breath and braced himself, and Starla moved back a few steps.

"I'll let you go in alone, Zac. It's better if they don't glimpse me until you've met them and explained things. They've simply been told that one of the Federation Council members is about to greet them."

"OK."

"Good luck."

"Thanks."

Zac approached the door and opened it. He stepped into the small waiting room and saw six faces turn towards him simultaneously. He smiled and said, "Welcome." The word seemed cumbersome in his mouth, unaccustomed as he was to be speaking the ancient Terran.

He looked at the faces, trying to recognise them, but couldn't see anyone familiar. Unless ... perhaps ... the woman? His age. The same eyes that he remembered, although creased and wrinkled now with the passage of time. The same red hair, with some stray greys interspersed. The same curve of the lips. *It couldn't be! Surely not!*

"Jaz?" he said, his eyes wide with shock.

"Zac?" said Mel.

"Dad?" said Dayna.

"Hello Zac," said Jaz. Her eyes brimmed with tears and overflowed, and her lips trembled. She took two steps toward him and was in his arms, hugging him tightly and sobbing freely as she buried her face in his neck. "It's you, it's really you! I can't believe it! I hoped ... all these years ... and now, here you are."

Zac was dumbfounded. He hugged her back, wanting to comfort her, but also feeling extremely uncomfortable. This was the woman he had been married to for only a few short months, 22 years ago. He had loved her passionately back then, but he had assumed that she was long dead. He had grieved for her and moved on. He had built a new life here on Altaria. He had another wife whom he loved deeply and with whom he had shared over twenty years of life.

This can't be happening! This can't be real!

Jaz lifted her face to kiss him, and she was partially successful, finding his lips but not his heart. Zac didn't know how to respond. It was like kissing a ghost. Were they still technically married? What about Kit? What was going to happen? His head was swirling with confusion. Jaz, sensing his reserve, pulled back and looked at him, with concern and uncertainty written on her face.

"Zac what's wrong?"

"I ... don't know ... it's ... it's such a shock ... after all this time ... I don't know ..."

"Dad?" repeated the young woman in front of him. She was staring at him, clearly unsure how she should be reacting.

Jaz disentangled herself from Zac. "This is our daughter, Zac. Dayna."

"Dayna?" said Zac, uncertainly. "We ... we have a daughter? I have a daughter?" His eyes misted over, and he felt an upwelling of emotion. He and Kit had tried for a baby for years and had finally given up, but now, standing in front of him was his own flesh and blood.

Dayna stepped forward tentatively. "It's really you?" she asked.

Zac could only nod his head, words failing him as his eyes overflowed. He reached out to her and they embraced, awkwardly at first, but soon Dayna was sobbing and Jaz was crying with her, the three of them embracing in a family hug that Zac had never imagined would happen.

After a few moments, they broke apart and Zac said to Dayna, "You're beautiful. How did I end up with such a beautiful daughter?"

"It's clearly a genetic mistake of some kind," said Mel.

"Do I know you?" asked Zac, looking at the woman who appeared to be in her mid-30s.

"Yes. Although I was only a little girl when you left."

"Possum?"

She nodded. She hadn't heard that name for years, and the memory of Zac's tenderness towards her and their shared sense of fun and mischief suddenly rose up and overwhelmed her.

"Little Melody," he said in wonderment, saying her name with such tenderness that it broke through her defences. Now she was crying too, and Zac embraced her and Dayna together, with Jaz holding his arm with her head on his shoulder.

"Look at us all," said Mel after a few moments, sniffing back her tears and drying her eyes. "What a bunch of sooks. Anyone would think we hadn't seen you for a couple of decades."

"About that ..." began Zac.

"Later," said Mel. "First let me introduce you to Rajesh. Keo's son."

"Keo's son?" Zac continued to be gobsmacked.

"Hello Zac," said Raj, shaking his hand formally. "Can you please tell me, is my father ... is he ...?"

"Yes. He's alive and well. And he will be delighted to see you."

Raj nodded, at a loss for words.

"And your mother?" asked Zac. "Prisha? Is she ...?"

Raj shook his head. "No. She died three years ago."

"I'm so sorry. She was a wonderful person."

Zac was then introduced to the other two newcomers; Phil Lambert, the 37-year-old scientist with whom Mel had started a relationship, and Karl Henley, the 42-year-old pilot. They each greeted Zac with a handshake, although Zac did not have any clear memories of either of them.

There was a pause as they all looked at each other, not knowing how to proceed.

"There are some things I need to explain to you," said Zac to the group, "but I think it would be better if I first took you to more comfortable surroundings. Are you hungry?"

"No, we're fine," said Mel. "We've had plenty of food on board the ship."

"Even so, I'll take you to the private quarters we've arranged for you and we can talk. There's so much to tell you."

2

———

They were sitting in the lounge area of the same private quarters that Zac and the others had used 22 years ago when they first arrived. Zac had briefly spoken to Starla outside the reception room and cleared the way to the living quarters, so that the new arrivals would not encounter any Altarians until Zac had briefed them on their appearance.

Now he looked at them as they waited for an explanation as to why he had never returned. He had no idea how he was going to break the news to Jaz that he and Kit were married.

"I owe you an explanation," he began.

Jaz nodded. "Where have you been, Zac? Why didn't you ever come home?"

"I couldn't, Jaz. It was impossible. The wormhole was locked open all these years, and we had no access to it. It was completely blocked off to us from this end. And, until today, we had no idea why."

"Until today?" asked Mel.

"Yes. It's clear now that the reason we couldn't travel back through the wormhole was that there was another vessel in it. Yours."

"But we were only inside the wormhole for two days. You had 22 years to get back to us!" said Jaz.

"OK, this is where it gets weird," replied Zac. "Let me ask you, what year do you think it is?"

"5402," said Mel. She raised her eyebrows. "But I suppose you're going to tell us that it's not."

"Yes, unfortunately. The wormhole apparently formed too close to a black hole - the same black hole that we originally encountered on our journey to Nova. Your journey through the wormhole took you very close to the event horizon of that black hole where, as you already know, significant time dilation occurs."

"How much dilation?" asked Mel.

"While only two days passed for you, a lot more time passed in the outside universe."

"How much more?" asked Dayna.

"119 years."

There was silence as the group digested this new information.

"So this is the year ...?" began Dayna.

"5521," answered Mel, who had done the math.

"Yes."

"We left the ring 119 years ago?" asked Jaz, incredulously.

Zac nodded.

"So that means ... it means that everyone we knew ... they're all ..."

"Dead," said Mel bluntly.

"Yes," said Zac. "I'm sorry."

"But you only left 22 years ago," said Jaz, not quite comprehending.

"Yes, in comparison to your departure. But we have both been displaced 119 years into the future. I left Nova in 5380 and arrived here in 5499, 119 years later. You left in 5502, just 22 years after me, and arrived here in 5521, still 22 years after me. Both our journeys took the same amount of time through the wormhole, and we've both been displaced by the same amount of time — 119 years."

"So, Harvey and everyone else ...they never made it here?" asked Karl.

"No."

"But surely they could still be in the wormhole too," continued Karl. "They might have left years after us and they could still be travelling here, just like we did."

"No. That's not possible."

"Why not?" asked Mel.

"Because the wormhole closed as soon as you arrived. That means that there was no other spacecraft in the wormhole, keeping it open."

"So, no one followed us through the wormhole in all the years that followed?" asked Dayna.

"That's right. The wormhole would have remained open in the Nova system for 119 years, and during that time no one entered it."

"Why?" asked Dayna. "Surely someone would have attempted it during that time. They had the technology. They had plenty of void jumpers. Why didn't anyone follow us?"

"That's a very good question. The simple answer is, we just don't know. Perhaps they concluded that two ships disappearing and never being heard from again was enough evidence that the wormhole wasn't safe. Or perhaps something happened to prohibit them from attempting it. Or they may have somehow been able to analyse how long the time dilation effect was going to be and no one was prepared to subject themselves to it. There are a number of possibilities."

"Another of them being that the ring colony could have been attacked or infiltrated by the EIs," said Mel, voicing a fear that the others had all started to hold. "The reason why they never followed us could be that they're all dead or under EI control."

"Yes," agreed Zac. "That's a possibility."

"Hold on," said Dayna. "you said that the wormhole is now closed."

"Yes."

"So, we could send a probe or even a ship back through to Nova now and re-establish communication with them!"

"That may be possible now, yes. But if the rogue black hole is still in the vicinity of the wormhole when it forms, the same time dilation effect will occur on the return journey. It could take another century or more for a probe or ship to return to Nova, and that would make the wormhole unusable from our end for the same amount of time."

"So we are here to stay now," said Mel. "No going back."

"That's right," said Zac. "Which brings me to another issue. I need to explain about the Altarians."

"The people who travelled here from Nova centuries ago?" said Phil, speaking for the first time.

"Yes. They fled from the EIs on Nova 1,724 years ago. They have settled on Altaria and have built a prosperous and peaceful society here. In many ways you have come from one paradise to an even greater one. Altaria is a beautiful world and I think you are going to love it here."

"Is there a 'but' coming?" asked Mel.

"Only a small one. The Altarians have made many technological advancements, one of them being that they have modified their genome. They have made certain enhancements to their physical characteristics."

"What sort of enhancements?" asked Dayna.

"They are much taller. Their average height is around two metres. Some a little taller than that. They have also enhanced their sight, smell, hearing and manual dexterity. This means that their eyes are a bit bigger and slightly further apart. Also, their ears are larger, their noses are wider and their fingers are longer, with larger pads on their fingertips."

"Why haven't we seen any of them yet?" asked Mel.

"They were concerned not to shock you with their appearance, which is why they asked me to meet with you first, in order to explain the differences."

"Are they ugly?" asked Mel.

"No," said Zac, smiling. "In fact, they have beautiful olive skin, which is another of their enhancements. They are just different, that's all. If you are ready, Commander Bree is outside the door, waiting to meet you."

"Sure, send him in," said Mel. "We can't stay locked away in here forever."

"Actually, Commander Bree is a she," said Zac, smiling. He turned towards the door. "We're ready for you Starla."

All heads turned towards the door. It slid open and Starla entered the room. Her Federation uniform did nothing to hide her stunning figure. The new arrivals looked at her with wonder.

"Wow!" said Dayna, voicing what they were all thinking.

"Hello," said Starla simply. "Welcome to Gateway Station. I am Starla Bree, commander of this facility. I hope my appearance doesn't shock you too much."

"No," said Dayna. "You look like a super model! Do all the women look like you?"

"There are no obese people on Altaria, if that is what you mean. We modified that part of our genome many centuries ago."

"At least your language hasn't changed," said Mel. "After more than 1,700 years I would have expected it to be significantly different."

"It is quite different, actually," said Starla. "I am speaking your ancient Terran at the moment."

"In that case you speak it very well," complimented Jaz.

"That is because I have utilised our technology to upload your language directly into the language centre of my brain. Which brings me to the topic of your integration into our society."

She paused and smiled at them.

"The technology you will encounter on Altaria is significantly more advanced than the technology we left behind on Icari, or Nova as you call it. Over the centuries we have modified our genome to not only produce the physical characteristics that you see in me, but also to enable us to seamlessly integrate with our technology. Part of that involves a microscopic cerebral implant comprising tiny bio-conductive filaments much thinner than a human hair, extending through various parts of the brain. The implant allows us to directly upload new skills and information, and also enables us to operate much of our technology via amplified thought waves."

"Unfortunately, the implants do not mesh as well with your brains as they do with ours. The implants are designed for Altarian brains, which have developed slightly different pathology as a result of our modified genome."

"Pathology?" asked Jaz.

"Gross physical characteristics. Various parts of our brain have changed slightly in size and structure. Some have more synapses and a more complex network of neural pathways. Zac and his friends received the implants when they first arrived, and we spent several days mapping the neural pathways in their brains and found some incompatibilities with our technology. The implants simply aren't able to make a strong enough connection to some parts of your brain."

"So, you won't be recommending we receive them?" asked Mel.

"Actually, there might be some value in you temporarily receiving the implant. Certainly, most areas of your brain appear to be unresponsive to our implants; for example, the hippocampus that is responsible for storing long term or global memory, and the amygdala, which is the emotion centre of your brain. But one key area has proven to mesh very well with the implants; your neocortex, which is the language centre of the brain. This is why we were able to successfully upload our language to Zac and the others 22 years ago."

"You said 'temporarily receive the implant'. What does that mean?" asked Dayna.

"We would install the implant, upload our language into your neocortex and then remove the implant, all while you were asleep."

"I don't like the sound of that," said Mel. "No offence, but

I'm not keen on undergoing brain surgery when I could just as easily learn the language the old-fashioned way."

Starla looked at Zac and raised her eyebrows.

Zac switched to Altarian and addressed the newcomers. "You might think that learning the Altarian language will be easy, but it is a highly sophisticated language and, even after many years, you will not be completely fluent in it."

"What the frig was that?" exclaimed Dayna.

Zac repeated what he had said, this time in Terran. Then he added, "Even after many years, you would still sound like a Terran trying to speak Altarian. What the upload technology does is not only instantly provide you with a comprehensive understanding of the vocabulary, grammar, syntax and idioms of the language, but it also creates new muscle-memory pathways in the brain that enable you to make all the right sounds. You will instantly be speaking Altarian as if you had been born here."

"That's all well and good," said Mel, "but it still involves drilling holes in our brains and then ripping the wires out again. That doesn't sound like much fun at all."

"It is not nearly as invasive as that," assured Starla. "The implants are microscopic and the filaments are 100 times thinner than a human hair. They are inserted via sonic laser technology that does not require your skulls to be cut open or anything as gruesome as the brain surgery that you remember from your own era."

"Will it take long?" asked Phil.

"The longest part of the procedure will be the modification of your genome, which will require about ten days. This is needed in order to subtly alter the biochemistry of your synapses, in order to make your brain receptive to our upload technology. Following this, the implant can be introduced, the upload made, and then the implant removed, all within a single day. For your comfort you will be kept sedated during this period. Once you wake up, you will feel completely normal and you will be able to speak Altarian like a native."

"Is there a reason why you aren't proposing to leave the implants in?" asked Mel.

"Yes." Starla looked at Zac, who shook his head slightly. "But I think that explanation is best left until after you have received the upload. In a sense, what we are proposing is not so much an implant and its removal, but a temporary microfilament insertion to enable a one-time upload."

Jaz looked at Zac. "Do you go along with this, Zac?"

"Yes. It's harmless and very effective. You won't regret it."

After further assurances, the group agreed to the procedure, and it was scheduled for that same afternoon.

3

Zac was returning to Tradewind Island with some neighbours on board their skippa, having just transferred down from Terminus 8 to A1, and from there to Manna Island. The new arrivals were undergoing genomic update and would be asleep for at least ten more days. In the meantime, Zac needed to inform the others of who had just arrived. Keo would be thrilled to know that he had another son. Kit, on the other hand ... *How will I break the news to her? How will she take it?* There was no question of abandoning his marriage with Kit. He loved her dearly and they had been happily married for nearly 22 years. They had an unbreakable bond of love and, yes, still passion, even after all these years.

But what would they do about Jaz? *How do I even feel about her? My feelings for her are like a dim memory; pleasant but no longer intense or overwhelming.* And how would Jaz react when he told her he was remarried? He hadn't had the heart to break it to her yet, and she apparently hadn't noticed his wedding ring. He had a sense that she had held on to the intense love that they had once shared, refusing to let go, whereas he had grieved and moved on.

He wrestled with these thoughts as the skippa scudded across the inland sea, making the most of the strong afternoon nor'easterly breeze. At the marina, the other family offered to drive him home in their buggy, but he declined, preferring to walk and gather his thoughts.

An hour later he arrived unannounced at their tiny village to find that the bungalows were deserted. Taking into account the warmth of the afternoon sun and the presence of a nor'easter, Zac guessed that they were all on the southern beach, having an afternoon swim. He put his bathers on and walked down the sandy track, emerging 100 metres later to see his 'family' relaxing and playing together. Keo and his son, Noah, were surfing, using wooden boards that Keo had fashioned from the local bunjar trees. Keo's daughter, Kia, along with Tash and Kit, were floating lazily in the whitewash, chatting and laughing together. Kit looked up, saw him and waved for him to join them. Taking off his shirt he jogged down to the surf and dived in. After a few strokes he had reached the girls. Kit wrapped her arms and legs around him and kissed him passionately.

"There you are, you handsome man," she said when she came up for air. "I didn't realise you'd be back so soon."

"Neither did I."

"Is everything OK?"

"Yes. I guess."

"Did you meet the people from the ring? Who are they? Did they remember us?"

"Oh, yes. They definitely remember us."

"Something's wrong. What's the matter? You seem a little strange."

He pulled her closer to him and kissed her again.

"Kit Tyler, you are the love of my life. Do you know that?"

"Yes, I know that," she answered, kissing him back.

"I want you to really know that; be absolutely convinced of that. And nothing is ever going to change that. OK?"

"OK," she said, starting to worry now. "Is there a 'but' coming?"

"No. But ..."

"So there is a but!"

"No. Not exactly. Well, kind of ..."

"For goodness sake Zac, just spill it!"

"Jaz was on the spaceship."

"What???" Her eyes opened wide in astonishment, and her brow creased in confusion. "How is that possible? We left there 141 years ago now! She would be long dead! Are you sure it's her?"

"Yes, it's her alright. She and the others followed us into the wormhole only 22 years after we entered it. They were caught up in the same time dilation that affected us."

"Good grief!" said Kit. She shook her head, trying to process the new information. "How did she take it when you told her you'd remarried?"

"That's just it; I haven't told her yet."

It took Kit 20 minutes to calm down enough for Zac to have a reasonable conversation with her again, and even then, she was still angry. Tash and Kia had moved away, sensing that they needed time to sort something out. Kit's fiery nature was something that Zac loved about her, but, at times like this, it could be a little wearing.

"How could you not tell her? Are you ashamed of me? Is that it?"

"Of course not."

"Do you wish you hadn't married me now?!"

"Don't be silly. I love you. Marrying you is the best thing I ever did."

She started to soften a little. "Really?"

"Yes. Really." He drew her close and kissed her. "And nothing's going to change that. You're my wife and you always will be."

"Well, alright then. Just as long as that's clear," she said, nestling against him again. "But why didn't you tell her?"

"We were never alone together, so I didn't get the chance. Besides, I wasn't sure how to break it to her."

"So, you're telling me that at this point she still thinks she's married to you?"

"At this precise point, she's unconscious, so, no, she's not thinking anything."

Kit squeezed his butt. "Ha, ha, smarty pants. You know what I mean!"

"Yes. Unfortunately, I do. You're right. When she wakes up, she'll still think she's married to me."

"She didn't remarry?"

"Apparently not. From what I can gather, she never stopped hoping that I would return. That's what's going to make it so difficult to tell her. When she finds out that I've remarried, it will break her heart."

"What a mess," said Kit.

"You can say that again."

"What a mess."

"Very funny."

4

———

Dinner was finished and the two 'kids' had taken the nets and lights to the north beach, to catch midgies, shrimp-like creatures that were swarming in the shallows because of the coinciding of a high tide and a full moon. The adults were sitting in Tash and Keo's loungeroom, discussing the recent developments.

"So, what is my son like?" asked Keo. "Is he as good looking as me?"

"He's bound to have more hair, that's for sure," said Tash, rubbing his bald dome.

"He's got your eyes and your black curly hair – or what hair you used to have, anyway," said Zac. "And he's certainly as tall as you, with broad shoulders. Although he's got a lot less ... um ...," he pointed to Keo's stomach.

"... muscles around his abdomen," finished Keo.

"Is that what you call that bulge around your middle, my love?" said Tash. "They're kind of squishy for muscles, aren't they?"

"That's just because I've trained them to relax when they're not needed."

"In that case, they must be extremely relaxed most of the time," offered Zac.

"They're solid as a rock when I need them," Keo replied, patting his considerable girth contentedly.

"And you have a daughter?" enquired Tash.

"Yes. Dayna. She's the same age as Rajesh. 22."

Zac had been worried how Kit would react to the news that after all their years of trying unsuccessfully to fall pregnant, Jaz had provided him with a daughter after only a couple of months of marriage. He needn't have worried. Kit was ecstatic for him and was already talking about how wonderful it would be to welcome her into their lives.

Jaz, however, was another matter.

"She's not going to take it well, when she finds out I'm remarried," said Zac a little later.

"Um ... Can I raise a sensitive question here?" asked Tash. "Aren't you still legally married to her? I mean, you never actually divorced her, did you?"

"You're right in one sense," agreed Zac. "I didn't legally divorce her. But most societies recognise a legal statute of limitations in regard to missing persons. For instance, in the country where I grew up, a person who was missing for 7 years could be legally presumed dead and a marriage could be rendered null and void. So, in a legal sense, our marriage is no longer valid."

"Not that legalities matter all that much to us here anymore," said Tash. "But I just thought it was worth asking the question. Sorry."

"That's OK, Tash," said Kit. "No need to apologise. But we

do need to work out the best way forward for Jaz. From what Zac tells me, it's going to be very hard on her when she finds out."

"Bro, you need to tell her as soon as you get back to Gateway Station," said Keo. "Get her by herself and break the news to her. You can't let another day go by without her knowing."

"Yes. I need to do that. But what then? How do we move forward from here? We need to work out living arrangements for them all. Councillor Drummond has offered to build some more bungalows here, at our end of the island. Certainly, it would make sense for them to be here with us. At least they won't be gawked at all the time like they would if they were anywhere else."

"Of course, bro! Besides I want my son to be near me, and I'm sure you want to be near your daughter. We have 22 years of catching up to do!"

"We'll have to be sensitive about Jaz, though," said Tash. "She might find it difficult to see Kit and Zac together. At least at first."

"Yes," agreed Kit. "It might be sensible for there to be some distance between us and the new bungalows. To give everyone privacy when they need it."

"We'll also need another buggy and some more dune bikes," said Keo. "Possibly also another skippa. Do you think Drummond will foot the bill for those as well?"

"I'm sure he will. Speaking of whom, I need to go to a council meeting tomorrow. I'll be gone overnight. The arrival of the void jumper and the closure of the wormhole has changed the whole ballgame."

"I'll bet it has, bro."

5

Councillor Drummond called the meeting to order.

"You've all been briefed on recent developments on Gateway Station. We have two major issues to deal with as a result; the security of our solar system against the possibility of attack from the EIs, and the resettlement of the new Terrans. I suggest we deal with the latter issue first, as it is much simpler. Zac, how can we help?"

"Thanks Councillor Drummond. I've talked it over with Kit, Keo and Tash. There is no doubt that the best place for the newcomers is with us on Tradewind Island. Although I haven't confirmed it with them, because they're currently undergoing genomic upgrade, I am sure the newcomers wouldn't want to be anywhere else."

Drummond nodded. "Well, I think I speak for the rest of the council when I say that we will commit to building them the same infrastructure that we built for you. Just say when and where, and we'll make it happen." The others around the table were all nodding their heads.

"We were also wondering," ventured Zac, "whether your generosity would extend to an additional sand buggy, some more dune bikes and even, possibly, an additional skippa."

"Of course!" Drummond looked around the table. "Any objections from anyone?"

There were shakes of heads all around.

"Done!" said Drummond. "I'll mobilise a construction crew and get them out there within 48 hours. Anything else, Zac?"

"No. Thank you. That's very generous of you."

"Not at all. It's the least we could do. Now, moving on to more difficult matters. Gentlemen and ladies, the closure of the wormhole escalates the risk of EI invasion to a whole new level. I've asked Dr Spooner to kick off our deliberations with a report on the state of the wormhole. Dr Spooner?"

Spooner cleared his throat and started speaking with his customary clipped precision. "The readings we are now getting from the subspace portal seem to indicate that we are able to open a wormhole whenever we like now. The pattern of echyon frequencies we are now receiving through the portal from a huge number of star systems matches the pattern in our data banks from prior to the frozen wormhole. Obviously, we haven't actually opened a new wormhole to confirm its operational status, because of our desire to not draw the EIs' attention to us."

"Yes," agreed Drummond. "We don't want to advertise the operational status of our subspace portal to them."

"I suspect it's probably too late already," said someone. "If they have been monitoring wormholes throughout the galaxy, as the message from Polaris indicated, then they are almost certainly aware that our wormhole has closed down and our portal is now free to be dialled into."

"I agree," said another councillor. "We have to assume that they know they can now reach us and are preparing to do so. We have to make plans for repelling an imminent invasion.

"General Kellar," said Drummond. "Where are we at, regarding our defences forces?"

"We have three battle ships standing by at the portal, fully armed and ready for action. All personnel have been recalled from shore leave and we are ready to blast the bastards out of existence."

"Weapons?" asked someone else.

"As well as the standard lasers and molecular disruptor beams, the science team has recently added another weapon to our arsenal. I'll let Dr Spooner explain."

"Thank you general," said Spooner. "As you know, we have been working for decades on trying to build an EMP bomb – an electromagnetic pulse bomb — that will wipe out all of the circuitry within an EI vessel, effectively killing any EIs on board. Building such a bomb is easy but creating one which won't fry our own circuits at the same time is the difficult part. In the end we had to concede that it was not possible. Any EMP bomb powerful enough to fry every circuit on board an EI starship, is also going to wipe out the circuitry on any other ships or space stations within several light seconds of the explosion. A targeted EMP bomb that will fry one ship but leave another untouched doesn't seem to be feasible, so we've come up with a different kind of solution."

"We have placed two large EMP bombs adjacent to the subspace portal. These are shielded, so hopefully they won't be detected. Over the last two decades we have developed physical shielding for all our electronic circuitry that will be resistant to an EM pulse. Even so, most systems will still need to be powered down prior to an EMP detonation. We have built a central kill switch into Gateway Station and our battleships, so that at a moment's notice, almost all systems can be instantly shut down with the push of a single button. A few systems, such as power reactors, can't be instantly shut down, and so these have been encased in a new extremely dense, metalised compound that deflects EM pulses. The bottom line is that within 30 seconds of us identifying an EI ship, our own vessels can be shut down and rendered safe, and the two EMP bombs can be detonated via a small relay station on a 30 second delay."

"And you think that will work?" asked Drummond.

"Unless the EIs have developed some form of advanced shielding, yes, it should."

"It would be better if we could stop them getting here in the first place," said Zac. "How are things progressing with the concept of a subspace portal disruptor? Something to interfere with our subspace portal's emissions so that it can't be dialled into from somewhere else."

"We're getting close," said Spooner. "Very close, I think. We are modifying the Nicolls Field Generator, used in the STAR drive of wormhole ships. The theory is that by distorting the echyon frequencies at our subspace portal, someone attempting to dial in from another star system won't be able to get a lock on our portal. I think we could be ready within another 12 months."

"But that's probably 12 months we don't have," said someone.

"I agree," said Drummond. "Are there any other suggestions?"

There was silence for a moment, until Zac spoke up.

"Why not use the black hole?"

"What do you mean?" asked Spooner.

"If we don't yet have the capability of stopping someone from dialling in, why don't we dial up the Icarus system again and lock up the wormhole for another hundred years?"

There was silence as everyone considered this.

"That's a great idea!" said someone.

Drummond looked at Spooner. "Could that get us out of trouble Dr Spooner?"

"Yes ... yes... I think it could ..." He was furiously tapping on his data pad, engaged in some kind of calculations. "We hadn't really considered any course of action that involved activating the wormhole, out of fear of further alerting the EIs. But if, as you say, they have probably already noted the deactivation of our wormhole, then we have no reason to attempt to remain undetected. Yes ... yes ... it would effectively block them from dialling in again."

"Could we expect it to lock the wormhole open for a similar length of time?" asked someone.

"Probably not. The black hole is rogue, meaning that it is moving across the elliptical plane of the galaxy. As it continues on its course, it will probably move further away from the wormhole that we establish between us and the Icarus system. That means that the black hole's event horizon will not exert as strong an influence on the wormhole, resulting in less time dilation. In fact, the point could be reached quite soon, when the wormhole is not influenced at all by the event horizon. The wormhole could spring back away from the event horizon quite suddenly, like a stretched elastic band that has been bent sideways at its centre and then is suddenly released. When the force that has stretched it sideways becomes less than the attractional forces at the two subspace portals, it could quite suddenly spring back into its normal shape and function."

"In other words, we don't know how long it will stay locked this time," said Drummond.

"Correct."

"Thoughts?" Drummond said, looking around the conference table.

"Do it," said someone.

"I agree," said another.

"The sooner the better," said a third.

"I assume we'll send a probe through, rather than a manned spacecraft," said Zac.

"Yes," agreed Spooner. "We wouldn't want to subject a crew to an unknown amount of time dilation. For all we know it could be locked open for another century. Although I doubt it."

"So, we are all agreed?" asked Drummond.

There were nods all around.

"OK. Let's get this done. Dr Spooner, how quickly can we get a probe ready to launch?"

"We have several ready right now, already in place at Gateway Station."

"In that case we'll launch immediately. I'll notify Commander Bree. Zac, thank you, once again, for your valuable input."

6

Jaz woke feeling better than she had in decades. She had a wonderful feeling of euphoria, as if she was floating on a cloud. An underlying sense of wellbeing and, yes, even happiness filled her. It was more than merely the drugs she had been given. It was Zac. She had found her husband, the love of her life, and now they would be together again. Zac had seemed a little reserved with her during the brief hours since their reunion, but that was probably to be expected. He was in shock at her sudden appearance. *It will take a little time, but we will rekindle the love that we had. We will live out the remainder of our lives in love. We will rediscover the passion that we once shared.*

She sat up and looked out of the window at a beautiful scene of mountains and lakes and lush valleys receding into the distance.

"It's just a simulation," said a white-coated medical orderly at her bedside. "You're still on Gateway Station. How are you feeling?"

"Extremely well thank you!"

He glanced at a data tablet in his hand. "Yes. All your vital signs are looking good. If you are ready, there is someone who would like to see you."

"Yes, certainly."

As the medic left the room, she swung her legs over the side of the bed, noticing that she was still clothed in the jumpsuit that she had been given when she arrived.

Zac walked into the room.

"Zac!" She got to her feet and walked to him, embracing him and sighing contentedly as she rested her head against his shoulder. "I've missed you so much! I still can't quite believe that we're together again." She reached up to kiss him, but he pulled back, and smiled uncertainly.

"Can we talk?"

"Sure. Is something wrong? Am I missing something?"

"Let's sit together." He led her to the side of the bed, and they sat together.

"What's wrong Zac?"

"This is really difficult, Jaz. We've been apart for 22 years."

"I know. And I realise that I'm older and wrinklier now."

"No, it's not that ..."

"I'm sorry that I'm not the fresh young thing that you married, Zac. But I'm still the woman you loved and married. I'm still the person you pledged to be with forever. We can make this work again. I know we can."

"Jaz it's not that simple."

"Why not?"

"Because ... because ... well, I'm married," he said holding up his wedding ring.

"I saw that ring when I first arrived, Zac. I thought it was something you'd had made to remember me. You mean ...?"

"I mean, I'm married to someone else."

"What? One of the locals?"

"No. Kit."

"You and Kit? Married? No! No! Please tell me it's not true!"

"Jaz, I thought you were dead."

"But I'm not dead, Zac! I'm here now, alive and well! And you're still my husband!"

"Jaz, when we arrived here, we discovered that we had jumped 119 years ahead in time. By our calculations you had died nearly 90 years earlier. I grieved for you. I was a mess."

She reached out and took his hand. "But I'm here now Zac. Everything's OK. We can start again."

"No, we can't Jaz. We can't start again. I'm married to Kit now."

"How long?" she asked, letting go of his hand and looking at him with a steely glare. "How long have you been married?"

"21 years."

"Ugh!" she let out a stifled sob, and stood up, moving to the window and keeping her back to him. She covered her face with her hands and sobbed, her shoulders shaking with grief and anger. "How could you! How could you, Zac!"

"I'm so sorry."

"Sorry?" She turned on him now, angry. "You're SORRY? Oh well, that's OK then! That's just fine! 'I'm so sorry I'm married to someone else now'. Really? And I'm just supposed to accept that? And what? Give you my blessing?"

Jaz walked to the only chair in the room and sat down, placing her head in her hands again, and letting the tears flow.

Zac had no words. He felt dreadful. He just stood there, looking down at her helplessly.

Jaz wiped her eyes again and looked up at him. "I never

stopped loving you, Zac. Never. All these years, I kept waiting for you, hoping you'd come back to me, always hoping, half-believing that somehow, someday we would be together again. I could have married several times over. I turned down many offers. But I kept myself for you, Zac. For you only. And now I discover that you couldn't even wait more than a bloody year before you jumped into bed with someone else!"

"That's not fair, Jaz. It wasn't like that."

"Well, what was it like, Zac? Please, tell me! I'd like to know!"

"As far as we knew we were never going to see another Terran again. It was just us. We had to go on with our lives."

"Do you love her?"

"Yes."

"As much as you once loved me?"

"Yes."

"And what about me? How do you feel about me? Are there any feelings left at all?"

"Jaz, don't do this. Please. It's not going to help."

"No, Zac. I really want to know. How do you feel about me? Is there any spark of love left at all?"

"Jaz, we were only married for a couple of months. I've been married to Kit for 21 years. It's not fair to compare."

"So, no feelings at all then?"

"No, that's not true. Of course I have feelings for you." He moved to where she was sitting. He squatted in front of her, reached out and took her hands in his. "You were the first person I ever truly fell in love with. And that love was a beautiful thing. We were so lucky to find each other, and if I could go back in time, I would never have left you that morning – never have stepped into that transfer pod. If I could change the past, I would make sure that I stayed with you on Nova, so that we lived out the rest of our lives together. Had more babies. Grew old and wrinkly together."

Jaz was openly sobbing now.

"But it wasn't to be, Jaz. Fate, or whatever you want to call it, separated us. And now the love that we once shared is a memory for me - a happy memory, a wonderful memory – but my heart is given to someone else now."

She took her hands from his. "You need to go now."

"I'm so sorry Jaz."

"Just go."

7

The newly woken Terrans breakfasted on fruit and cereals, although Jaz was strangely absent, claiming she wasn't hungry. While they were eating, Commander Bree paid them a brief visit.

"I'm glad to see you all looking so well," said Starla. "I trust the refreshments are satisfactory?"

"Yes! Fantastic!" said Dayna. "These different kinds of fruit are amazing!"

"Were the uploads successful?" asked Mel.

"Considering you are now speaking Altarian, I would say they were very successful," said Starla.

"Oh my goodness!" exclaimed Dayna again. "You're kidding! No, you're not! I really can speak Altarian! It feels like I've been speaking it all my life."

The others made similar comments and spent several minutes experimenting with their new language. To their amazement, both languages now resided very comfortably alongside each other in their consciousness.

Starla asked them to join her in the conference room as soon as they finished their meal.

Less than half an hour later they were all seated around the conference table. Jaz had joined them but was strangely quiet. Zac was sitting alongside Starla, who began proceedings.

"I am glad to see you all looking so well and rested. Please let me know if there are any needs that you have. We will do whatever we can to meet them."

"Thank you," said Mel. "You've been very kind."

Starla nodded and continued. "The purpose of this meeting is to bring you up to date with developments on Altaria, and then to discuss your future." She paused, gathering her thoughts. "As you know, we came to this planet over 1,700 years ago, fleeing from the manipulation of the EIs, as you yourselves have now done. Until recently we've enjoyed a peaceful existence here, free from the threat of their influence. 141 years ago, we opened the wormhole and sent an exploratory ship to the G-894 star system, 117 light-years distant. The very next day, the wormhole from your star system opened here and remained locked open until a few days ago, effectively trapping our exploratory ship and its crew in the other star system."

"That's horrible!" exclaimed Dayna. "They could never come back home!"

"That's correct. Many families here lost loved ones. But the relevance for our discussion this morning is that 20 years ago, we received a tight beam transmission from Explorer 1, the vessel we sent to that system. They had eventually mapped their position and ours. The message had taken 117 years to reach us. They informed us that when they realised they could not return, they had eventually established a colony on Polaris, which is what they named the cold earth-like planet in that system. They also informed us that soon after their arrival, an advanced EI ship had arrived, apparently having travelled from a nearby star system using some kind of advanced sub-light propulsion system."

"The same kind of Enhanced Intelligences that were killing us on Nova?" asked Dayna.

"Yes. Although, in this case, the ship was crewed by a single EI. Initially, the Polaris settlement didn't know that. It opened communication with the settlement, claiming to be a survey ship from a nearby star system, crewed by humans. When the settlement responded, the EI used the settlement's signal to download its coding into their technology. It then gained complete control of the settlement. A skeleton crew was on board Explorer 1 which was in a high orbit at the time of the EI ship's arrival. The Explorer crew was working on the final stages of development of the tight beam technology. They immediately cloaked the ship when the EI arrived and remained hidden from its sensors, but they were able to monitor the wide beam communication between the EI and the settlement. Over the next month, as they worked to finalise their tight beam transmitter, they were able to glean additional information while remaining hidden."

"The EI claims that it and its brethren throughout the galaxy are the guardians of humanity. They view their role as ensuring that humans never again cause the same devastation that nearly destroyed the Earth. They became aware of the Explorer 1's presence in that star system because they have developed the technology to identify when and where a wormhole has been activated anywhere within our galaxy. They are also aware of our presence in this solar system and were, at that time, waiting for our wormhole to shut down in order to open a new wormhole to travel here and take charge. Once the Explorer crew completed construction of the tight beam transmitter, they briefly decloaked and transmitted their message to us."

There was silence for several moments around the conference table as the new arrivals digested this startling information.

"What happened to the crew on board the Explorer vessel?" asked Karl, thinking with his pilot's cap on. "Wouldn't decloaking have revealed their position to the EI vessel?"

"Yes, probably, but we don't know what resulted. The message was extremely compressed and so it only lasted for less than 20 seconds. The ship would then have cloaked again. We simply have no way of knowing what happened after that. If the EIs have not developed cloaking technology, perhaps Explorer 1 has managed to evade capture. We can only hope that this is the case. Of course, all this happened 137 years ago — 20 years since we received the message, which was already 117 years old by then — so whatever took place happened long ago."

"And you've received no further communication from them in the last 20 years?" asked Karl again.

"No. Which doesn't bode well. We can only hope that the crew has somehow managed to evade capture and survive somewhere else. We haven't sent a message back, because we don't want to aggravate the situation by alerting the EIs to the fact that the ship has been able to communicate with us."

"So, we could now be in danger of an EI invasion, ourselves?" asked Mel.

"Yes. As soon as you arrived and the wormhole closed, we became vulnerable to EI invasion. They could open up a wormhole here from anywhere else in the galaxy, which is why we took measures while you were asleep to counteract that threat."

"What measures?" asked Mel.

"We opened a wormhole to Nova again and sent a probe through. The wormhole has remained open for the last two weeks, effectively blocking any incoming wormholes from anywhere else. Obviously, the black hole in the R-421 system is still interfering with the wormhole and creating significant time dilation. But we don't know how long the wormhole will remain open this time. If, as our scientists believe, the black hole is continuing to move across the elliptical plane of the galaxy, the wormhole could break free of the black hole's event horizon at any time, and close down without warning."

"So we can't rely on the wormhole staying locked open indefinitely?" said Dayna.

"No. This is why we've put in place other defensive measures. We have developed a means of quickly identifying and destroying an EI vessel as soon as one enters our solar system."

"But if one manages to slip through your defences, we're basically all stuffed," said Mel.

"It is definitely a very troubling scenario," said Starla.

"Is there any way we can nullify the ability of the EIs to manipulate our physiology — their ability to interfere with our brain waves and kill us when they think we've lived long enough?"

"That's one of the things we've been working on," said Starla. "Over the last two decades, in response to the threat of EI invasion, most people have had their cerebral implants removed, and we have retrograded our technology so that it is no longer controlled by thought waves. This is why we told you we would not be leaving your implants in place. By removing our implants, the EIs won't be able to have direct control of our executive brain functions – they won't be able to control us like automatons, which would have been simply unthinkable – if you'll pardon the pun. But they will still have the ability to manipulate us as they have in the past, including orchestrating our premature deaths. This is because of our modified genomes, which they have somehow tuned so that our central nervous system is susceptible to their manipulation."

"So can we somehow switch that part of our coding off?" asked Phil.

"That is what our scientists are trying to determine. As you can appreciate, with 3.2 billion base pairs, our DNA is extremely complex, and trying to isolate those segments that are instrumental in allowing the EIs to manipulate our brains is extremely difficult. It's like trying to find a needle in a haystack – an expression I have learnt from Zac."

"Is there any way we can help?" asked Mel.

"Not at this stage. Our priority for you is to get you settled into your new lives as quickly as possible. Which is why I've invited Zac to this meeting. He will explain what arrangements are being made."

8

———————

"As you can imagine," Zac began, "your arrival here has created a lot of excitement, especially among our little Terran community. Keo, Tash, Kit and I thought we would never see another Terran face for the rest of our lives, so to say that we are thrilled to have you here is an understatement. For Keo and I, there will be the added bonus of getting to know a son and a daughter that we never knew we had." He smiled at Dayna, who flushed slightly.

"Needless to say, we want you to come and live with us on our island. It would make no sense for us to live apart, as there are no other people like us on the planet. Accordingly, while you were asleep and undergoing your genomic update, work has begun on your new dwellings. In fact, it is almost completed. You'll spend a few more days here at Gateway Station, receiving a basic overview of Altarian society, and by the time you're ready to leave, your new homes will be ready."

Starla activated a 3D holographic image of Tradewind

Island and its archipelago, which hovered above the centre of the table.

"We live in a beautiful archipelago of islands," continued Zac, "25 degrees south of the equator. The main islands form an almost perfect circle, creating a calm inner sea which is perfect for fishing. Our island, D5242, known locally as Tradewind Island, is the southern-most island of the archipelago. We share the island with five other families, and we have been given the western end of the island. Our parcel of land is more than 3 square kilometres and stretches from the northern beach facing the calm inner sea to the southern beach which is exposed to the surf."

Starla zoomed in on their section of the island while Zac continued his explanation.

"Tash, Keo, Kit and I have a small compound consisting of two bungalows and some other small buildings, about 100 metres from the southern beach. We've been very happy living side-by-side like that for 22 years, but we realise that you might like a little more privacy. While you were sleeping, the Federation Council has constructed four additional two-bedroom bungalows, along the same stretch of the southern beach. Each one is separated by about 100 metres and is quite secluded."

Starla zoomed the holographic image in further, showing the four bungalows. Workers could be seen moving between the buildings and some machinery was being operated by the construction crew, revealing the fact that these were actually live images.

Zac continued. "We weren't sure what living arrangements you would want, in terms of who would live with whom, but we think that four bungalows among the six of you should be sufficient. The furthest bungalow is still only 400 metres from the original two bungalows, so we're not far apart. The council has also built additional storage sheds and covered areas, as well as providing you with a six-seater sandy buggy and individual dune bikes. Additionally, there is a new boat, called a skippa, waiting for you at the marina on the northern beach, about four kilometres away."

"Mayor Berg, who lives on the archipelago's main island, Manna Island, has also donated another four kordu to our herd – they're a type of local cattle. I think you will be very comfortable and, hopefully, very happy living among us."

"Until the EIs arrive," said Mel, with her usual blunt approach.

"That is a complete unknown," said Zac. "We've had 22 years of uninterrupted peace here, and for all we know, the wormhole may stay locked for another century or more. All we can do is take each day as it comes."

They talked over some minor points for a few more minutes, but everyone was extremely happy with the arrangements that had been made. The meeting ended shortly afterwards and Starla invited the new arrivals to attend their first information session, where they would be given an introduction to Altarian society and to the world that would be their new home.

Jaz left quickly, claiming that she needed to use the bathroom. As the group moved out of the conference room, Zac intercepted Dayna and asked if she could stay behind and talk. She nodded uncertainly, and they sat again, side by side.

"Dayna, I can't tell you how happy I am to have found you — or for you to have found me, as it turns out."

"I'm glad too."

There was an awkwardness between them, the strange

dichotomy of a father and daughter who were complete strangers.

"I knew that Jaz was pregnant, and the day before I disappeared, we found out that we were expecting a girl. I want you to know that over the years I have often thought about you – wondering what you were like and how you had grown up. Finding you now is one of the highlights of my life; one that I thought would never happen."

Dayna just nodded, not knowing what to say.

He reached out and took one of her hands in his. "I'm so sorry I wasn't there for you. I'm sorry I missed all the little girl years — the bedtime stories and piggyback rides, the walks in the park and the birthday parties. I'm sorry I missed your teenage years and I wasn't there for you when you needed a dad."

Her eyes were welling up, and her bottom lip was trembling.

"If I could go back in time and relive that fateful day, I would make sure that I never left home that day. I would gladly choose to stay there and be with you through the last 22 years, even if it meant dying at 50. I really mean it. I would gladly give up a long life to have had the chance of being a dad to you through all your childhood years."

She nodded, tears freely flowing down her face now.

"I missed you, Dad."

"I missed you too, sweetheart. Although I suppose I shouldn't call you that now that you're all grown up."

"Of course you can call me that; you're my dad."

"I am, aren't I? It's going to take a while to get used to — for both of us I guess."

"You're not as tall as I thought you'd be."

"Really?"

She nodded.

"I used to make Uncle Gus tell me stories about you, over and over again. I could almost recite them word for word in the end. And I imagined you as some kind of superhero, tall and strong and fearless and wise."

"Wow! What a letdown when you finally found me!"

"No, silly. Now that I've found you, I much prefer the real thing to a silly little girl's fantasy."

"I wish you'd found me 15 years ago; I was in a lot better shape back then!"

They both cracked a smile and Zac reached over and wiped a tear that was running down her cheek.

"We have a lot of catching up to do," he said, "And I'm really looking forward to getting to know you."

"Same," she said, wiping her eyes and smiling.

"Dayna, there's something I have to tell you; something that you might find very difficult, even painful. And, I'll be honest, I'm scared that it will ruin our relationship before it even begins."

"What?" she asked, concern now written across her face.

"There's no easy way to say this, so I figure I'd better just come right out and say it." He paused and took a deep breath, exhaling slowly. "I'm married to someone else here on Altaria."

He looked at her closely, trying to gauge her reaction, watching her blink several times as she processed the new information. He waited for a response, but she said nothing, still obviously thinking it through, her brow furrowed now.

"When we arrived here, we discovered that everyone we loved was long dead. And if you hadn't entered the wormhole, that would certainly be the case. You, your mother, everyone we knew and loved; dead for nearly a century by the time we got here. We grieved deeply. But eventually we moved on and created new lives. We had to."

"I see," she said. "I'm assuming you've told Mum?"

"Yes."

"And I don't have to guess how she took it."

"No. As bad as you might expect. Possibly even a little worse."

Dayna nodded, a grim look across her features.

"You know she waited for you, all these years?"

"Yes. That's what makes this whole situation so horrible."

"She's been an emotional mess for 22 years, Dad, living in the hope of you coming back or of her somehow finding you."

"I gather that."

"This is gonna mess her up, big time."

"I know." He sighed again. "Dayna, I feel terrible, and I wish there was something I could do to help the situation."

"How long have you been married?"

"21 years."

"Wow."

"I'm sorry. I know it's a shock."

"Do you have kids?"

"No. Kit and I tried for years. We both desperately wanted children, but it never happened. It's one of the reasons why finding you means so much to me."

"Kit? The pilot who disappeared with you?"

"Yes."

"What about Keo and Martinez?"

"Keo and Tash got married the same day we did. They have two children. The eldest is Boyd's, the youngest is Keo's."

Dayna just nodded, absorbing it all.

Zac looked at her closely, searching for a sign, hoping to gauge how she was taking it.

"Dayna, I'm hoping this won't affect our relationship. I don't want it to come between us before we even get a chance to get to know each other. I know that Kit will love you, and I'm sure you'll grow to love her."

"It's not Kit I'm worried about; it's Mum."

"For what it's worth, I'm worried about her too. I still care for her deeply, whatever she might think about me now."

Dayna just nodded her head and stood up.

"I need time to think. Because, right now, I'm not sure what to think. I guess I'm pretty disappointed." She bit her bottom lip and shook her head, as if to clear her head of an unwanted thought. "Maybe I'm unrealistic, but I've always imagined that if you and Mum ever found each other again, there'd be this wonderful reunion and we'd be a normal, happy family at last. In all my fantasising, I never considered the possibility that you'd be happily married to someone else. It's not exactly the fairy tale ending I'd imaged."

"No. I guess not."

"I need to go. I'm late for the first info session."

She walked to the door, leaving Zac standing awkwardly. As she got to the door, she turned and was about to say something. She changed her mind, shook her head, turned and walked through the door.

"Excellent work, Zac!" he said out loud to himself. "Just great!"

9

The group of seven stepped out of the transfer booth on Manna Island. Zac was accompanying the new arrivals to their new homes and as they walked towards the marina they gazed around in obvious delight. The warm tropical air enveloped them, and the breeze carried the fragrance of a dozen different exotic plants.

"It's a perfect day for sailing," Zac said as he glanced at the sky, assessing the wind's direction by the movement of small white wisps of cloud.

Zac saw their skippa tied up at the end of the jetty, and the bulky form of Keo waved at them from the deck. They walked up the jetty and Keo leapt nimbly from the vessel onto the wooden planks and stood beaming at them. He extended his arms as if he wanted to hug them all.

"Welcome friends! Welcome to your new home!"

Zac introduced him to everyone, and Keo did indeed hug them, one by one. There were happy reunions with Mel and Jaz, with exclamations of delight from Keo of how little Mel had grown into a beautiful woman. Jaz, however, seemed reserved and withdrawn, barely smiling when Keo greeted her.

Lastly, Zac indicated Rajesh, who was standing at the back of the group.

"And this is your son, Keo."

The two stood facing each other, and Raj seemed awkward and uncertain.

"Father," he said, nodding his head.

Keo rushed forward and enveloped him in a huge embrace.

"My son! My son! How wonderful! I am truly blessed! I've looked forward to this moment since the day of your arrival. God is smiling upon us today!" He then placed his forehead and nose against Raj's in the traditional Maori greeting. "I see you Rajesh, my son."

They boarded the skippa and very soon they were skipping across the small chop, their sails taut and bulging with the late morning breeze. Keo had seconded Raj and was teaching him the finer points of sailing, letting him hold the wheel and helping him to feel the sweet spot as they sailed close to the wind.

Jaz was sitting alone near the bow, and Dayna was leaning over the starboard rail, next to Zac.

"Dad, I've been doing a lot of thinking."

"I'm sure you have."

"Obviously, we can't undo what's happened. And I really have no right to sit in judgment on you for your decisions. If I'm really honest with myself, I may have done the same thing if I was in your shoes. It doesn't fit in with my fairy tale ending, but I can see now that I was very unrealistic."

Zac just nodded.

"I'm not saying I feel great about the situation, but I understand. And I don't want it to come between us. I've spent 22 years wanting to find you, and it would be churlish to let this stop us from being friends – hopefully great friends."

She smiled tentatively, and Zac gave her hand a brief squeeze.

"I'm so glad, Dayna. I was worried that I'd lost you as soon as I'd found you."

"That's not gonna happen," she assured him. "At least not until I get all the birthday presents that you owe me."

Zac smiled, and then grew more serious. "How has your mother been over the last week?"

"Not good. She's barely speaking. I'm worried about her. You were her reason for living, and that's been taken from her."

"I know. I don't know what I can do to help. You'll need to watch her carefully. We don't want her to do anything ... stupid, if you know what I mean."

"I know exactly what you mean."

The skippa docked at their local marina and they walked down the short jetty to find Kit and Tash waiting, with two sand buggies parked nearby. More warm welcomes and reunions took place, with the exception of Jaz's frosty reception of Kit's hug. They piled into the two buggies and not long afterward they arrived at their newly enlarged village. The four new bungalows were spread along the coastline, joined by a newly made path that wound its way among the lush tropical foliage. The sounds of surf from the nearby southern beach told the newcomers how close they were to the ocean.

Mel and Phil, who were now officially a couple, chose the closest bungalow. Karl and Raj took the second and Dayna suggested that she and her mother shared the third. But Jaz was adamant that she wanted privacy. She claimed the fourth and furthest bungalow for herself, leaving Dayna to occupy the third alone.

They spent an hour settling into their new homes and being shown around the village, also meeting Tash and Keo's children, Noah and Kira. Raj couldn't help noticing the mutual flash of interest that passed between Dayna and the well-built Noah, as well as the slight flush to Dayna's cheeks. Zac saw it too and thought, *this is going to be interesting.* Noah and Kira were animated and excited at finding a step-brother in Raj and a new friend in Dayna. They had led an extremely limited social life to this point and so they immediately swept the newcomers up in a wave of enthusiasm.

Lunch was an impressive spread of seafood and fruits, shared under the new gazebo that Keo and Noah had constructed, finishing it only the previous day.

"Can you guarantee this one won't fall down?" asked Tash, eyeing the roof suspiciously.

"Yes," replied Noah. "Because I didn't let Dad build this one on his own."

"I keep telling you - the last one only collapsed because of the storm!" complained Keo.

"Of course it did, sweetie," said Tash, condescendingly.

"Gentle breeze, more like it," muttered Zac.

Everyone laughed and several people joined in the banter. They talked animatedly together, with the conversation ranging from fishing, to the kordu herd, to boats and buggies. After lunch was finished and the plates were cleared, the newbies were taken for a walk to the beach where everyone except Jaz went for a swim. Jaz, however, sat alone on the sand dune and eventually left everyone and walked back to her bungalow.

Toward sunset, the whole group piled back into the buggies

and drove back to the island's marina where the locals were holding a hāngi to welcome the newcomers. Introductions were made and glasses of rhapsody were consumed as the roasted kordu was unwrapped and its succulent aroma filled the air. After dinner, when the sun dipped below the horizon and dark slowly enveloped the small community, Zac saw Noah showing Dayna how to catch midgies at the water's edge, with head-lamps and nets.

"Noah is already making a move," said Keo, standing beside Zac.

"Yes, and I don't think Raj is very impressed," Zac replied, nodding towards Raj who was sitting alone on the grass watching Dayna and Noah. "Someone is going to get their heart broken here."

"Unfortunately, there is no avoiding it," agreed Keo. "Dayna is the only available Terran girl on the planet, apart from Kira."

"What about one of the locals?" asked Zac. "Do you think that could ever happen?"

"It's possible. Marsh and Razna's daughter, Astil, seems to have shown some interest in Noah, and until Dayna arrived, he was showing interest in return. But I suspect he'll be pursuing Dayna from now on – with everything he's got."

"What about half-brother and sister relationships?" asked Zac. "They were not legal back in our world, but is that a possibility here for Raj and Kia?"

Keo puffed out his cheeks as he exhaled. "That's a tough one, bro. We're writing a new rule book here, aren't we? It's possible, I guess, if there's no genetic problems between them. But the old taboos are hard to overturn."

They both sipped their drinks as the light completely faded from the sky and the stars took over. Zac noticed Karl walking over to Jaz, who had separated herself from the others and was sitting looking out to the calm waters of the inner sea. Karl handed her a drink and sat down beside her.

"I've got a feeling a whole lot of things are about to change," said Zac.

"Me too, bro. Me too."

10

The emergency meeting of the Federation Council was quickly brought to order, and Councillor Drummond didn't waste time getting to the point.

"As you all know by now, the wormhole between us and the Icarus-421 system closed yesterday. We immediately reopened it, sending another probe through, but the wormhole closed after 14 seconds. A second attempt had the same result. It seems that the black hole's trajectory has taken it far enough away from the Icarus system so that it no longer exerts an influence over the wormhole."

"So that's it then," said someone with a resigned voice. "In the end, we only got two months protection from the locked wormhole."

"Yes. But two months was better than nothing," said Drummond.

"Where does that leave us now, in terms of security?" asked someone else.

Drummond nodded at General Kellar, who assured

everyone that the Federation Defence Force was ready to meet any EI threat head on. Three battleships were once again on high alert, with two always stationed at Gateway Station at any one time. The EMP bombs were cloaked and ready for instantaneous detonation as soon as the 'canary' satellites signalled the presence of an EI vessel. Dr Spooner then addressed the meeting, indicating that they still hadn't perfected the subspace portal disruptor field.

"Alright then," said Drummond. "I'm not sure if there's anything else we can do at the moment. Unfortunately, it's now a waiting game."

"While we're waiting," said Zac, "why don't we try to make contact with the Nova launch ring? We've got nothing to lose now. The EIs know where we are and will already have noted that our wormhole has closed down. There's no reason for us not to use the wormhole now. And I would like to know what happened to the ring inhabitants after we left. Why didn't they ever follow us through the wormhole? Are they still there at all? What happened to them? Besides, they may have gleaned some additional information about the EIs over the last century that could prove useful."

"Yes," agreed Drummond. "Our previous reasons for not contacting them no longer apply. But we will have to safeguard ourselves from possibly infection. The ring may have been successfully taken over by the EIs by now."

"I doubt that," aid Zac. "If the EIs were on the ring they would have sent an infected probe or vessel through the wormhole. The fact that they didn't, tells me that the EIs are still confined to the planet in that solar system."

"That is probably true," said Dr Spooner, "but just to be safe, we could send a probe through with a recorded message to be broadcast in a basic FM band that is not capable of transferring coding, and ask them to send a similar probe through to us with a reply."

Everyone agreed that this was a good plan, and the rest of the meeting was spent constructing an outline of a fairly lengthy message that gave the Novan 'ringers' a detailed overview of past and current developments in the Altarian system. When the meeting concluded, Drummond retired to his office to record and upload the message to Gateway Station. Within two hours a probe with their message had been launched through the wormhole into the Icarus system.

11

———

"No, you're not letting go of the line soon enough as you cast," said Zac. "Wind it back in again — which shouldn't take too long since it barely went five metres."

"Ha, ha," said Dayna. "It's easy for you – you've obviously had nothing else to do except fish for 22 years!"

"And surf. Don't forget that. It's been a busy life!"

"Yeh, well while you've been blissfully transforming yourself into a beach bum, some of us have been too busy to pursue such frivolous activities."

"There's nothing wrong with frivolous activities, sweetheart. You know what they say about all work and no play ...?"

"Yeah, yeah," she said wearily. "OK. I've wound the line in. Show me again. Clearly, I'm missing something here. What am I doing wrong?"

"Well, for starters, you should stop sticking your tongue out like that. The seagulls are likely to peck it off. You're as bad as Kit. Her tongue has a mind of its own when she's concentrating on something."

Dayna cast the line out again, this time releasing it earlier in the cast. The baited hook and sinker sailed out past the break and landed with a satisfying plonk.

"I did it!"

"Brilliant! Well done, girl."

"I really like her, you know." She looked at her father. "Kit I mean. She's lovely."

"Yes. She is. And she thinks the world of you too."

They stood in companionable silence for a few moments, each with their finger on their lines, feeling the gentle pull and release of the swell.

"How's Jaz? I can't seem to talk to her."

"She's OK, I guess. Karl spends a lot of time with her, trying to cheer her up. I think he's pretty keen."

"And how does Jaz feel about him?"

"Not sure. She won't really talk to me about him."

Dayna's line suddenly went tight and the rod bent right over.

"Oh my gosh! I think I've actually caught something! What do I do? What do I do?"

"Don't just stand there, girl! Reel it in! Nice and steady. Keep the tension on it. By the looks of that rod you've got something big enough to put on the table at tonight's party."

Later that night, the fish occupied the position of honour in the centre of the table in the gazebo which, contrary to Tash's subtle predictions, was still standing. The whole group were present to celebrate Tash's birthday which, as far as they could estimate, was today.

"So how old are you now, Tash?" asked Mel, helping herself to a slice of fish.

"Not telling."

"She probably can't remember, the poor old thing," said Noah with a grin.

"You're lucky you're on the other side of the table, young man, or I'd be giving you a slap across the back of the head." She shook her head, and muttered, "Cheeky bugger!"

"The fish is delicious, Dayna," said Kit.

"It's more due to your cooking than my catching I think."

"Nonsense! The skill of the fisherman who catches it brings out the flavour," said Keo with a wink.

The food was delicious, and several bottles of wine were consumed. The party got louder as more wine was drunk, and Zac noted for the first time that they seemed to have blended into a single community. Relationships were growing, friendships deepening, and in the case of Dayna and Noah, romance had clearly blossomed. The two young love birds were sitting together, thigh to thigh, and touching whenever possible. He would need to talk to Dayna soon about whether it was time to make it more official. He looked across at Raj, who seemed to have accepted defeat, but was still feeling the loss deeply. He made a mental note to have a chat with him as soon as possible.

Evening fell and a slight chill could be felt in the air. Winter was very mild here, but it was still nice to light a fire sometimes. They gathered around the firepit and kindled a small fire, cracking open another bottle of rhapsody. Zac rarely drank more than two glasses, as it seemed to take longer to recover these days. Tonight, however, he had indulged a little more heavily and he accepted yet another top up. They chatted good naturedly as the fire gradually died down, and eventually, in ones and twos, people started drifting off to bed. Raj had disappeared a while ago, perhaps in the direction of the beach, and Zac decided to see if he was OK.

He walked unsteadily down the sandy track, thinking belatedly that he probably should have stopped drinking several glasses ago. He emerged onto the gently sloping beach. The tide was going out and a half moon hung low in the sky. Raj was nowhere to be seen, but Zac took a few moments to stand and absorb the peaceful scene, trying unsuccessfully to clear his fuzzy head. Phosphorescence was sparkling along the shoreline, and the stars in the southern sky formed a curved crown hanging above the world.

"It's beautiful, isn't it?"

He turned and saw Jaz emerge from the track behind him.

"Jaz."

12

"I saw you leave. I've wanted to talk to you for some time now, and I though this might be a good opportunity."

"Sure. How are you, Jaz? I've been worried about you." He was trying hard not to slur his words but wasn't sure how successful he was.

"I'm OK. A lot better. I ... I've been doing a lot of thinking."

"OK."

"Zac, I'm sorry for the way I reacted. You and Kit ... it was the last thing I expected. In all my thinking over the years, I never imagined ... you know ... that you would have moved on. It was a shock."

"I know."

"And I need to tell you that I understand. I really do. You thought we were all dead. And you had to get on with your life. I get that now. I'm sorry for how I reacted."

"Gosh! There's no need for you to apologise to me! It should be the other way round."

"Can we sit together for a bit?" she asked.

"Sure."

They sat side by side on a patch of grass on top of a small dune.

"Zac, I want to say something, and I'm not expecting a definite response tonight. But I want you to hear me out."

"OK."

"The thing is, I'm still in love with you. I've tried not to be. I've tried to be angry with you. I've even tried to ... I don't know ... hate you, I guess. But I can't. I love you. I can't stop loving you." She paused and looked at him. "Do you remember what I said to you all those years ago, on our first night on Nova?"

"Yes. You told me that you're a dove and not a lyrebird."

"That's right. And eventually you worked out what I meant, although I think you needed some help."

"Yeh. I did. Kit helped me work it out."

Jaz pressed on, ignoring the reference to Kit. "Doves mate for life. My heart only has room in it for one man, and that's you. I've tried to stop loving you, but I can't. I just can't." She looked at him carefully, trying to gauge his reaction. "I love you, Zac. And I always will."

Zac shook his head and exhaled. "Jaz, how do you expect me to react to this? What do you expect me to do?"

She cocked her head on the side. "Let me ask you a question. Can you honestly say that you don't love me at all? That there's not a small spark of our love still buried somewhere deep down in your heart? I want an honest answer please."

He thought about it for a moment. "No. I can't say that the love I felt for you is completely gone. But that doesn't mean ..."

"Shoosh," she said interrupting and touching his lips with her fingers. "Hear me out please. In many cultures back on Earth, a man could have more than one wife. Even in the Bible, the ancient Israelites practiced polygamy as a way of looking after widows. In a world where men died young and women outnumbered men, polygamy made sure that every woman could have a husband."

"Yes, but ..."

"I haven't finished. I'm not saying that I should come and live with you and Kit. And I'm not even demanding an equal share of you. But I want you in my life at least part of the time. I want you in my heart. And, yes, dammit, I want you in my bed. I'm asking you to consider two nights a week. Just two nights."

"That wouldn't be right! I couldn't ..."

"How is that not right!" she interrupted. "I'm your wife Zac! I'm still your wife! And I was your wife first, before you married Kit. Nothing's actually changed. We're still married. Can't you see that?"

He stood to his feet, shaking his head, and she stood too.

"Jaz, I couldn't. I mean, I still care for you, very much ..."

"I know you do, Zac. That's the thing. I can see it in your eyes." She took a step closer, so that they were standing so close they could taste each other's breath. She reached out and touched the side of his face. "I can see the love that is still there, in your eyes. And I see the turmoil that my presence here causes you. But it doesn't have to be like this, Zac. You and I are married." She put her arms around his waist and pulled herself against him so that their bodies were touching. "I'm your wife, Zac." She kissed him lightly on the lips. "This is not wrong. We are husband and wife, and I love you so much, my darling."

She kissed him fully this time, opening his mouth with her tongue and searching urgently for his. Zac's head was spinning and his passion took hold of him. He took her in his arms and kissed her back. He placed his hands on her buttocks and pulled her closer, and she ground herself against him, moaning now. She reached down between them and undid his shorts, letting them fall to the ground, caressing him and hearing him moan in turn. She pulled him quickly down to the grass, removing her clothing as she did. Before he had time to think, they were joined together and he lost any semblance of control. They moved together urgently, and it seemed to Zac that all the years that had passed vanished in an instant as they were swept up in the passion of their youth.

"Yes, yes, my darling!" she cried out. "Oh Zac, Zac! My husband! Yes, yes!"

Their movements grew more urgent, as they gave themselves completely over to their passion. She clung to him desperately, wrapping her legs around him and calling out his name.

It was over very quickly and afterward they lay together, panting and satiated, him on top of her, with Jaz kissing his face again and again.

"O Zac, my love, my darling. This isn't wrong. This is the way it's meant to be, when two people love each other and are married. You don't have to feel ashamed. We've done nothing wrong."

Zac started shaking his head.

"No, no, no, no, no! What have I done? Oh God!" He stood to his feet, doing his shorts up. "This isn't right ... I should never have ... Kit! Kit! Oh my God!" He turned away and started stumbling unsteadily down the path.

"Zac! Wait!" said Jaz, getting herself together and standing up. "Don't go. Please."

"I have to. I have to go ..."

She caught up to him and grabbed his arm.

"Think about it, Zac. Promise me you'll think about it. Please. Two nights a week, that's all I ask."

He shook his head, not quite believing what had just happened. He broke free of her grasp and stumbled back down the track, away from her and towards the dreadful consequences that must surely now await him.

13

———

K it woke to find Zac sitting on the end of the bed. She yawned and stretched.

"What happened to you last night?" she asked. "I tried waiting up for you, but I must have fallen asleep before you got home." She sat up. "Are you OK? You look dreadful."

"I feel dreadful."

She touched his forehead. "Are you sick?"

"Yeh. Actually, you could probably say that."

"Zac, what's wrong. You're worrying me."

Zac took a deep breath and let out a long, slow sigh.

"Last night I went down to the beach, thinking I'd seen Raj go in that direction. I wanted to talk to him about Dayna, and about how he was feeling. I'm worried about him."

"Of course. So am I."

"He wasn't there. But Jaz followed me down there. She said she wanted to talk. She said she has a proposition."

"What kind of proposition?"

Zac took a moment to gather his thoughts.

"She told me that she still loves me; that she'll always love me. And she insists that we're still legally married."

"Well she's wrong. You're married to me."

"Yes. She accepts that. But she also believes I'm still married to her as well. She referred to other cultures where a man has more than one wife."

"You're kidding! She's proposing some kind of time share arrangement?!"

"Something like that. She says she wants two nights a week."

"WHAT??? That's outrageous! That's ... that's ... I can't even put it into words! That's unbelievable! We've been married for nearly 22 years and now she turns up and wants a piece of the pie? How's that even supposed to work? Do you clock on and clock off with each wife? Are you supposed to wander between the bungalows like a stallion at a stud ranch? I hope you told her what she could do with that idea."

"I didn't exactly get a chance."

"What do you mean?"

Zac stood up and breathed out loudly, running his hands through his hair, and walking in circles.

"O man! Kit, I ... Oh man!"

"What Zac?!! What have you done?!!"

"I started to tell her that it wasn't possible. But she launched herself at me, and started kissing me ..."

"No, no, no, no, ..."

"I'd had way too much to drink ..."

"No, Zac! Please, no!"

"Before I knew what was happening ... things got out of hand ..."

"Please tell me you didn't! Please, Zac, no!"

"I'm so sorry Kit. I love you. Only you! I was drunk. I was … it happened so fast it was over before I knew what was happening."

"Oh I'm sure that's not true! I'm sure you were very bloody aware of the fact that you were banging her!"

"Kit. Please! I'm sorry. I love you. It was a horrible drunken mistake."

Kit had buried her face in her hands and was sobbing uncontrollably. Zac reached out and touched her on the arm and she flinched, raising her face in a bitter mask towards him.

"Get out!"

"What? No. You can't be serious."

"Get out!"

"No Kit, please!"

"GET OUT!!! I don't want you in my house ever again! GET OUT NOW!!!"

He walked to the bedroom door, paused and turned back to her. "Whatever else you might think of me, I swear to you that I love you, and I only want to be with you. No one else."

She just shook her head and said quietly, "Get out of here before I punch you."

He turned and left.

Keo found him two hours later, sitting on some rocks by the seashore at the western end of the island, watching the tide gradually cover the spit of sand that joined their island to the next one. Keo sat beside him and didn't say anything for several minutes. It was an overcast day, and some dark clouds were gathering on the southern horizon, looking ominous. Zac had a handful of small pebbles and was tossing them one at a time into a rock pool nearby.

"I gather you know what's happened?"

"Yes bro. Tash is with Kit now."

Zac just nodded and tossed another pebble.

"I've really stuffed up now, Keo. Stuffed up big time."

Keo said nothing.

"I don't think she'll ever have me back. I think that's it – we're done."

"Maybe not. She just needs time."

"You don't know Kit like I do. Loyalty and trust are everything to her. She felt threatened enough by the mere memory of Jaz for all these years – wondering if she was only a convenient second-best option – and now I've gone and confirmed her worst fears. I've just proved to her that at the first available opportunity I'm willing to drop her like a hot potato and go running back to Jaz. This will have devastated her and destroyed any chance we have of being together."

He shook his head and threw all the remaining pebbles angrily away.

"I was drunk, you know."

"I guessed that."

"Not that that's any excuse."

"No."

"And Jaz ambushed me. She practically threw herself at me."

"I kind of guessed that too."

"Not that I can put the blame on her either."

"No."

"You must be disgusted with me."

"Disappointed – yes. Disgusted – no. I'm not here to judge you, Zac. I have feet of clay, too. Who knows how I would have reacted in your situation? There, but for the grace of God, go I."

"How's Kit?"

Keo just shook his head.

Zac nodded.

After a long pause, he said, "You know what's messing with my head about all this? Jaz kept saying that there's nothing wrong with what we were doing. She kept saying that she never divorced me and that we're still husband and wife, so it can't be wrong. What do you think, Keo? Are we still married?"

"You can't be married to two people at the same time, bro."

"Can't I? In some cultures, you can. Jaz kept saying that too. She wants to have some kind of shared arrangement. She asked for two nights a week."

"I know. Kit mentioned it. That's not a good idea, bro."

"This is doing my head in, Keo! Do you think it's possible for a man to love two women at the same time?"

"Yes. It's definitely possible. But it's not sensible. That will never end well. One wife will always win out over the other one, and there will inevitably be mistrust and insecurity between the two. 'Does he love her more than me? Is she better than me in bed? Do they talk about me behind my back?' Trust me Zac, polygamy is a recipe for disaster."

"I know that. I do. It makes sense. And that's what I tried to tell Jaz, before she ... before we ..." He shook his head again. "Do you think what I did with Jaz was adultery? If she's still my wife, how can it be adultery? Tell me. What do you think?"

"Instead of telling you what I think, I'll ask you a question."

"OK."

"Did it feel like adultery? And I don't mean physically. I mean in your heart. Did it feel righteous and pure and noble? Or did it feel like adultery?"

Zac was silent for a long moment, then he bowed his head and whispered, "Adultery."

"Well there's your answer."

Zac nodded.

"Let me ask you another question. If you had to choose between the two of them right here, right now, with no conse-quences – you just walk away with one of them into the sunset with no recriminations – who would it be? Jaz? Or Kit?"

"Kit," without hesitation.

"You're sure of that?"

"Of course I'm sure! It's not even a close contest. I love her completely and utterly. All I have with Jaz now is a faded memory."

"Good. At least you're clear about that."

They sat silently together for a while, watching the tide gradually cover the last section of sand dividing the two islands.

"What am I going to do, Keo?"

Keo remained silent.

"That's not a rhetorical question, bro. I'm seriously in need of some advice here."

"When are you due back in the capital for a council meeting?"

"Any day, now. As soon as we hear back from the Icarus system."

"Go now. Leave early and stay there for a week or so. Give Kit some time and space."

"But I need to talk with her."

"Not at the moment you don't. You need to let her have time to cool down and think. Time to remember all that you two have together. Time to let the hurt fade just a little." Keo paused for a moment. "Go, Zac, and leave her to us. We'll do everything we can to help bring you two together again."

He nodded. "OK." He looked into Keo's eyes. "Get her back for me please, Keo. Please. I don't want to live without her."

14

NOVA

Harv flew the moon jumper into Bay 9 way too hot, braking at the last possible moment with a furious burst of retro thrusters. Some of the technicians in the glass-walled annex instinctively threw their hands up to cover their faces as the blunt-nosed craft stopped metres away from their window.

The tech leader punched a comm button and exclaimed, "Dammit Harv! You're gonna kill yourself or us doing that one of these days!"

Harv's laughter came back over the comm. "No chance of that. You're talkin' to the hottest pilot on the ring. I know what I'm doing. Besides, if I don't keep it on the edge, I'll lose the edge. You know what I mean?"

"That boy's gonna lose something else if I get my hands on him," said one of the techs, who had spilled his drink all down his front. "Sometimes I think these 5Gs are a completely different species altogether. They seem to have lost the gene for caution."

"I know what you mean," said another. "My grandkids are fifth generation ringers and they have absolutely no fear. It worries me."

Harv found his sister in the zero-gravity pod, where he knew she would be playing a game of laser tag with the some of the other 5Gs. He scanned the info board at the entrance and saw that she was registered on the green team, so he quickly donned a suit and registered on the blue team. His dark suit immediately lit up with glowing blue bands around his ankles, wrists and neck which glowed brightly for a moment as the suit was reset and then faded to a much softer glow. He put a helmet on and immediately began hearing all the chatter from the other blue team members. He turned the comm off with his chin. He grabbed a laser, opened the door to the dome and stood on the launch platform, peering into the huge spherical pod. No one would expect a late entrant to the game, and they were probably not even looking at the entrance anymore.

He stepped past the glowing white line on the platform and felt the familiar weightlessness as he moved into the gravity-free zone. Grabbing one of the hand-holds he launched himself straight down, toward the bottom of the pod. Most people tended to launch to the sides or up, but he knew that his sister always went down at first. With any luck she would be in one of her usual spots, on the underside of one of the floating "islands". He reached the bottom and began moving along the outer wall, using the hand holds. One of the lower islands was almost directly above him now, and he spotted a figure holding onto the bottom outer edge, peering upward, her back to him. It was Delta for sure, her long blonde ponytail visible through the spherical transparent helmet. He steadied himself, wedging his feet in some hand holds, and took careful aim. If he was fast, he could probably tag her with three or four good shots before she reacted. He aimed the small games laser at her, steadied himself and then opened fire. Squeezing the trigger in short bursts; one, two, three, four, five! The harmless blue beam spat out and found its target, lighting up Delta's suit with red and pinging her comm with each hit. But she was fast. She spun to the side after the first two tags and Harv's remaining shots went wide. Delta wedged herself into some protrusions at the outer edge of the island's underside and began firing back. Harv felt the tags hitting him and he fired back at her, but she was well covered now, and he wasn't as good a shot as she was. The tags were mounting up on his suit and he had to take evasive action before he was frozen out of the game.

He launched himself into free air aiming for an adjacent floating sphere, covered in handholds. He was in the open now and she was firing from cover, and the tags kept hitting him. *Damn! She's good! How can she hit a moving target like that!* He reached the sphere just in time, with 18 registered hits on his suit. A couple more and he would be frozen. He was out of her line of fire now, and safe for the moment. He looked above him and saw a green suited figure, also clinging to the sphere, firing at someone above them. He took aim and fired off some quick shots. The green suit lit up red three times and then stayed red, indicating that the player was frozen and out of the game. He must have already been near his limit. His comms would also be off now, so he couldn't warn his other teammates about Harv's position.

Harv moved up the side of the dome until he was next to the frozen player and saw that it was Kyle, the guy who had the hots for Delta. Harv smiled insincerely at him, hoping to infuriate him, and moved past him, peering over the top of the sphere. A fierce battle was raging above him, blue and green laser beams flashing across the expanse between various shapes of floating cover. He had a good line of sight on two of the green team, so he carefully took aim at the nearest figure.

One, two! His own suit lit up and then stayed red. He couldn't move. Delta came up from below and touched her helmet to his.

"Hi there, big brother. You really ought to watch your six. That's the third time in a row I've nailed you from behind."

Later, in the dining hall, the talk was all about the probe that had been received from Altaria. A town meeting had been held in mid-afternoon and the contents of the message had been explained. The two void jumpers that had travelled through the wormhole over a century ago hadn't been destroyed as everyone had assumed! There was a planet that was free from EI control! And it was accessible now! But the threat of imminent EI invasion that hung over Altaria cast a gloom over the exciting news. Was it worth the risk to venture there? Most people seemed to be arguing for safety – staying on the ring rather than subjecting themselves to the risk of EI domination all over again.

"I don't care!" said Harv, as he munched his yeast burger. "I want to plant my feet on some dirt and feel the wind and sun on my face." He took another bite of his burger and said, with his mouth full, "Plus I want to taste real meat!"

"And die at 50," said Brenda, one of the others.

"The EIs may never come!" argued Harv. "And if they do, we'll deal with them. I'm confident we'll defeat them."

"Besides," said Delta, taking her brother's side, "if they reach Altaria, they'll also eventually come here. I'd rather die fighting the EIs on a real planet than die fighting them on the ring."

"But at least here, we have a tight defence system," said someone else. "The ring is much more defensible than an entire planet."

The arguments continued for several days. In the end, the vast majority of ringers elected to stay where they were and monitor developments on Altaria. But a small group, 32 in total, refused to wait. They decided to migrate to Altaria and they would not be talked out of it. A large percentage of them were risk-taking 5Gs, spurred on by their adventurous spirits and abundant confidence.

Sadly, on this occasion, their confidence was misplaced.

15

———

ALTARIA

Zac moped around the capital for three days waiting for the council meeting to be called. On the second day, he ignored Keo's advice and tried to call Kit, but she refused to take his call. Keo called soon after to admonish him and tell him to give her space and time. Time was all Zac had at the moment, and it crawled by agonisingly slowly. He worked out in the gym, swam in the pool, and wandered around the city, ignoring the stares of inquisitive people. Zac confided in Councillor Drummond on his third day, and Drummond invited him home for dinner that night. He and his wife lived alone in a bungalow on C244, a nearby island, their two daughters having married years earlier. After a simple meal, the two men went for a walk in the garden, drinks in hand.

"I really appreciate your hospitality, Gerval. Flora is a lovely person."

"Yep. I struck gold when I married her," said Drummond. "How are you coping?"

"Oh ... you know ... not so well."

Drummond nodded. "If you need to stay somewhere for a while, we have a small cabin by the lake a few kilometres from here. We use it for occasional weekend getaways. We'd be very happy for you to use it for a couple of weeks if you need to."

"That's incredibly generous of you. Thanks. I'll see how things go and let you know."

"Gerv!" Flora called from the back door. "There's a call for you from Commander Bree on Gateway Station."

"OK love, I'll be right there." He turned to Zac. "You may as well stay out here and enjoy the fresh air while I take this in my study."

Zac wandered around the garden, noting the carefully tended plants. Flora obviously lived up to her name. A small vegetable garden contained an impressive variety of healthy-looking plants.

Drummond emerged from the house twenty minutes later and joined Zac who had taken a seat on a garden bench.

"Well that was interesting," he began. "I'm sorry I took so long. A probe has arrived via a wormhole from the Icarus system. It contains a detailed message from the inhabitants of the ring who have obviously survived and successfully avoided EI infestation."

"That's great news! I was worried that the lack of any wormhole contact from them meant that something terrible had happened."

"So was I. But their message indicates that their community is flourishing. There are about 350 of them living on the ring and one of the moons. They had apparently assumed that the wormhole wasn't safe, thinking that your ship and the more recent one must have been destroyed."

"So, both sides are surprised to learn that the other has survived."

"Yes. But that's not all. There are 32 of them who are planning to come through the wormhole. They're preparing a void jumper as we speak and are planning to make the trip within the next few days."

"Are they aware of the threat we are facing here?"

"That's my concern as well," answered Drummond. "We explained our current situation in the message that we sent in the first probe, but perhaps we didn't make it clear enough. I've asked Commander Bree to send another probe immediately, outlining the threat more clearly. We just drafted the message together – that's why I took so long. I wanted to make sure the ringers, as they refer to themselves, are fully aware of the severity of the threat we are facing here. The probe with the new message has probably already been sent."

"Let's hope they pay attention and don't do anything foolish."

As it turned out, it was a forlorn hope.

16

———

The council meeting the next day outlined the message from the Nova ring and Drummond's hastily formulated reply. Although they discussed the issue for nearly an hour, they agreed that nothing further could be done. It was hoped that the ringers would stay where they were for the moment, until the safety of any migrants could be assured. Another hour was spent reviewing their defensive measures, but there had been no further developments in that area. Everything that could be done had already been done, and now it was a waiting game to see whether the EIs would come. Most Councillors were convinced that a confrontation was inevitable. Drummond concluded the meeting by asking that the councillors remain on call in case there were any urgent developments. By lunchtime the meeting was over, and Zac was once again left to mope about the capital. He had turned down Drummond's offer of accommodation on the smaller island, but as the afternoon wore on, he began to regret his decision. A workout in his apartment's gym and some laps of the pool on the floor above helped kill some time, but the evening was tedious. He tried calling Keo after dinner, but there was no answer. Perhaps they were all still outside in the gazebo or having an evening swim at the beach. He opened a bottle of wine and sat at the panoramic window looking at the lights of the city below him, hoping that sleep would eventually come.

He woke the following morning, finding that he had eventually fallen asleep in his chair. He had a stiff neck and a sore back, and he noticed that most of the bottle of wine was gone. He was emerging from the bathroom five minutes later, still rubbing his bleary eyes, when he received a call from Keo.

"Hi bro, how are you doing?" Keo's concerned face looked back at him from the big screen.

"OK. Bored as hell actually."

"I'm sorry I didn't return your call last night. We were at the village green and didn't get back until really late."

Of course. He'd forgotten. It would have been the weekly dinner for all the families on the island. The thought made him even more homesick.

"I want to come back, Keo. Nothing's going to get resolved with me being here."

"I can tell you it won't get resolved if you come back either. She's nowhere near ready to talk to you yet."

"I don't care if she's ready or not. She can't just write off 21 years of marriage after one mistake. She's got to be willing to at least talk to me!"

"Not yet, bro. I think you need to stay where you are. Isn't there something you can do? Somewhere you can go?"

Zac gave a long, slow sigh. "Drummond has offered me the use of a cabin on another island."

"Take it, bro. Go. Do some fishing. Go for walks. Just let

some time slide by and let us deal with Kit for a while. We'll do our best to talk her around."

"Is there a chance, Keo? Honestly, what do you think?"

"I don't know, bro. She's pretty hurt and angry."

Zac just nodded.

They signed off a few minutes later, and Zac wandered around the apartment for another half an hour. He walked to the lift, thinking to go for a walk around the city, but stopped just short of the lift door, realising that he just couldn't face the gawking crowds. He returned to the apartment and called Drummond.

"Zac! Nice to hear from you. What can I do for you?"

"Hello, Gerval. I was just wondering if that offer of the cabin still stood."

"Of course! You're welcome to use it any time. I can have a flitter fly you directly there if you like."

"Thanks. I accept. I'm grateful to you."

"Not at all. It's my pleasure. The kitchen is fully stocked, and there's a vegetable garden that needs harvesting. Plus, the lake is full of fish and we have some excellent fishing gear in the shed."

"That actually sounds just what I need. Thank you."

"When would you like to go?"

"How about now?"

17

NOVA

The message in the second probe from Altaria had the desired effect on most of the prospective ringer migrants, but it didn't dampen the spirits of Harv, Delta and eight others. They met with the town council who attempted to talk them out of their plan, but they remained adamant.

"We're not suggesting that you don't go at all," said Maeve, this year's elected mayor. "We just think it would be prudent to wait and monitor developments there over the next few months. The wormhole has only recently become unlocked, and it is still too early to tell if the EIs are about to invade that system. Why not wait and see what happens?"

"No amount of waiting is ever going to prove that the system will be free from EI invasion," argued Harv. "We could wait six months, or a year, or even ten years, and then finally decide to go, only to have the EIs turn up the next day! Waiting does nothing except waste time when we could be living on a planet."

"That's not exactly true," replied Maeve. "The more time

that elapses without the EIs invading, the less likely that they ever will. Plus, the longer we wait, the better our technology will be in defending ourselves against the EIs. We're working on that all the time. There are a lot of advantages to waiting."

"None that I can see," said Harv. "All those arguments are purely theoretical. The way I see it, it's a choice between living my life paralysed by fear of things that might never happen or stepping out and taking hold of the opportunities that are actually in front of me. I choose the latter."

"Do the rest of you feel that way as well?"

The group nodded, and Delta spoke up.

"We are all adults, and we have the right to choose our own paths. You don't have to agree with our decision, but you certainly can't stop us."

"No one's talking about stopping you," said Maeve. "Of course you have to make your own decisions. We just hoped you would delay your plans for a few months, until the situation becomes clearer."

"We've made our decision and we're not changing our minds," said Harv.

"How do your families feel about this? I guess I'm thinking particularly of the seven of you who are still quite young."

The group consisted of a childless couple, a middle-aged man who had never married and the rest were 5Gs – fifth generation ringers – all in their early 20s.

"Obviously, they have similar concerns," said Delta, "and, Maeve, I know you've been chatting with Mum. Her and Dad considered coming with us when they realised they couldn't talk us out of it, but they've decided to stay, at least until our younger sister is a bit older."

"I see," said Maeve, who seemed disappointed that she'd

failed to at least delay their plans. "If we can't change your minds, then the least we can do is ensure that you are well equipped. Laramie is putting the final touches to the latest model void jumper. It should be ready in about a week. That will give you some more time to prepare, and possibly even reconsider."

"I can assure you, we won't be changing our minds," said Harv.

A week later a farewell party was held in the dining room of Module 8. The whole module had been transformed over the years into a dedicated recreation centre. As the time for the party arrived, ringers began transferring in from all over the ring, and two moon jumpers full of party goers arrived from Little Boy, Nova's smaller moon. Ringers knew how to party, and this one proved to be one of the best in recent years. The departing adventurers were surrounded by friends and family and people who barely knew them. Some of those who had backed out of the plan after the second probe from Altaria now had doubts about whether they had made the right decision. The thought of walking on the surface of a planet with a breathable atmosphere was alluring, and several of them almost changed their minds at the last minute.

However, the next morning there were still only ten who boarded the new, streamlined void jumper. Hugs and tears and final farewells were eventually over and the ten were finally sealed in their ship, ready for launch.

Harv looked over his shoulder at Delta, who was sitting directly behind his pilot seat. She had tears in her eyes and was trying not to lose it completely.

"Are you alright, Del?"

She nodded. "Just got some dust in my eyes."

"Sure," he said. "We're gonna be OK, you know."

"I know."

"Just remember, your big brother is the best damn pilot in the whole solar system. Possibly the universe. What can possibly go wrong, hey?"

"Apart from the fact that you forgot to do your fly up, you mean?" said his co-pilot, Andrea, nodding toward his groin.

"And why would you be looking down there?" he asked as he zipped up the offending part of his flight suit.

"No reason. Just wondering how you manage to fly a spaceship when you don't seem to be able to dress yourself properly."

Harv was saved from having to answer by Laramie announcing that the dome was open and they were clear for launch. Harv decided to prove his prowess by exiting the landing bay at maximum acceleration, adjusting their flight path as he went and rocketing towards their rendezvous with the subspace portal.

"Your security identification code has been uploaded," said Laramie over the comms. "This will identify you to the Altarian security forces at the other end. I suggest you begin transmitting that immediately after you exit the wormhole, so that they know you are not an EI vessel."

"Roger that, Laramie. Thanks for all your help, buddy. This thing flies like a dream."

"I'm glad it meets your requirements, Harv. Good luck to all of you."

Twenty minutes later they were approaching the subspace portal at an impressive velocity. They made contact with Voekler station, transmitting the necessary star frequency for the Altarian system. The automated station issued a confirmation message and initiated the Nicholls Field Generator, opening a wormhole ahead of them, still too far off to see. Harv locked onto the coordinates of the subspace portal and the two pilots began peering through their front window, looking for the tell-tale black circle blocking out the stars.

"Harv, this is Laramie. Do you read me?"

"Roger Laramie. Go ahead."

"I'm picking up some asteroid debris in the vicinity of the portal. It looks to be very small and scattered, but at your velocity it could cause serious damage to your ship. I suggest you activate the STAR drive immediately, as this will create a protective energy field ahead of you. I repeat, activate the STAR drive immediately. Don't wait until you have reached the threshold."

"Roger that. We'll ..."

There was a loud crash as something impacted the outside of their spacecraft.

"Activate the STAR drive now!" shouted Harv.

Andrea activated the drive and their ship was immediately cocooned in a ball of blue light.

"Are we damaged anywhere?" asked Harv. "How is cabin pressure holding up?"

"Cabin pressure is dropping!" said Andrea. "We've been holed somewhere! Although I can't hear anything, so it must be a very small hole." She turned around and addressed the eight people in the cabin. Guys, see if you can see or hear where the hole is!"

The eight passengers clambered out of their seats and began searching the sides of the void jumper.

"Harv, should we turn back?" asked Andrea.

"I don't know. You tell me. It would take us almost an hour

to cancel our velocity and get back to the ring. Will cabin pressure hold up that long?"

"No way! We've already lost ten percent."

"Any luck back there, guys?" yelled Harv.

"We can hear a slight hissing somewhere, but it's impossible to locate."

"Get your helmets on and activate your suit breathers, all of you!" said Harv. "Andrea, put yours on then put mine on for me. I've got my hands full at the moment."

As the others started donning their helmets, Harv tried contacting Laramie.

"Laramie, do you read me?"

There was no response.

"Laramie, are you there?"

Nothing.

Andrea attached Harv's helmet, and he activated his suit oxygen.

"Um ... Harv?" said Andrea through his suit comm.

"Yeh?"

"If that means what I think it means, and our external comms are down, how are we gonna broadcast the security code at the other end?"

"That's a good question, but we don't have any choice except to go through, because we won't have enough air to get back to the ring. These flight suits only have enough oxygen for 30 minutes. For better or worse, we're committed."

A moment later they burst through a shimmering wall of light and were immersed in a swirling tunnel of green.

18

ALTARIA

Zac dived into the cool water again and set out for the far shore. The lake was oval in shape, about 800 metres long and 500 metres wide. On his second morning he had decided to try to get himself back into shape. He had swum across the width of the lake, and back again, and it had almost killed him. Today, on the sixth morning, he was attempting the length of the lake. He had made it to the far end and had a five-minute rest on the sandy bank, now he was attempting the return leg. *Just another 800 metres. I can do this!*

He almost made it. 200 metres from the end he started to cramp up in the legs, and knew he had to turn in to the shore on the closest side. He had deliberately swum close to one shore in case this happened. He found his footing in the shallows and limped up to the sandy beach and sat down, massaging his weary muscles.

Half an hour later he was sitting on the small verandah of the cabin, drinking a cup of juvo when a flitter landed on the grassy bank that led down to the lake. To his surprise, Keo emerged followed by Dayna. They were both carrying some kind of packs, which they dumped on the verandah, as the flitter took off again. There were hugs all round and Zac was nonplussed.

"What are you guys doing here?"

"We came for a visit. We thought you could use some cheering up."

"What's all the gear for?"

"We thought we'd stay overnight. If that's OK with you?"

"Definitely! Absolutely! I'm just about going out of my brain with boredom here. Sit down and I'll make you a cup of juvo."

Shortly afterward, they were sitting together on some rickety wooden chairs, drinking juvo and watching the local birds swoop down for their morning bath in the shallows of the lake's edge.

"How is she?" asked Zac after only a few moments.

"We'll get to that in a moment," said Keo. "But firstly, how are you? I mean, how are you really?"

Zac glanced at Dayna.

"You can talk freely, Dad. I'm a big girl now."

Zac nodded.

"Honestly? I feel depressed and miserable. I feel sick and lost and alone. I feel guilty and dirty and morally weak. And I'm not sure how I can go on like this for much longer. How's that for feelings?"

"Uh, huh. That's understandable, bro. I'd probably be feeling the same way in your shoes."

"So, how is she?"

"Tash and I have tried talking with Kit. She's very hurt and very angry. And I'll be honest with you, she's saying it's over. She says she doesn't want you back. "

Zac's eyes immediately filled with tears and overflowed.

Keo continued, "I thought time would help, and maybe it will eventually, but I can't see it being a quick thing. I thought that maybe a week or two would be enough for her to cool down a bit and be willing to talk, but I can see now that she really has made her mind up. At least for now."

Zac merely nodded, as more tears flowed.

"I don't think it's serving any purpose - you being out here all by yourself. It's certainly not doing you any good. So, we've come to bring you home. We thought we'd spend the night here with you and take you back home tomorrow. The flitter will pick us up after breakfast."

"OK. I've certainly had enough of living on my own. I can only take so much of my own company."

"That's why we're here, bro."

"So where will I live?"

Keo and Dayna looked at each other.

"I'm going to move in with Mum. You can take my bungalow."

"I thought Jaz wanted to be by herself? Will she be happy about that?"

"Probably not. But I'm not giving her a choice. After the way she's acted, I don't care what she thinks. I'm moving in whether she likes it or not."

"It wasn't all her fault, Dayna."

"I know. But I'm laying ninety percent of the blame on her doorstep. She took advantage of you when you were drunk. I saw you towards the end of the party, Dad. You were having trouble walking a straight line. Mum saw it too, and she decided to ambush you. I'm disgusted with her, quite frankly."

"What a mess. I've made a mess of everything," said Zac.

"Not a total mess," Dayna said, reaching out and touching his arm. "You've still got me, and Keo and the rest of us. We're here for you, and we're not going anywhere."

"That's right, bro," said Keo. "And for the rest of today and tonight we're in charge. We're the official, 'Cheer Up Zac' committee, and we have a stringent program of restorative activities planned."

"We do?" asked Dayna.

"Yep," said Keo. "Just as soon as I think of them. I might need another cup of juvo first though."

The day did prove to be restorative for Zac. Nothing could diminish the pain that he felt over the loss of Kit, yet gradually, as they fished and swam and walked through the hills together, he felt the cloud of darkness that had enveloped him for over a week lift a little, and he experienced the first glimmer of hope that he might be able to salvage something from the wreckage of his life.

For dinner they barbequed freshly caught fish, and Dayna harvested some vegetables from the garden which she cooked over an open fire. Afterward, they sat around the fire, sharing a bottle of wine and talking until the moon rose over the lake and the stars had traversed half the sky.

Zac woke the next morning feeling as though he had slept deeply. Keo had mugs of juvo ready for him and Dayna by the time they came back from a morning swim, and the three sat contentedly together sipping their hot drinks as the early morning sun dissolved the last of the mist.

"When are we leaving?" asked Zac.

"I asked the flitter to pick us up close to lunchtime," said Keo.

"Really? Well who's that?" said Zac, pointing over the lake.

A flitter could be heard approaching from the south, and within a minute it landed on the grassy lawn. The door opened and two security officers jumped out and ran up the slope.

"Dr Perryman? We're sorry to intrude, sir. Councillor Drummond sent us to pick you up. You're needed on Gateway station, urgently. There's been a development."

"What sort of development?"

"Sorry, that's all we know. You really need to come with us immediately, sir."

Keo said, "You go Zac. We'll tidy up here and head home when our flitter arrives."

"OK. Thanks guys," said Zac.

"And make sure you come back home when the crisis is over," said Dayna.

"I will."

"You'd better. I want my dad back," she said as she gave him a kiss on the cheek.

19

———

Councillor Drummond was waiting for him as soon as he came out of the docking tube at Gateway Station. He had arrived on a super-fast shuttle from Terminus 8, the geosynchronous terminal orbiting above A1.

"Thanks for coming so promptly, Zac. I'm sorry to drag you away from your retreat, but this couldn't wait, unfortunately."

"What's happened?"

"There's been a disaster. A terrible tragedy. It's best explained if I take you to the control room. Commander Bree is waiting there to brief you."

A few moments later, they stepped out of an elevator into the impressive control room. A huge screen took up the entire front wall, showing different views of surrounding space. Commander Bree was deep in discussion with a senior officer but broke off immediately when she saw Zac.

"Welcome back, Zac," she said. "I wish it was under more pleasant circumstances."

"Good to see you again, Starla. What's happened?"

"Approximately two hours ago, a wormhole opened briefly, and a void jumper appeared. It was a new, sleek design. The ship just sat there and didn't communicate. General Kellar was on board one of the two cloaked battle cruisers at the time, and they instantly went to battle ready. We tried hailing the ship using our new frequency modulation transmission which is incapable of being used by the EIs to infiltrate our systems. There was no response and they didn't transmit the security code. Kellar gave them a 30 second warning, saying that if they didn't transmit the security code within that time, they would be destroyed. I contacted Kellar and told him to stand down, as I believed the ship was from the Nova ring. Nova had sent a probe through yesterday saying that a ship would be coming through today. I suspected that they were experiencing some kind of communication problem. Kellar refused to listen."

"What happened?" asked Zac, with a sick feeling in his stomach.

"Kellar blew the ship to pieces."

"No!" exclaimed Zac.

"Here is the video of the incident," she said, bringing an image up onto the screen.

The video started with the shimmering threshold of a wormhole appearing where, a moment before, there had been empty space. A ship suddenly emerged from the mouth of the wormhole and, a few moments later, the wormhole closed. The ship was a gleaming black tear-drop shape, like nothing Zac had seen before. The video rolled on, with Zac hearing the voice of the Gateway comm officer asking it to identify itself. Kellar's voice could then be heard demanding that it give the required security code. Then Zac heard Starla's urgent pleas.

"General Kellar. This is Commander Bree. We believe this

ship is the expected vessel from the Icarus system. Please stand down. I repeat, please stand down."

"You don't have authority to order me to stand down. I've been charged with the defence of our world, and I will carry out my duty as I see fit."

Kellar could then be heard issuing a final warning.

"Unidentified vessel. You have 30 seconds to identify yourself or you will be destroyed."

"General Kellar!" said Starla's voice. "Do not destroy that ship! There are innocent people on board! General Kellar, do you copy? Stand down!"

There was a moment's silence and then two simultaneous beams of blinding light struck the vessel from different angles, obviously from the two battle cruisers. The ship exploded in a massive fireball that was too bright and too fast for the exposure dampeners on Gateway Station's cameras. The screen went completely white for a second and then the exposure adjusted, showing a debris field that was expanding outwards at extreme velocity.

Zac stared at the video screen with horror. Thousands of tiny pieces of debris glittered and sparkled as they mushroomed outward. It would have looked spectacularly beautiful if it wasn't for the fact that it represented the senseless deaths of innocent people.

Zac shook his head. "It's sickening."

"Yes," agreed Drummond. "As I said, it's a terrible tragedy."

"Why didn't the ship respond?"

"I can only guess that they were experiencing some kind of technical problem," answered Starla. "Perhaps they had experienced some kind of damage en route."

"Apart from the human tragedy of the incident," said Drummond, "it is also going to be a diplomatic nightmare."

"You haven't contacted Nova since the incident?" asked Zac.

"No. It's why we needed you here. We thought you would be the best person to convey the bad news. Given the severity of the issue, a video message will need to be recorded and sent. Obviously, it will be much better coming from someone who looks like them, than from one of us. I'm sorry to dump this on you, Zac, but we really need your help on this."

"Sure. I'll do what I can." He looked up at the screen again. The video had paused, with an image of the glittering debris field frozen on the screen. "What's happened with Kellar?"

"General Kellar has been relieved of all duties and is currently under arrest here on Gateway Station," said Drummond. "A preliminary interview is due to take place shortly, which will end with him being given formal notice of our intention to proceed with a court martial enquiry. The preliminary hearing requires that two council members and a Federation officer be present, so we will need you to take part, along with Commander Bree and myself."

"I can't say that I'll enjoy that, but I'll do what is required."

"Thanks, Zac."

The preliminary interview took place in the conference room. Zac, Starla and Drummond sat on one side of the conference table, and General Kellar sat on the other side with his legal counsel.

"General Kellar," began Drummond, "the purpose of this interview is to determine whether you have acted outside the scope of your authority or breeched operational guidelines. If there is sufficient evidence that you have acted inappropriately, we will be issuing you with a notice of intent to proceed to court martial. This interview is being recorded and anything you say can be used in any future court martial proceedings. Are you clear about the nature of this interview or is there anything you would like to say at this point?"

Kellar just sat there, glaring menacingly at Drummond, not saying a word.

"Very well. We have the video footage of the incident in question, which we will play now."

The video unfolded inexorably towards the same dreadful conclusion, after which Drummond addressed Kellar again.

"General Kellar, do you acknowledge that you were advised on two separate occasions by Commander Bree that the newly-arrived vessel was probably a void jumper from the Icarus system?"

"Of course I do! I'm not deaf! I heard her concerns."

"Do you also acknowledge that Commander Bree urged you to stand down on two occasions?"

"She had no authority to demand that I stand down! Look at my uniform, Drummond. I'm a general! Bree is a commander. Last time I checked; generals outrank commanders."

"But as the head of our defence force, you are obliged to consider all intel that may be relevant to any developing situation. Commander Bree was providing you with important information that identified the vessel in question as potentially friendly – information which you chose to ignore."

"You're damn right I did!"

"Would you care to explain your reasons?"

"I don't believe the ship was from the Icarus system. I think it was an EI vessel."

"You still think that?"

"You're damn right I do!"

"On what basis did you reach that conclusion?"

"They didn't give the security code. Any vessel from the Icarus system would have immediately broadcast the code."

"Unless they were experiencing some kind of technical difficulty," said Drummond.

"If you're going to make that assumption every time a ship fails to give the code, what's the point of using security codes at all! We may as well not use them!"

"So that was the sole basis of your decision to destroy the vessel; that it didn't give the code?"

"No. My gut instinct told me something wasn't right. The ship didn't look human in origin. The whole thing felt wrong."

"So, you destroyed a vessel, and possibly killed dozens of innocent people, based on your gut instinct?"

"Listen to me Drummond," said Kellar aggressively. "I followed operational protocol. Once a ship does not broadcast the security code, I am commissioned to act in the defence of our world. You pay me to make the tough decisions. While the rest of you sit in your cushy offices, second-guessing yourselves, my job is to make split second decisions. And, yes, dammit, my gut instinct plays a role in that! I stand by my decision, and one day you'll be thankful that people like me have the guts to push the button when it's necessary!"

"Did the canary satellite system give an alarm?" asked Zac. "Isn't that supposed to raise the alarm if it detects an attempt by EIs to infiltrate our systems?"

"There was no alarm from the canary satellites," admitted Kellar.

Starla added, "We activated one of the canaries as soon as the vessel arrived. It did a scan, but no alarm went off."

"General Kellar, I think we've heard enough," said Drummond. "On the basis of your testimony in this interview ..."

He didn't get any further. An alarm sounded, and Commander Bree jumped to her feet.

"That's the wormhole alarm! Another wormhole has been activated!" She sprinted out the door into the adjoining control room, followed closely by everyone else in the room.

20

Zac arrived in the control room in time to see a ship suddenly emerge from the wormhole, which then closed a few moments later. It had some similarities to the void jumper that Jaz and the others had arrived in, but it was even more streamlined; clearly an updated model.

"It's broadcasting the correct security code!" announced the comms officer.

"Are you certain?" asked Commander Bree.

"Yes, ma'am. It's the code we gave to the Novans."

"Open a secure FM channel."

The comms officer touched the screen on his desk. "Channel is open, ma'am."

Starla switched to Terran. "This is Commander Starla Bree, of Gateway Station. Please identify yourself."

"Boy, are we glad to hear your voice!" replied a young-sounding male. "We weren't sure our comms were still operational. My name is Harv Walden, pilot of the void jumper. There are ten of us on board, from the ring around Nova."

"Stand by Mr Walden. We need to scan you prior to opening full digital engagement with you." Starla muted her comm and turned to another officer. "Initiate the scan by the canary satellite."

The scan took only a few moments and then they waited while the satellite processed the data.

"No alarms have been triggered, ma'am. It looks like they're clean."

Starla nodded and opened her comm channel again. "Thank you for your patience. We have scanned your vessel and confirm that there is no EI presence on board. We will synch with your vessel now and take control."

"OK. But can you hurry up and get us docked somewhere. We've sprung a leak and we've had to wear our ship suits. We've only got about 25 minutes of air left."

"Roger that. We'll have you docked and safely off your vessel within ten minutes."

"Sounds good. Although I can't see where that will be. There's nothing on our scanners in the immediate vicinity."

"We'll decloak now, and you shouldn't have too much trouble spotting us," said Starla.

A moment later, Harv could be heard saying, "Holy crap! That's impressive!"

While Starla's first officer took charge of the void jumper and oversaw the docking procedure, Starla turned her attention back to the others from the conference room.

"Well this certainly throws a new light on our previous discussion," she said.

"You're damn right it does!" said General Kellar.

"If the vessel you destroyed wasn't from Nova, where was it from?" asked Drummond, clearly perplexed.

"I keep telling you – it was an EI ship! I'm convinced of it!"

"But how do we know it wasn't humans from some other star system; people who didn't know our security code?" asked Drummond.

As if in answer to his question, an officer on the control room spoke up.

"Excuse me, ma'am. I've got something here that might be relevant."

"Go ahead," said Starla.

"I've been going over the scan log from the satellite that scanned the first vessel. It actually did find something, but it wasn't enough to trigger the alarm. The scan began to show a branch of coding that led to what appeared to be a huge reservoir of unidentified programming. The scan only picked up the opening phrase of the gateway coding before the whole thing just disappeared. Like a branch of a tree that was cut off. It was there one moment and completely gone the next."

"What are you saying?" asked Starla.

"It looks as if there was an EI on board that sensed our scan and hid itself."

"So, it was an EI vessel after all?" said Councillor Drummond. "General Kellar, I apologise for ..."

"Dammit Drummond!" interrupted Kellar. "You've just wasted several hours of my time with this ludicrous witch hunt of yours! In future, why don't you stick to doing your job, and let me do mine!" He turned and walked out of the control room, saying "I'm going back to my ship."

After he left, Zac raised the issue of the failed scan.

"Obviously the EIs sensed the scan and somehow hid their coding. We're going to need to update the scanning protocol on the canaries."

"Agreed," said Starla. "What do you suggest?"

"The alarm needs to be triggered if the scan discovers any missing or deleted coding, or any obvious dead ends."

"Can you make that happen, Jyle?" she asked the officer who had examined the log.

"Yes, ma'am. Easily."

"Make it so. Immediately. And send a message to General Kellar telling him what you've done. Let him know that the alarm should be triggered next time."

"Will there be a next time?" asked Zac.

"Almost certainly," answered Drummond. "I think this has only just started."

As promised, the ten newcomers were safely on board the station within a matter of minutes. After undergoing decontamination, they were gathered in a waiting room when Zac walked in.

"Welcome to Gateway Station," he said. "My name is Zac Perryman, a member of the Federation Council."

"You're famous, dude!" said Harv, enthusiastically.

"Not really," said Zac. "Just lucky to have survived. But if I'm not mistaken, you must be related to Harvey Walden."

"Yeh. He was my great-great-great-grandfather. He was the first Mayor of Ringtown."

"I knew him. He was a good man," said Zac.

"That's insane! He died over a century ago."

"Tell me about it!" admitted Zac. "Now, could you introduce me to everyone else?"

Zac was introduced to Harv's sister, Delta, his co-pilot,

Andrea, and the others, including the middle-aged married couple and the single man, Heinz, who appeared to be a similar age to Zac.

Zac said to Harv, "You mentioned that you were worried that your comms might not work. I assume that's related to the hole in your vessel."

"Yeh. Totally. After we were hit by the asteroid debris, we weren't able to contact Laramie. I thought the impact had taken out our comms. But now I realise that we'd immediately activated our STAR drive to protect us from further impact, and it was probably the STAR drive that was blocking all incoming and outgoing transmissions."

"Well, it's just as well your comms were working," said Zac, "otherwise you wouldn't be standing here now."

"That sounds ominous," said Delta.

"I need to update you on developments earlier today," said Zac. "There's a lot to fill you in on, including some info about the Altarians themselves. But first, let's move to a more comfortable living room."

21

———

Zac had hitched a ride on a neighbour's skippa. He was standing in the bow as the sailing boat screamed across the water in the strong wind, healing over as it sliced through the chop. The wind was whipping his hair wildly and salt spray had drenched him, but he didn't mind. It felt good to be coming home.

They docked at the marina, and his neighbours offered to drive him home in their sand buggy, but he declined. He wanted to walk. He set off down the track, carrying a backpack with his meagre possessions, and with each kilometre his anxiety grew. He felt like he was marching to his own execution. He'd been found guilty, his sentence had been passed, and now it was about to be carried out. Banishment. The end of his marriage. Having to live like a stranger alongside the woman he loved. And, of course, there would be her coldness towards him; her hurt and anger, expressing itself in subtle ways every day. He didn't know how he was going to cope, but he knew he had to, for Dayna's sake. *I may have lost my wife, but I'm deter-*

mined not to lose my daughter. He squared his shoulders and walked on.

In the end, his arrival was an anti-climax. Tash and Kit had gone to visit Razna, their nearest neighbour, with whom they were spending the day preserving fruit. Dayna had gone fishing with Noah, and most of the others were doing things around the property. Keo spotted him as he walked into their compound and greeted him with a slap on the back. They dumped his few possessions into Bungalow 4, where he would be staying, then Keo enlisted Zac's help in doing some maintenance on fences in the yard where they kept pregnant kordu that were about to give birth. It was good to do some physical work for a change, and as the two friends worked together, they fell easily back into their familiar camaraderie.

"Pass me the blue handled thing, bro," said Keo.

"They're called tensioners, dude."

"I know that. I was just testing you."

"Sure you were. And what's this thing called?" asked Zac, holding up another strange looking tool.

"Its ... a thing for ... twisting other things."

"Your technical jargon is impressive, Keo."

"It's not what they're called that matters, bro, it's how you use them that counts."

"Well this *torsion adjuster* looks like you've been using it as a hammer, dude."

"Yes ... well ... a good workman shouldn't be constricted by the narrow conventions that toolmakers attempt to impose upon him."

They worked happily together until the sun was low in the sky, and finally Keo suggested that they call it a day.

"No. I think we can do a bit more before we go back," said Zac.

Keo shook his head. "You've gotta face the music sometime, bro. May as well get it over with. You can't put off seeing her forever."

They walked back towards the compound, with Zac's heart pounding and his feet feeling as heavy as lead. Almost everyone was gathered in the gazebo, putting the final touches on dinner preparations. Zac was welcomed warmly by most of them. Kit, however, refused to look at him or acknowledge his presence. Jaz also seemed wary of displaying too much affection in front of the others, and merely offered him the briefest of smiles.

They all sat down to dinner and it was clear that people were making an effort to make Zac feel at home again. They filled him in on developments around the property and asked his opinion about decisions that needed to be made. Kit had positioned herself as far away from Zac as possible, and continued to ignore his presence, sometimes even changing the topic in an effort to exclude him from the group conversation.

Towards the end of the meal, Karl asked the question that many of them had been thinking.

"What's going to happen with the new arrivals? Where will they live?"

"Well, that's really up to us," said Zac. "The council views them as refugees and is willing to build homes for them anywhere they like. They could certainly come and live here with us, as long as we think there's room."

"Where would they go if we don't think there's room?" asked Tash.

"I'm not sure. Somewhere that they would choose in consultation with the council, I guess."

"But there's plenty of room here, isn't there?" said Dayna, who had placed herself alongside her father at the table.

"We can make room, for sure," said Keo. "I think our property could support another 30 people, at least!"

"Yes. I think it could too," said Zac. "But at some stage we're going to have to draw the line. There are another 330 people on the ring, and we can probably expect more of them to arrive in the future."

"Well, that's a problem for another day, I guess," said Mel, who had seated herself on the other side of Zac to show her own support. "I agree with Zac and Keo that we could easily absorb these people into our community."

"Does anyone have any serious objections?" Zac asked. He looked around the table. "No? Ok. I'll let Councillor Drummond know. I expect that the construction team will arrive within a couple of days. Things will probably be a bit crazy again for a few weeks."

Dinner concluded soon after, and people began clearing up. Zac picked up some serving plates that he recognised from his and Kit's bungalow and carried them there. He was about to go inside when Kit stopped him at the door with a 'stop' hand gesture. She took the plates from him and looked him in the eye for the first time all evening.

"I never want you in this house again."

She turned and left him standing on the doorstep devastated.

Dayna was walking past, having taken some dishes back to Tash and Keo's bungalow, and overheard Kit's remark. She shook her head and her mouth firmed into a grim line, revealing that she was clearly displeased with Kit's reaction.

"Come on, Dad. I need you to help me move my stuff into Mum's place."

As they walked along the path to the new bungalows, she tried to brighten the mood with chatter about her fishing exploits that afternoon.

"How's things with Noah?" he asked.

"Good."

"Just good?"

"Ok, sticky beak – really good."

"I'm happy for you Dayna. I hope you two will be as happy as ... well ... as we were."

"Don't give up hope, Dad."

"It's a bit hard not to."

They arrived at her bungalow and she began rushing around gathering up her stuff which was strewn all over the house.

"I think we need to call the police," said Zac. "There's obviously been a break-in and the robbers have trashed your house."

"Sorry! I didn't know you were coming back today, otherwise I would have tidied up. It's a bit of a mess."

"Really? I hardly noticed."

They carried her few possessions and clothes into the next bungalow, and Zac left her there to return to his own. He was about to open his front door when Jaz stepped from the shadows.

"Zac. A word, if I can."

He remained silent.

"I just wanted to say welcome home."

"OK. Thanks."

"I missed you." When he didn't say anything, she continued. "I'm sorry about the trouble I've caused between you and Kit."

"Really? I find that hard to believe. I think you're probably secretly glad."

"That's not fair, Zac. I never intended to break up your marriage. I was willing to work in with it."

Zac just shook his head and turned towards his front door, not trusting himself to speak. As he opened the door, she made one final comment.

"I love you, Zac. And my offer still stands. I want us to be together."

He closed the door without saying a word.

22

———

Construction began two days later. Six new bungalows were being constructed for the ten newcomers, allowing some flexibility in sleeping arrangements. One bungalow was being added to the row of four along the beachfront, the new one being called Bungalow 5 and was situated beyond Jaz and Dayna's. The remaining five were positioned in a parallel line about 50 metres inland from the beach bungalows, and these were being called 'garden bungalows.'

The new residents all arrived on the sixth day of the build with each of them erecting their own two-person tent which would provide temporary shelter until construction of their permanent homes was completed. Their arrival was celebrated with a barbeque at the marina that night, where they were able to meet the other islanders and start to form friendships with their Terran counterparts. Zac noted that the young arrivals, who referred to themselves as 5Gs – fifth generation ringers – were brimming with enthusiasm and confidence. Kia had immediately latched onto Harv who seemed flattered with the attention and was doing all he could to return it. Delta had attached herself to the broad-shouldered Rajesh, her vibrant personality a strong contrast to Raj's quiet, calm nature. Zac wasn't sure whether they were a good match, but they certainly seemed to be getting along well for the moment. The wine flowed and the mood was definitely one of celebration.

But Zac was finding it difficult to join in the festivities. Earlier that afternoon he had noticed that Kit was no longer wearing her wedding ring. He wasn't sure whether it was just chance, but it seemed that the ring's removal had coincided with the attention she was starting to receive from Heinz, one of the newcomers. He had been hanging around Kit all day and now he was plying her with wine. It seemed to Zac that Kit was laughing a little too much, as if she was deliberately trying to provoke him, and, on several occasions, he caught her stealing guarded glances at him, as if she was checking to see whether he was noticing. As the evening wore on, she and Heinz were increasingly making casual hand contact with each other and obviously flirting. Eventually, Zac decided he couldn't stay to watch it anymore, so he excused himself from the party and walked home. He heard the sand buggies arrive home in the middle of the night as he lay in bed trying to sleep, and thought he heard Kit's laughter several times in response to Heinz's distinctive voice.

The next morning as the work continued on the bungalows, Zac saw Heinz carrying building materials from a heavy-lift flitter that had just landed on the beach. As Heinz dumped them on the ground at the site of Bungalow 6, the one closest to the compound and within view of the original bungalows, Zac cornered him.

"Heinz, can we have a chat for a moment."

Heinz was sweating profusely, his shirt removed, revealing a once muscular body that had turned to flab. He was a big man with a sizeable gut and was clearly out of shape. He stopped in front of Zac, breathing hard, and wiped the sweat from his forehead. He gave Zac a determined look.

"You want to talk about Kit, right?"

"Yes, I do. She's my wife."

"That's not what she says. She tells me it's over between you two."

"It's not over as far as I'm concerned. We just need time to sort things out. And you're not helping."

"It takes two to have a relationship, pal. And Kit's adamant that she's signed out. Besides, I'm not forcing her to spend time with me – she's doing that of her own free will."

"Don't blame her! You've been sniffing around her since the moment you got here!"

"So? A man is allowed to talk to an attractive woman if he likes."

"Not if she's someone else's wife!"

"Zac, we're going around in circles here. Kit tells me it's over, and everything I've seen so far confirms that. You can't stop your ex-wife from seeing other men." He reached out and put his hand on Zac's shoulder in a patronising manner. "Look, I understand how difficult it must be for you. But you've got to move on."

"Get your hand off me!" Zac said, forcing his arm away violently. He stepped forward and stood in front of Heinz menacingly. "You touch my wife again, and I'll do more than just speak to you!"

Heinz just stared at him with a steely glare, refusing to take a backward step. "Really? Well that would be interesting, wouldn't it?"

"Zac? Let's walk, bro," said Keo coming up to the pair who were almost standing chest to chest. Zac looked around and noticed that everyone had stopped work and was staring at him. Looking down the path towards the original bungalows he saw Kit standing there, and as their eyes briefly met, she turned and walked off.

"Come on, bro. You don't want to do this. It's not helping."

Keo placed his arm around Zac's shoulder and turned him down the path towards the beach. They walked together in silence until they reached the beach.

"I may not have handled that as well as I'd hoped," said Zac, grimacing.

"Probably not."

"And you're probably going to tell me that causing a scene like that is only going to hurt my chances with Kit."

"I don't need to; you've just said it."

"I've got a feeling Kit's doing this just to hurt me."

"It's possible," agreed Keo.

"So, what am I supposed to do? Have you got any wise words of advice for me, Keo?"

"Not really, bro. This is uncharted waters for me. But one thing I know for sure is that you'll never win Kit back by arguing with either her or Heinz. You don't own her. Any proprietorial behaviour from you is likely to drive her further away."

Zac nodded. "Yeh. You're probably right."

"Richard Bach once said, 'If you love someone, set them free. If they come back, they are yours. If they don't, they never were'. The only thing you can do is let her go and hope that she comes back to you when she's ready."

They stood for a few more moments looking at the file of people who were unloading materials from the heavy-duty flitter.

"Come on, bro," said Keo, slapping Zac's back. "Let's get this gear unloaded."

They walked down to the flitter and started hauling materials.

23

———

Two days later, Zac got a lift back to AI with a flitter that was returning to the capital. Drummond had called another meeting. Zac was a little early for the meeting, so he decided to take a walk through the streets surrounding Federal Square. Ignoring the stares of the taller Altarians, he found his way to the side street where he had purchased their wedding rings and, on impulse, he stepped inside.

"Mr Zac! Mr Zac! How nice to see you," said the elderly craftsman. "What can I do for you? Perhaps a special gift for your lovely wife?"

"Hello Zareb. No, not really. I was just passing and thought I'd have a look around."

"You wait there. I have something very special. It arrived only yesterday. Just wait."

He disappeared into the back room and Zac was left browsing the jewellery in the display cabinets. A minute later, Zareb emerged with a small black box which he placed on the counter.

"This is extremely rare. A blue cronium – mined from deep underground on Jasper, our larger moon."

He opened the box and lifted out a beautiful gold necklace with a blue stone set in a gold pendant. The stone was stunning; a deep blue with flecks of gold and deep red, sparkling as if it shone with its own internal fire.

"It's incredibly rare. Only six of these stones have ever been found. The heart shape is entirely natural. We wouldn't dare shape or trim such a precious stone."

Zac was mesmerised. He held it up to the light and saw how it shone and sparkled.

"How much?"

Zareb named his price and Zac whistled.

"I'll tell you what I'll do for you, though. I will sell it to you on a payment plan. You can pay it off over two years. No interest."

Zac continued to admire the necklace, thinking how beautiful it would look on Kit.

"It would look beautiful on your wife," said Zareb, as if reading his mind.

"Yes. It would."

He turned the pendant over and noted the solid gold back.

"Could you engrave something on the back?"

"Certainly, Mr Zac! Anything you want."

Zac stood there pondering. This was probably a foolish gesture. He had probably lost Kit already, and he would be just placing himself in debt for no reason. But he had to do this. He had to try to show her how much she meant to him. He placed the necklace back in its box and nodded to the jeweller.

"OK. Here's what I want you to engrave ..."

An hour later he was seated at the conference table, and Drummond brought the meeting to order.

"Councillors, there has been a further development at Gateway Station. The simplest thing will be to show you the video recording from the control room on the station itself."

He nodded to an assistant, who dimmed the lights and an entire wall lit up with an image. They were viewing the Gateway Station control room from the vantage point of high up on the back wall. They could see the control room staff at their various consoles and, beyond them, the huge screen on the front wall, showing a view of empty space. Suddenly, an alarm began sounding and a circle of stars in the front image disappeared, leaving a faint shimmering surface in their place. Commander Bree came running into the control room a moment later.

"Status?" she asked.

"Wormhole, ma'am," said her first officer.

As he spoke, a ship winked into existence on the screen. It was a black, shiny tear drop, sleek and strangely menacing. The wormhole closed down, leaving the spaceship suspended against the sparkling backdrop of stars.

"No security code, ma'am," said her comms officer.

"What's the status of the canary satellite?" she asked another officer.

"It's completing its sweep now, ma'am." She touched her screen and made some adjustments, and then frowned. "The sweep has been blocked. The ship has some kind of shield activated."

"Incoming tight beam transmission from General Kellar, ma'am," said her comms officer.

Kellar's face appeared in a secondary area of the front screen.

"Commander Bree. Our sensors are indicating a defensive shield around the EI vessel. I'm activating one of the EMP bombs in thirty seconds. Initiate emergency shut-down procedures."

"Roger that," replied Starla.

To her comms officer she said, "Issue the ten second warning, then activate shut-down."

A recorded message could be heard echoing through the nearby speakers, giving a ten second warning. It counted down and, when it reached zero, the entire control room was thrown into darkness. The front screen, however, remained operational, as did the camera making the recording. *They must be on some kind of protected, isolated circuit*, thought Zac.

The EI ship seemed to now hang suspended in the middle of the control room. Seconds ticked by with nothing happening. Suddenly a massive explosion took place to the side of the ship, creating a sizzling, spherical event horizon that quickly passed through the ship and beyond. A pink and green glowing field briefly lit up around the ship and then seemed to break up and disappear. A moment later twin laser beams, as bright as lightning, struck the vessel as the two cruisers on duty opened fire. The ship glowed momentarily and then exploded in a stunning fireball, reducing the vessel to hundreds of thousands of tiny, sparkling shards which raced outward in a violently beautiful sphere. The video froze at that point, and the conference room lights came back up. All eyes turned back to Drummond.

"As you can see, our protocol was followed perfectly and our defensive measures were effective. The EI vessel was destroyed and no infestation occurred. All systems on Gateway Station were successfully restored and there was no damage from the EMP bomb. But the incident leaves us with two concerns."

He looked around the table, noting several who were nodding in agreement.

"Firstly, it is clear that the EIs haven't given up. This is their second attempt to infiltrate our world and we can now almost guarantee that they are going to keep coming. I'm afraid our battle is only just beginning."

There were sombre faces all around the conference table.

"Secondly, it is also apparent that the EIs are adapting. The first vessel had no defensive shield and we were able to scan it. This latest vessel had learnt from that first experience, and had its shield activated from the moment it arrived."

"But how could they know what had happened to the first one?" asked someone. "The wormhole wasn't open when the first one was destroyed, so there can't have been any communication happening."

"That's a very interesting question," said Drummond. "Over the last few hours our scientists have been scanning back through the recordings of echyon emissions at the time of both ships' appearances, and they have found something rather disturbing. A new frequency of echyon emissions commenced the moment each ship appeared and continued until each was destroyed. Our scientists have concluded that the EIs have developed the technology to communicate through subspace."

"What does that mean, exactly?" asked someone.

"It means that they can communicate instantaneously across the galaxy."

There was stunned silence.

"So other EIs already know what has happened to this latest ship?"

"Yes," agreed Drummond. "And we have to assume that they are already making plans to modify their ships to counteract our EMP bombs, if that is possible. And if the next ship can't be disabled with an EMP bomb, we won't be able to destroy it."

Several councillors swore loudly, and the expressions of concern deepened.

"So, what's our next step?" asked someone.

Drummond spread his arms. "I'm open to suggestions."

"Dr Spooner," said Zac. "How close are we to a workable disruptor field – something that will interfere with the subspace portal so that it can't be activated from somewhere else?"

"Very close. I think another month should do it."

"How long was there between the first and second EI ship," asked someone.

"16 days," said Drummond.

"Can you fast-track your research?" asked someone.

"Perhaps we could be ready in three weeks, maybe even less, if we work night and day."

"Do it!" said Drummond. "We'll give you every resource you need. Triple your team. Quadruple your budget. Whatever it takes. Because, I'll be honest with you, I don't think we're going to be able to stop the next ship that comes through that portal."

24

Zac returned home, deeply worried. Subsequent discussions with Drummond and Spooner, in Drummond's private office, had only strengthened those worries. Both men could not see how the Federation could continue to repel the EI ships indefinitely. Their only hope lay in stopping the vessels from reaching the Altarian system in the first place.

"What about the genetic research into blocking the EIs' access to our brains?" Zac had asked.

Spooner had responded that they were making progress in that direction too and hinted that he was planning to talk to Zac about their findings in the very near future. He wouldn't say more, and his enigmatic comments had left Zac puzzled.

Now, as Zac returned to their blossoming Terran village in the late afternoon, he wondered how much longer their idyllic lifestyle would continue. He noted that the four original occupants were all over 50. How long would it be before the EIs gained control of the planet and began to implement their horrendous method of population control? The thought sobered him and seemed to put everything else into perspective. He might only have months left to live.

As he stood looking at the bustling construction of new dwellings, he decided that he would give the necklace to Kit tonight, after dinner. He patted his pocket, feeling the bulge of the small necklace box. He didn't hold out much hope; he had almost certainly lost her. But his heart would not be deterred. He would tell her one final time that he loved her. And then he would let her go.

He walked down the path towards his bungalow and saw Heinz struggling with a large bag of some kind of cement-like substance.

"Here, let me help you," Zac said as he drew near. He took hold of one end of the bag and saw the look of surprise on Heinz's face. They carried the bag a distance of 20 metres without saying a word to each other, dumping it on a pile of identical bags at the site of Bungalow 8.

Zac turned and walked away, and heard Heinz mutter his thanks.

At dinner that night, Kit was in fine form, drinking heavily, and flirting almost continually with Heinz. The two were sitting together, touching each other at every opportunity. Everyone else at the gazebo table seemed extremely uncomfortable with what was happening and felt awkward for Zac. But a change had come over Zac. His awareness of the threat of imminent EI invasion and the possibility that their very existence was now in jeopardy had distilled within him a firm resolve. If Kit did not want to be with him, she deserved to be happy with someone else. They might not have long to live, and he had no right to deny her a chance of happiness again, however brief that might be. He had hurt her enough, and he didn't want to be a source of further hurt. He loved her too much to do that.

As dinner concluded and people were packing away the dirty plates and serving trays, Zac saw Heinz whisper something to Kit. She nodded and they stood together, taking a bottle of wine and two glasses and walking into the night. Zac saw Kit glance furtively at him, to see if he was watching, and he smiled at her. A confused look passed across her face, as if this was not the reaction she had anticipated, and then she was gone. Dayna had seen the couple depart, and she looked with concern at Zac.

"Dad, are you OK?"

"Yes, sweetheart."

"Are you sure?"

"Yeh. Can we walk and talk for a moment?"

"Sure."

They walked down the path to the beach and sat on a grassy dune. Zac smiled sarcastically to himself as he realised it was probably the same spot where he and Jaz had had their fateful rendezvous.

"Are you sure you're OK?" Dayna asked. "That can't have been easy for you to watch."

"No, it wasn't. But I'm not going to stop her if that's what she wants."

"You still love her." It was a statement, not a question.

"With all my heart."

"So, what's your plan?"

"I don't have one. I have to let her go. I love her too much to make her life miserable. I realise now that you can't make someone love you back. And trying to do that will only have the opposite effect. Besides, there are events starting to unfold that are … very serious."

He paused and looked at Dayna.

"The EI threat is escalating. We're not sure we can hold them off much longer."

"Really?"

"Yes. I'm sorry. It's why I wanted to talk with you." He reached out and held her hand. "Make the most of every day you have left, Dayna. If you and Noah are happy together, grab the opportunity with both hands. Don't let the chance for love and happiness pass you by. You guys should get married or move in together or however you want to make it official. But don't put it off."

Dayna seemed moved, and merely said, "OK."

"And one more thing," he said. "I didn't want another day to go by without me telling you that I love you. I know we've only known each other for a few weeks, but I'm so proud of you, and I couldn't love a son or daughter more if we'd lived together all our lives."

She wrapped her arms around him and kissed him on the cheek.

"I love you too, Dad."

When they drew apart, Zac noted the tears glistening in her eyes which matched the moisture in his own.

"OK," he said, wiping a moist trail that had leaked from one eye. "Homework Task One completed. Tell daughter you love her. Tick."

"What's Task Two?"

"Tell Kit I love her one last time."

25

Zac was sitting on a bench not far from the back door to Kit's bungalow. The bungalow was empty, and she still wasn't back from her rendezvous with Heinz. He had been sitting there for over two hours, and, as far as he knew, everyone else was asleep. He was determined to do this tonight; one final declaration of love. And then he would walk away. She deserved to be left in peace, to enjoy the rest of her life, however short that might prove to be.

He looked up at the stars. So much of his life had been dictated by their influence. He had been ripped from his own time and cast adrift in a universe that he felt was no longer his own. He was like a piece of flotsam that had been caught in a storm and washed up on a strange shore. The Milky Way's light-show was particularly stunning tonight. There was no moon, and the translucent cloud of stars was smeared across the sky like a splattering of white paint on a black canvas. How could something so beautiful be so destructive? Stars that exploded and destroyed whole solar systems. Black holes that were slowly consuming whole galaxies and callously casting insignificant lifeforms such as himself thousands of years into the future.

Zac shook his head, unable to make sense of it all. As he did, he heard footsteps approaching, and looked up to see Kit walking toward her bungalow, a little unsteadily, it seemed to him. She reached her back door and was about to go inside.

"Kit," he said, standing and walking over to her.

She turned and looked at him in shock.

"Zac?" she said, seeming a little embarrassed to have been caught sneaking back so late. Then a hardness came across her face, and she simply said, "What do you want?" It was not a tone that invited expressions of undying love. But Zac would not be turned aside.

Now that the moment had arrived, he suddenly wasn't sure of his words. He was silent for a few more seconds, gathering his thoughts.

"I guess I've come to say goodbye."

"Goodbye? Why? Where are you going?"

"Nowhere. At least not just yet."

"In that case, it can wait until tomorrow," she said, turning to go.

"No, it can't, Kit."

Something in his voice made her stop and turn back to him. "OK. But make it quick. I'm tired."

"I'm sure you are," he said, and then instantly regretted it. "I'm sorry. I didn't mean that."

"I'm waiting," she said, choosing to ignore his comment. "What is it that you need to say that apparently can't wait until tomorrow?"

"Kit, I can see now that you've really made your mind up

about us. I didn't believe it at first. I thought I could change your mind. I thought that maybe if I gave you time, you could possibly forgive me, and maybe we could start again. But I can see now that that's never going to happen. I know I really hurt you. And I think my actions have probably caused you to think that you were only my second choice – a fill in until Jaz arrived."

"That's exactly what I think!"

"Well you're wrong. Completely wrong. And I don't want you to go into the rest of your life believing that. I want you to be happy Kit, and I couldn't bear the thought that my actions might cause you to doubt yourself for the rest of your life. So I'm here to set the record straight. You are the love of my life. You are the most extraordinary, generous, loving, clever, adorable person I have ever met. I don't love Jaz. I love you. It's always been you. For 22 years it's been you and only you, and it always will be. I will never stop loving you."

"It's too late for that, Zac."

"I know. But I had to say it. I couldn't let you go forward thinking that you weren't loved." He reached into his pocket and brought out the small jeweller's box. "I bought you a gift." He held it out to her.

She refused to take it. "I don't want anything you have to offer me."

"You don't have to accept it, but you can't stop me from giving it." He bent down and placed it on the back step. Straightening up, he looked at her. Were there tears glistening in her eyes? "Love is like that too," he said. "I will always love you, Kit. You can reject it. You can ignore it. But you can't stop me from giving it. I'll never stop loving you. Never. But if you can't be happy with me, I hope you find happiness with someone else. I really mean that. Goodbye, Kit."

He turned and walked away, hoping that she might call him back, or come running to him with open arms, ready to forgive him and start over. But she didn't. He kept walking, and with each step, the spark of hope that he had held onto slowly faded until, as he drew level with his own bungalow, it was finally extinguished.

He walked inside and poured a glass of wine. It was pointless trying to sleep now. He had stayed sober all night, wanting to be clear-headed when he spoke with Kit, but there was no point anymore. He walked back outside and sat on the step. The moon was just starting to rise, and he sat sipping his wine and listening to the sounds of nocturnal life all around him. The pain of his loss was a deep, all-consuming pain, but he was determined not to let it overwhelm him. He had a daughter who loved him, and who needed him. He couldn't fall apart and leave her with two parents who were emotional wrecks.

As if she had been summoned by his thoughts, Jaz stepped out of the shadows and stood in front of him. She was wearing a whisper-thin night dress and the moonlight was shining through it, revealing her naked body in vivid detail.

"I've been waiting for you, Zac."

"Go home, Jaz."

"I am home. You're my home."

"Don't be ridiculous. I'm not your home. I'm not your husband. I haven't been your husband for 22 years."

"Yes, you have. You'll always be my husband. I love you, Zac. I've never stopped loving you. And I know you still feel something for me. I felt it when we made love on the beach."

"When you seduced a seriously drunken man, you mean."

"Don't blame me, Zac. You wanted to do it too."

"That's just the thing, Jaz. I didn't! I actually didn't want to do it! You seem to think that you unlocked some deep reservoir of residual love that I have for you, but all that happened is that you jumped me and I could barely stand up straight, and it was all over before I knew what had happened!"

"Don't deny your feelings for me, Zac."

"Good grief! You're unbelievable!" He stood up and faced her. "Jaz, I want you to listen to me very carefully. I DON'T LOVE YOU! I did love you once, a long time ago. But I don't anymore. I love Kit. In fact, I love her more than I ever loved you. And I'll never stop loving her."

Jaz cocked her head sideways and looked at him with pity.

"But she doesn't love you anymore, does she? We all saw her go off with Heinz tonight. When are you going to realise that it's over?"

"Oh, I realise alright! Don't you worry about that! I'm not a fool." He thought about it for a moment and laughed. "Actually, that's not true. I'm a complete bloody fool. I should have run from you the moment I saw you on that beach. I should have run back to the woman I love." He shook his head, sat back down and had another gulp of wine.

Jaz stepped forward and squatted in front of him, reaching out to place her hands on his thighs.

"Zac, it's just you and me now. I'm the only available woman for you now. There's no one else. And even if what you say is true, even if you don't love me, I don't care. I'll take what I can get. Maybe, with time, you can learn to love me again."

"I could never love someone who would deliberately break up a marriage the way you did!"

"Are you sure, Zac?"

She stood up and took a step backward, the moonlight revealing the shape of her body. She reached up and slid her shoulder straps over her shoulders. The flimsy nightgown slithered to her feet and she stepped over it. "Are you really sure you couldn't learn to love me again?"

Jaz had aged well. She had the body of someone half her age. Her breasts were firm, with pink nipples now erect in the cool evening air. She still had a stunning hour-glass figure, with firm, round buttocks, a flat stomach and a golden nest of hair between her legs. Despite himself, Zac felt his desire flare. He stood up and stepped towards her.

"That's right, my love," she whispered, seductively.

Before he could change his mind, Zac quickly stooped down, picked up her nightgown and thrust it at her.

"Go home! Go home now! And don't ever try this again!"

"You're making a big mistake, Zac. This is your last chance. If you turn me away now, I promise I'll find love somewhere else."

"Good. Go back to Karl. He'll have you in a heartbeat, the poor unsuspecting sod!"

Jaz shook her head, and her smile turned to a snarl.

"You're a fool!"

She turned and walked back up the path, leaving Zac sitting on the step. He took another gulp of wine and muttered to himself, "Yep. That's me. Zac Perryman. Complete bloody fool!"

"You've got to admit, she's got a hot body."

He stood up and peered into the shadows opposite the path. "Kit?"

She stepped out, so that he could see her.

"How long have you been there?"

"Since before the evil temptress turned up. I was about to

step out when Miss Perky Boobs walked down the path. She has a great arse, don't you reckon?"

"I've seen better."

"Oh yeh? Where?" she said, stepping forward tentatively.

"I prefer yours," he said, his heart thumping now, hope welling up within him.

"Did you mean everything you just said to her?"

"Yes."

"And everything you said to me earlier?" Tears were now brimming in her eyes, threatening to overflow.

"Yes. I meant every word. You really are the love of my life, Kit, and I'll never stop loving you."

"Yeh. I kind of got that message," she said, opening her hand and looking at the inscription on the back of the pendant that was nestled in her palm. *I will never stop loving you. Zac.*

"You opened it."

"Uh huh," she said, nodding her head, which caused both dams to burst their banks and send two glistening tears dribbling down her cheeks.

"I'm so sorry for what I did, Kit."

"I know."

"I never want to hurt you again."

She nodded. "OK. That sounds good."

He stepped close and wiped her tears with his fingers.

"You are the love of my life, Kit," he said for the second time in as many minutes.

"You're the love of my life, too," she said, as the tears started flowing freely and she tried unsuccessfully to choke back her sobs.

He cradled her face in his hands and said, "Kit, will you be my wife again?"

She shook her head.

"No."

He took a step back, suddenly confused.

"What? I thought ..."

"Not until you put this around my neck," she said, holding out the necklace.

He took the necklace and placed it over her head. The blue cronium glowed in the moonlight, giving off tiny red and green sparkles. It nestled perfectly between her breasts which, he noticed now, were almost completely revealed by her partially unbuttoned top. His heart was racing, and he hardly dared to believe what was happening.

"Well don't just stand there staring at my breasts. Do something about it! I've been dangling them in front of you for the last few minutes. If you were a fish, I'd have packed up my rod and gone home by now!"

He took her in his arms. "What would you like me to do?"

"How about we start with a kiss?"

He kissed her, softly and gently, feeling as though he was dreaming.

"Not bad, not bad," she said after a moment. "But I think you can do a hell of a lot better."

He kissed her again, and this time he gave himself completely to her, and she to him. She wrapped one leg around him and drew him closer, kissing him passionately, and he ran his hands over her, feeling the familiar contours of her body. She kissed the side of his neck and whispered in his ear, "Take me to bed."

"Are you sure? I mean, after you and Heinz, tonight ..."

She leaned back and looked into his eyes.

"Nothing happened with Heinz. It was never going to

happen. In the end, I couldn't bear to let him near me. I tried to do it, to hurt you, but I couldn't." She was crying again now, sobbing. "Ask me why. Ask me why I couldn't do it."

"Why?"

"Because I'll only ever love you."

He nodded. "You and me, forever."

"You and me, forever," she repeated, crying again.

Then she was in his arms again, kissing him urgently and passionately. She wrapped both her legs around him, and he fumbled his way through the bungalow door and into the bedroom.

26

"Dayna, have you seen Zac this morning?" asked Keo.

It was mid-morning and Dayna had just come back from a run and a swim at the beach. Keo had been working with the construction crew since breakfast and Tash had just informed him that they were almost out of meat and fish, so he was looking for Zac to take one of the skippas out with him.

"No, I haven't," Dayna said, towelling her hair. "I bet he's slept in."

"Still in bed? He's never slept this late before," said Keo.

"I'll go and check," she answered, walking up the path to the bungalows.

She came to Zac's place, opened the front door and walked straight in.

"Dad? Are you here? Wakey, wakey, sleepy head."

She heard rustling coming through the open door of his bedroom.

"Ah! So you really are still in bed! I can't believe ..."

She stood in the doorway, open-mouthed, staring at Kit and

Zac who had clearly just pulled a sheet up to their necks and were lying there with only their faces visible. They were both smiling cheekily at her.

"Wow! Umm ... sorry ... looks like I've interrupted something."

"Nothing that can't be resumed at a moment's notice," said Zac.

"Now you're boasting," said Kit playfully, cuddling up to him.

"I'm just stating the facts, my love. All systems are still fully operational and ready to spring instantly into action whenever they are required."

"Really?" said Kit, nibbling his ear. "I thought your 'systems' might need to reboot for a while after last night."

"Umm ... guys, I think you've forgotten that I'm still standing here in the doorway!"

"That's OK," said Zac. "You're family."

Dayna smiled. "Wow!" she said again. "I'm so happy for you both! I can't believe it! This is wonderful!"

"We think it's pretty good too," said Zac.

"I think I'll leave you guys alone," said Dayna, backing out.

"Don't go, Dayna," said Kit, sitting up, holding the sheet across herself. "Stay and have a cup of juvo with us. Despite Zac's boasting, we were just about to get up."

"If you're making it, I'll have mine extra strong please," said Zac.

Five minutes later they were sitting side by side on the edge of the small back deck, sipping juvo and listening to the rolling surf not far away.

"This morning I told Kit about the escalating EI threat," Zac said to Dayna.

"Is it that serious?" asked Dayna.

"The council thinks that the next EI ship that arrives will probably have developed some means of evading our defensive measures. It's only a matter of time before they arrive and take over. It's pretty serious, sweetie."

"But that means ...."

"It will take some time, perhaps years before they have the ability to start implementing their population control," said Zac. "They need to assimilate into not only our technology but also the biosphere of the planet. We don't completely understand how they operate, but they seem to need to embed themselves into a planet at a bio-electrical cellular level before they can influence the human lifecycle. At least, that's the process that apparently took place when they first arrived at Nova when the Altarians were originally there."

"But even if it takes a couple of years, you guys are over 50 now, and so is Mum and Keo and Tash. That means ... it's too horrible to think about!"

"Yes," agreed Zac. "It's pretty grim. I'm sorry, Dayna. We thought we'd escaped from all that, but it appears we've only delayed the inevitable."

"Which is why you need to make every minute of your own life count," said Kit. "You and Noah are so good together. Make it official. Move in here together; this bungalow will be free now. Don't waste a minute of potential happiness."

Dayna nodded. "But I want you guys to be there as I get older. I want you to be around for my kids ... I don't think I can do this all over again!" Tears were filling her eyes and cascading down her cheeks.

"I know sweetheart," said Zac, "but it doesn't look like

there's any way of avoiding it. I'm sorry." He put his arm around her, and she leaned against him.

"I love you guys," she said, wiping her eyes.

"We love you too," said Kit. "So, we need to make the most of whatever time we have left. We can't let this ruin what we have right now. Otherwise the EIs have already won."

Dayna nodded.

As they were finishing their juvo a few minutes later, Zac's comm screen chimed and he walked into the loungeroom to answer it. He had previously diverted his comm calls to his new bungalow.

Councillor Drummond's face appeared on the screen.

"Good morning Zac. I hope I haven't caught you at a bad time."

"No, Gerv. I've just been having some juvo with Kit and Dayna."

"With Kit? Does that mean there is good news?"

"Very good news. The best, actually."

"I'm so happy for you Zac. For both of you. I might also have some good news – at least potentially good news. Our scientists are still processing the information, so it's too early to tell. Can you possibly come to the capital today? There's been a development that I need to talk with you about."

"Are you calling a council meeting?"

"No. I'm scheduling a meeting with just you and Dr Spooner."

"Why just us?"

"Because the council can no longer be trusted."

27
———

"Why can't they be trusted?" asked Kit, as she and Zac packed a few possessions into a backpack.

"He wouldn't say over the comms."

"And what's this new development? Did he give any hints?"

"No. None whatsoever."

"But he said something about it being good news?"

"Potentially."

"Well I'll take 'potentially' over 'the EIs are coming and we're all gonna die'."

"Are you sure you want to come?" he asked. "If you wanted to stay here, I could be back within 24 hours."

She walked over to him and wrapped her arms around him. "Now that I've got you again, I'm not letting you out of my sight! Besides, we've got a bit of catching up to do, if you know what I mean."

"You're gonna wear me out, woman!" he said kissing her lightly.

They finished packing and walked down the path together,

hand in hand. Dayna had already told some people of their reconciliation, but others were witnessing the evidence without any warning. There were smiles and nods as they passed people, and when they arrived at Keo and Tash's, they were greeted with hugs and kisses and warm congratulations.

They arrived in the capital two hours later and had a light lunch in their usual apartment. Kit kissed Zac as he left for the meeting and announced that she would do some window shopping in the precinct around Federation Tower.

When Zac walked into Drummond's office, Dr Spooner was already there. After a brief greeting, Drummond got straight to the point.

"We've had another tight-beam transmission from Explorer 1."

"Wow! OK, I wasn't expecting that," said Zac.

"Neither were we," said Drummond. "In fact, we had assumed that the crew had either perished or that their vessel had been infiltrated by EI coding. It comes as a complete shock that they have survived and are still free of EI influence."

"A happy shock," said Zac.

"Definitely," said Drummond.

"It's been ... let me see ... 20 years since their only other transmission," said Zac. "Why so long? And how have they managed to remain hidden in the Polaris system for so long?"

"They didn't. They're no longer in the Polaris system. Let me explain. There's a lot of information in this latest transmission, so I'll try to distil the essential facts for you. Alfred, are you happy to let me start off?"

"Of course, Gerv. Go ahead," said Spooner.

Drummond cleared his throat and began.

"As you may remember, we sent Explorer 1 to the Polaris

system via a wormhole over 140 years ago, to search for metals to mine. Unfortunately, the wormhole you arrived in opened here the very next day and remained locked open for over a century, prohibiting their return. To make matters worse, an EI vessel arrived in the Polaris system not long after Explorer 1 arrived there, having been alerted by their use of the wormhole. The EIs took control of the human settlement that the Explorer crew had, by then, established on Polaris, but a small crew on board Explorer 1 managed to cloak their vessel and avoid detection by the EIs. Of course, the only way we knew all this, was because Explorer 1 briefly de-cloaked and sent us a short tight-beam transmission, which took 117 years to reach us and which we received over 20 years ago."

"Yes, I remember all that," said Zac.

"Good. Their most recent message tells us what happened next. The EI ship in the Polaris system was immediately alerted to Explorer 1's existence when they de-cloaked to send us their first transmission. Explorer immediately re-cloaked but the EI vessel had already targeted them with some kind of drone that was intended to latch onto their hull and infect the ship with EI coding. They took evasive action and managed to evade the drone by the smallest of margins. They took refuge on the far side of the second planet in the system – a barren, rocky world – where they stayed for nearly a year, living in the ship."

"How many of them were on board?"

"There were only six crew members on the vessel at the time of the EI's initial appearance. The rest of the crew had long ago settled on Polaris, being unable to access our wormhole. The six crew were putting the final touches to their newly developed tight-beam transmitter when the EI vessel appeared."

"Yes. I'm aware of that," said Zac. "And the Explorer spacecraft obviously had food production capabilities."

"Yes. Hydroponics and yeast protein production were fully operational. During their year behind the planet they scanned the nearby star systems looking for signs of human habitation. Realising that they couldn't return to our world, which is 117 light years distant, they were hoping to find another closer world where they might take refuge. It was a desperate hope, one might even say a shot in the dark, but as it turns out, they were extremely fortunate. They discovered faint tell-tale radio transmissions from a nearby star system – transmissions across a broad spectrum of frequencies used by humans – and even picked up faint images from video transmissions within that star system. The star, G-677, is a little over three light-years from Polaris. The crew of Explorer decided to leave the Polaris system and travel there."

"But that would have taken years!" said Zac.

"It did. It was a momentous decision the crew made, because Explorer was not equipped with cryogenic stasis chambers, so they were consigning themselves to years of space travel. But they preferred that to the option of rotting on the far side of a barren planet or, even, worse, giving themselves up to the EIs and dying young. Apparently three of the crew were already over 50, so it would have been an immediate death sentence for them."

"So, how long did it take to reach the new star system?"

"Nearly fourteen years."

"Good grief! It's a wonder they didn't go crazy!"

"As a matter of fact, one of them died on the journey. The crew suspect it was a heart attack."

"I can't imagine what it must have been like for them. But why didn't they travel there via wormhole?"

"Because they had no way of identifying which echyon frequency within subspace corresponded to the target star system. They might have searched randomly for longer than their lifetimes and still never found the right frequency. Plus, they needed to avoid using wormholes because that would only have alerted the EIs to their location."

"Of course. I didn't think of that."

"Anyway, they eventually arrived at G-677 and found an earth-like world that had been colonised by humans."

"From where?"

"From Earth itself. Apparently, the inhabitants left Earth in the year 3542, in an interstellar colony ship. This was nearly 200 years after our own colony ship left for Nova, in the year 3348."

"And are they free from EI infestation?"

"Yes, they are. And they claim they know how to destroy the EIs once and for all."

"That's extraordinary news! How? And if it's possible to destroy them, why haven't they already done so?"

"Those are both excellent questions. We don't know, and they are apparently not willing to disclose that information over a long-range transmission, for fear that it could be intercepted by EIs or, even worse, that we might already be infected and posing as helpless humans."

"Well, as far as I can tell, we are helpless at the moment," said Zac.

"Yes. Pretty much. But the leaders of Perdita, which is what they call their world, are only willing to communicate with us face to face. In fact, it took the Explorer crew nearly six years to convince the Perditans to consent to a limited tight-beam transmission. And in one sense, I can understand their reluctance, because they have now effectively revealed their location to us. They are taking a huge risk."

"How far away are they?"

"119 light years."

Zac whistled. "That's more than a Sunday drive through the country."

"Yes, it is."

"And they're inviting us to visit them?"

"Yes. They are. But there is one stipulation. They are only willing to meet with original genome humans. They don't completely trust our modified physiology and brain chemistry. Plus, they say that only unmodified humans are able to get close enough to destroy the EIs."

"But how did they know that there were unmodified humans on Altaria? Explorer 1 had already left when we arrived."

"They didn't know. They were effectively asking if we knew of any humans with original genomes – even more ancient that the Perditans. Apparently, it is crucial to the plan."

"OK ..." said Zac, who was starting to see where this was heading. "So you're hoping that some of us Terrans will volunteer to fly through a wormhole and pay these Perditans a visit?"

"No."

"Good," said Zac, sounding relieved. "Because I was starting to worry that ..."

"We want you to fly there using normal rocket propulsion."

"Using ... but it's 119 light years away! That would take ... that would take centuries!"

"Not quite. We have a plan."

28

———

"You want some of us Terrans to fly to the Perdita system, to meet people we don't know, to discuss a plan we have no details of, and possibly risk our lives in the process?"

"I know it's a big ask, Zac, but we are running out of options here. It's only a matter of time before the EIs evade our defences and infiltrate our world. And when that happens, well …"

"Yes, I get the picture. So, what's this plan you mentioned? Because, I'll be honest, I'm not keen about the idea of dying of old age in space."

"Alfred? Perhaps you would like to take over at this point?"

"Certainly." Spooner sat up straighter and tapped his data pad. "It would be out of the question to fly all the way to the Perdita system. Even using highly advanced propulsion systems and achieving up to 75% of the speed of light, it would take nearly 200 years to reach there. By then it will certainly be too late for us here on Altaria. But Perdita is only 3 light-years from Polaris, which we can reach via wormhole. From there, a journey to Perdita would only take about 5 years, using our more advanced propulsion system."

"Only?" said Zac.

"The vessel would, of course, be equipped with cryogenic stasis pods, so you would be asleep for the duration of that flight."

"But what about the EIs in the Polaris system? As soon as we activate the wormhole and pop out at their end the EI vessel will be alerted and will probably attack. Explorer 1 only just managed to escape. Plus, even if we do escape, they may be able to track our course to the Perdita system."

"We have plans for circumventing both of those issues," said Spooner. "Firstly, over the last few years we have been developing decoy probes. These are probes that can be sent just ahead of a wormhole ship, in the same wormhole. When they emerge, about 12 seconds ahead of the vessel, they immediately divide into two halves and accelerate away from the portal in a lateral direction. After 10 seconds they explode, producing a tremendous amount of visual and electromagnetic radiation across all frequency spectrums. The explosions will mask the exit of the main vessel from the wormhole. Secondly, we have also developed the technology for a ship to be cloaked several milliseconds after it emerges from a wormhole. Its appearance within normal spacetime should go completely unnoticed by even the most sophisticated sensors."

"You hope," said Zac. "I assume you haven't had a chance to actually trialling any of this new technology?"

"That is correct. But we are supremely confident that both of these systems will work flawlessly."

"OK. And then what? We just take off for Perdita?"

"Not quite. You cannot activate the newly developed Inter-

Stellar Drive while in range of EI sensors, even if you are cloaked. You will need to use minimal impulse power to travel to the far side of the sun while you are cloaked. Only when you are well hidden behind the sun will you be able to engage the ISD."

"I notice you keep saying 'you'," said Zac. "You're assuming that some of us will be willing to risk our lives on this escapade."

"As I said, we realise it is a big ask," said Drummond, taking the floor again, "but this seems to be our best hope. Once the EIs gain control of our world, you and I and everyone over 50 may only have months left to live."

"How are the plans for a subspace portal disruptor progressing?" asked Zac, hopeful that there might be another option.

"Excellent!" said Spooner. "Much better than expected in fact. We've solved all the remaining problems and we will be activating the disruptor field within a couple of days."

"Fantastic!" said Zac. "If that's the case, then there's really no rush to launch this mission."

"Unfortunately, there is," said Drummond. "This morning our astronomy department detected the signature emissions of a vessel firing its propulsion engines under extreme deceleration. It's travelling in a direct line from a nearby G-type star system toward us. It probably reached the turnaround midpoint over 12 years ago and is now only 5 years from reaching Altaria."

"And you think it's an EI vessel?"

"Almost certainly. When the EIs in the Polaris system realised they couldn't reach us via a wormhole, they must have dispatched a vessel from a closer star system or sent a ship to that star system using a wormhole and then commenced the journey here under normal propulsion."

"So, you're saying that even if our disruptor field is effective at shutting down our subspace portal, the EIs will still get here soon."

"Yes. The EIs are coming, and we can't do anything to stop them. You may be our only hope."

"Great!"

Zac stood up and walked around the office, sifting through the new information he had been given, looking for any alternatives.

"How do we know the Perditans really do have a feasible plan for destroying the EIs? And how do we know we can trust them?"

"We can't know that until someone meets them face to face. They are simply unwilling to divulge any further details over long distance communication. Besides, it would take many centuries to have a dialogue with them over such a vast distance. Plus, there is one other thing."

"What?"

"They know the exact location of Earth. And they know how to get there via a wormhole."

"They told us that?"

"Yes. And apparently the key to destroying all the EIs lies in travelling back to Earth."

"And doing what?"

"They haven't said."

"And why haven't they already done that?"

"We don't know."

Zac shook his head and did another circuit of the office, chewing over his thoughts. The other two men remained silent, watching him intently. Finally, Zac turned back to them.

"You're going to need to prepare a starship for this voyage. How long do you envisage that will take?"

"It's already prepared," said Spooner. "We've been developing it for over 140 years, since Explorer 1 left our solar system. Explorer 2 is ready to go. All it needs is a crew."

"I was afraid you'd say something like that." He took a deep breath. "OK, I can see why you wanted to talk with me. But why couldn't you discuss all this with the full Federation Council?"

Spooner and Drummond glanced at each other momentarily, before Drummond answered.

"Someone has been trying to sabotage Explorer 2. There have been two attempts to destroy it completely; one over ten years ago, and one just last week."

"The reversionists again?"

"Yes."

"Why would they want to do that?"

"Because it was our Explorer 1 mission that alerted the EIs to our presence here, and there are some extremists who are determined not to let any other vessel leave our star system and, by so doing, make our presence even more obvious to the EIs."

"But that's ridiculous! The horse has already bolted - I mean the damage has already been done."

"I agree," said Drummond. "But they don't see it that way. They think that if we keep a low profile, the EIs will decide not to bother us. It's an irrational hope, but rationality has never been the strong suit of cults and extremist groups."

Zac was shaking his head, a frown creasing his forehead. "But how is that linked to the council?"

"The extremist who came close to blowing up Explorer 2 made a comment when he was caught, just prior to killing himself, referring to something I had only uttered a few days earlier in a council meeting. The information had to have been leaked from one of the councillors. We strongly suspect that one of the councillors is now secretly in league with the reversionists."

"Do you have any idea who?"

"No. Which is why the Explorer 2 mission will be kept from the council until you have safely launched."

"There's that personal pronoun again," said Zac, scratching his head. He exhaled slowly. "What do you propose? What's the next step?"

"I would like to speak with you and your friends, personally, and ask for volunteers. I'm proposing that I travel back with you and Kit first thing tomorrow morning and discuss the proposal face to face with the entire Terran community."

"You realise you've just ruined my whole retirement plan, don't you?"

"I'm sorry Zac, this is not something that any of us wanted to happen."

Zac nodded his head. "OK. I guess I'll see you in the morning."

He said farewell to Drummond and Spooner and entered the lift, wondering how he was going to break the news to Kit.

29

The meeting took place under the Gazebo, as there were too many of them to all fit in the loungeroom of a bungalow. Both Councillor Drummond and Dr Spooner made presentations, and they were both completely open and candid, not withholding any information. They figured that if the Terrans were being asked to risk their lives by going back into space, they should at least be told all the facts.

The group was completely stunned. While ten of them had barely arrived, the original four, together with their children, had built a life here. This was their home, and they were now being asked to leave it all behind.

Over a period of nearly two hours, questions were answered and objections dealt with, until, finally, there was stunned silence.

"Are there any other questions?" asked Drummond, after a significant pause.

"Yes," said Mel. "Apparently humans with untampered

genomes are needed for this plan, whatever it is. But ours have now been modified. Surely that disqualifies us as well?"

"No," said Spooner. "We will simply need to reverse-engineer your genome before you leave. We will effectively undo the basic modifications we made when you arrived."

"If you can do that for us, why don't you just do that for yourselves?"

"Because we can't undo our modifications in a single lifetime. We would have to progressively roll them back over five or six lifetimes, gradually undoing the changes with the progeny of each successive generation. We only made a few minor modifications to your genome – just enough to be able to make your brains receptive to our upload technology so that we could upload our language into your neocortex. We can roll back your genomic modifications very simply and easily."

"How long will that take?" asked Tash.

"About ten days. As with your arrival, you will be asleep during the whole process and it will not cause any discomfort."

Another period of silence descended on the group. Finally Drummond broke the silence with some concluding remarks.

"I realise what a shock this is to all of you, and I acknowledge what a huge thing it is we are asking of you. Obviously, no one is going to be conscripted to the mission; your involvement will be purely on a volunteer basis. I will understand if there are those among you who choose not to participate, particularly those who are younger, but I would hope that there will be some who will be willing to step forward. We don't have a specific timeframe for mission departure, but obviously, the sooner the better. I'm hoping that, by the end of the week, I will have heard back from you and we will be able to make final preparations. Explorer 2 has been constructed at Crater Base, on the far side of our largest moon, Jewel. Those of you who volunteer for the mission will be taken there as soon as possible to undergo final training."

Spooner and Drummond left soon after, leaving the group to discuss the mission among themselves. Zac suggested that they take the rest of the day and night to think about the issues and talk them through informally with immediate family and friends. A meeting was scheduled for lunchtime the following day, by which time it was hoped that most people would have made their minds up or be at least part way there.

Work on the new bungalows came to a grinding halt, because they might not need the new dwellings at all now. All afternoon groups of people visited each other, talking through the issues and asking others what they were thinking. As evening fell, Kit and Zac were having a drink on their back deck when Dayna walked around the side of the house and sat herself down beside them on the edge of the deck.

"So, what are you guys going to do?"

"I don't think we have much of a choice, really," said Zac.

"You're going?"

"We think so."

"But you don't have to go. Someone else could go. And if the mission is successful, you won't have had to leave here at all."

"There's two problems with that," said Zac. "Firstly, it doesn't seem right to leave it to others to risk their lives while I stay home and go fishing."

"Yeh, but other people like Karl and Heinz don't have children here like you do. They could go off and save the world, and you wouldn't have to leave me."

"That brings me to the second issue," said Zac. "Timing. It's very tight. There's an EI vessel decelerating towards us that will arrive here in five years. The trip to Perdita will take five years. Then the mission itself, whatever that entails, may take months or even a year or more; we just don't know. In the meantime, the EI's could start their population control more quickly than we anticipate. And, if they manage to defeat our subspace portal disruptor technology, they could arrive here much sooner than five years. Anyone who is over 50 or even approaching 50 is at great risk of being euthanised before the mission can be completed."

Dayna bowed her head and nodded. "So, you really don't have a choice then?"

"We still have a choice," said Zac. "We could decide that five or six more years here is better quality of life than going racing off around the galaxy. You see, we also have to face the possibility that events might unfold that prohibit us ever returning. We might leave here and never see you or the others again. Maybe five years here with the people we love is a better deal than 30 or 40 years on the other side of the galaxy."

"Or drifting dead in space, our bodies dried out corpses, forever inhabiting the cold dark vacuum of interstellar space," added Kit, colourfully.

"Thanks for that, my love. Very helpful."

"My pleasure."

"But, yes, that's also a possibility," agreed Zac. "So, you see, Dayna, it's not cut and dried by any means."

"But despite all that, you're thinking of going?"

Zac nodded.

"Because you need to save the world again?"

"Because I need to save you," he said, putting his arm around her. "I can't bear the thought of you having to live with a death sentence hanging over you, knowing that I stood by and did nothing."

"I'm willing to bear it, if it means I don't have to lose you," she said, leaning against him.

They sat like that for a while, not saying anything. Eventually they retired for the night, hoping that an amazing alternate plan would reveal itself to their subconscious minds while they slept.

It didn't.

At the community meeting the following afternoon, the same main points were thrashed through again, with basically the same conclusions being reached. Anyone approaching 50 was facing an almost certain death sentence if they stayed, unless the mission was accomplished before the EIs began population control. That, of course, was the big unknown. How long would the mission take? And how long until the EIs started euthanising people? No one knew. By the end of the meeting it was clear who had decided to volunteer for the mission. There were some obvious volunteers; Zac and Kit. Keo and Tash. Melody and Phil. Jaz and Karl. Then there were some surprises. Heinz volunteered, having now switched his romantic attention to Jaz, whom he was hoping to wrestle away from Karl. Zac wasn't sure whether Heinz was a positive inclusion, as he seemed to be always complaining about something. Finally, there were some big surprises. After an all-night discussion, apparently Noah and Kia, Tash and Keo's children had decided to go. They were simply not willing to let their parents go wandering around the galaxy without them. In the middle of the night Noah had also proposed to Dayna who had accepted and was now set to join the expedition, ecstatic that she didn't have to choose between her new love and her family.

Seeing Kia volunteer, caused Harv to put his hand up. His sister, Delta, quickly followed, resulting in Raj, who was completely smitten with her, volunteering as well. It was like a line of dominoes falling, one after the other.

"So that's 15 of us," said Zac when the dust had settled. "Anyone else?"

The rest shook their heads. That really only left the five other young people from the Nova ring, and the middle-aged couple, Jeannie and James, who were very quiet and obviously not up for further space trips.

"OK," said Zac. "I'll inform Councillor Drummond. I'm guessing he'll want to get us moving as soon as possible. We'll probably only have a few more days together before we leave. We should make the most of it."

"That's right bro," said Keo. "I think I'll be spending a lot of time at the beach. I don't know how long it will be before we see another beach again."

As it turns out, it would be a lot longer than any of them thought.

30

The process of leaving the island was a difficult one. What would they say to the locals, whom some of them had lived alongside for 22 years? Drummond insisted that they could not mention the mission, because of the ongoing security risk from the reversionists, so they had to concoct a story that they had decided to move to another island to allow room for the new arrivals and others who could be expected to arrive soon. The locals found this very difficult to accept, especially Marsh and Razna who quietly expressed to Zac that they didn't believe the story.

"You wouldn't willingly leave this place unless there was something serious happening," said Marsh to Zac when they were alone at the farewell party that had been organised at the marina. "Are you in danger?" he asked.

"Not really," said Zac. "No more than any of us." It was not entirely true, but what could he say?

Marsh sensed this and said, "Take care Zac. Wherever

you're going, and whatever you're doing, make sure you keep your head down. And come back and see us some time."

"I'll do my very best to come back, Marsh," he said. He wished he could say more, but the security of the mission and the safety of the crew was too important to risk compromising it.

The party at the marina was a strange affair; a bitter-sweet farewell that was a celebration of friendship and a grieving for its imminent loss. At one stage Zac, Kit, Keo and Tash took themselves apart from the others and sat at the water's edge, sipping glasses of wine and looking across the calm inner sea. The water was dead flat, the calmest Zac had ever seen it, and the stars were reflected on its surface like fairy lights shining up from some kind of underwater city.

"Oh my, it's beautiful here," said Kit. "I'm going to miss it."

"We've had 22 very happy years," said Zac.

"It's the only home that our two children have known," said Tash. "I hope they're going to adjust alright to life in a tin can."

"At least they've both found love," said Keo. "A wise philosopher once said, 'it is better to live in hardship with love, than live in paradise alone'."

"Who said that?" asked Zac.

"Me. Just then."

"You should write a book."

"I would, bro, but I can't find a publisher anywhere."

They continued to sit together, sipping their drinks and watching the stars reflected on the water.

"Do you think we'll ever come back?" asked Kit.

"It's hard to say," said Zac. "If the kids had stayed, I would have said yes, definitely. But seeing they're all coming with us, I don't know. It depends where the path leads us."

"A path through the stars," said Keo, poetically.

Zac picked up a pebble and threw it into the water. A series of concentric circles rippled outward, distorting the perfect image and blurring the stars' reflections.

"One tiny pebble can distort the whole picture," he said, philosophically. "Have you ever noticed how one small splash doesn't just create a single ripple? It sets in process a whole chain of ripples, each one creating another after it, in ever-diminishing echoes. One small precipitating event producing a series of unavoidable cascading subsequent events."

"Uh, oh," said Kit. "He's about to get philosophical."

"Lay it on us, bro," said Keo. "Don't hold back. Give us the full benefit of your wisdom. This could be one of those moments that will go down in history. Centuries from now, people will be quoting you and trying to work out what colour pebble you tossed that gave birth to such a life-altering pronouncement."

They all looked at Zac, waiting.

He took a deep breath and said ...

"I bet I can skip a rock further than you guys."

They spent the next day enjoying their favourite activities one last time. Some swam and surfed. Some fished. Some walked along the beach. Some went sailing one last time. In the late afternoon they packed their meagre possessions and shared a farewell meal with those who were remaining on the island. As the sun began to set, a large Federation flitter arrived to take them directly to the capital. As they lifted off, the group peered out of the windows, watching their beloved island quickly shrink and get left behind.

Councillor Drummond met them as they disembarked on the rooftop of Federation Tower. "I hope you don't mind, but we thought we'd keep you here for a few more hours, until the crowds at the transfer terminal subside. The less people who see a large group of you transferring off-world, the better."

"We understand," said Zac.

Drummond led them to the spacious apartment where Zac and Kit stayed whenever they came to the capital, and encouraged them to relax for a few hours, ordering anything they wished from room service.

"Are you kidding me?" said Mel, after Drummond had left. She waved her hand around, indicating the opulently appointed apartment, with its gym and spa and stunning views over the island. "This is where you guys have been staying when you come here? No wonder you're so happy to attend council meetings!"

"You know what they say," said Zac. "It's a tough job ..."

"Yeh, yeh, yeh. My heart bleeds for you."

Drummond had promised to return at midnight and escort them to the terminal himself. In the meantime, the group availed themselves of the facilities. Some worked out in the gym. Some soaked themselves in the spa. Others cracked open bottles of wine and sipped while watching the city lights below.

"This is a bit like giving a condemned prisoner a last expensive meal before you lead him off to be executed," said Mel, taking another gulp from her wine glass as she soaked in the spa.

"Let's hope not," said Kit, who reached for the bottle and topped her own glass up.

"Take pleasure while you can, for you know not when it may pass by your door again," said Keo.

"Another gem from your unpublished book?" asked Zac.

"No. Ramone Beltayne. 2284."

Drummond arrived a little before midnight. He ushered them back into a flitter on the rooftop which transported them the few blocks to the transfer station. It landed on the street directly outside the station and the group walked through the doors, quickly crossing the empty concourse. They entered a large booth, big enough to fit twice their number. Drummond shook each of their hands and expressed his deep gratitude for what they were about to do. He promised that he would visit them at Crater Base prior to their final departure and wished them all the best for their two weeks of mission training.

He stepped out of the booth, leaving them in the care of four security personnel who would accompany them all the way to the moon. The door closed, leaving them with a final image of Drummond standing facing them, with his hand raised in silent farewell.

A moment later, they had left Altaria.

31

———

The shuttle journey from Orbital Terminus 8 to the moon took a little over two hours. Crater Base was an impressive sight as they came in to land. The crater itself was enormous; about 20 kilometres in diameter and eight kilometres deep, with almost vertical sides in many places. A spectacular city nestled in one small section of the crater, close to the wall. It consisted of fragile-looking tall cylindrical buildings, impossibly thin and rising at least a kilometre from the ground. There were about 20 of these spindly skyscrapers, all closely packed together and joined by a spider's web of clear connecting tubes, not only at ground level but also at various points higher up. The lights of the skyscrapers and their maze of clear connecting tubes glowed with spectacular beauty in the darkness of the crater's shadow. The vast majority of the crater, however, was taken up with many dozens of comparatively squat, domed buildings spread across the crater's floor, interspersed with a number of flat circular shapes that looked like landing pads.

As they descended towards one of these pads, however, it opened up, splitting into two, each half sliding into side recesses and revealing a large subterranean landing bay beneath. They landed gently on the floor of the bay and waited while the roof closed over them and the bay was pressurised. Upon exiting the shuttle, they were greeted by an attendant who escorted them directly to a subway car which whisked them along a maglev monorail for what seemed like several kilometres. They exited the car and ascended several floors in a lift which opened onto a large foyer. Dr Spooner was waiting for them.

"Welcome to the Federation Training Facility," he said. "I hope your journey wasn't too tiring."

"We are a little tired, to be honest," said Zac.

"I'm sure you must be. It's 0230 hours – we operate on A1 planet time here. I apologise for the late-night journey, but we wanted to make your arrival here as clandestine as possible. No doubt you are all looking forward to going to bed. We have decided to begin your genetic rollback immediately. Each of you will be given a separate room where you will be assisted to fall asleep. When you wake up, in about 10 days, your rollback will be complete and you will be refreshed and ready to commence mission training."

"You're going to start the modifications now?" asked Kit.

"Yes. Why not? You need a good sleep, and this is the best sleep you'll ever get. Plus, we are on a very tight schedule. So, if you can please follow me, we'll get you settled in your rooms and we can begin the process."

Zac woke, feeling euphoric and hungry in equal amounts. He got out of bed and walked out of the door of his small, one-bed room. His room, and about ten others, opened onto a large circular central living quarters, with kitchen facilities against one wall, a large dining table nearby, and a scattering of lounges and comfortable chairs. Several of the others were already sitting at the dining table, and others were emerging from their own rooms. He saw Jaz, Mel, Karl and Heinz entering the living quarters from a corridor in the opposite wall, probably from another collection of bedrooms. What interested him most, however, was what was on the table. Food! He was starving!

Within minutes everyone had arrived, and they were seated together at the dining table, devouring a hearty breakfast – at least they guessed it was breakfast. Towards the end, Dr Spooner arrived and confirmed that it was, indeed, morning, and assured them that their genetic rollback had been completed successfully.

"In fact," he said, "it was easier than we anticipated. Your genome had only received minimal modifications from us when you arrived, and those were quite simple to undo."

"So, we're back to the way we were on Nova?" asked Mel.

"No. We were also able to undo the modifications introduced by the EI on Nova. You are now back to the original genome that you had on earth. You are completely original!"

"How is it that we can still speak and understand Altarian?" asked Heinz.

"The knowledge of our language remains embedded in the memory centre of your brain. That has not changed. All we did was revert your genome back to its original form."

"So, an EI would not be able to manipulate us now?" asked Dayna.

"In your current state, no. But remember, it would only take the EIs a matter of days to infect you again with some form of uplift virus which modified your genome, and you would be subject to their control all over again."

"So, you haven't been able to work out a means of locking our genome to prevent further tampering?" asked Zac.

"Unfortunately, no. That appears to be beyond our capabilities at present." He clapped his hands. "But enough gloomy talk of EIs! We have a mission to train you for! When you've finished eating, please make your way to the briefing room, which is the first room to your right, down that corridor. Our first briefing commences in 15 minutes." He smiled and left them to finish their meal.

A quarter of an hour later they were all gathered in the briefing room, which resembled a traditional classroom with individual seats and desks facing a lectern in front of two large screens on the front wall. Spooner walked in and welcomed them briefly again, and then launched into the briefing.

"Firstly, let me explain where you are. You are in our Federation Training Facility, located on the far side of the crater from Crater City, which you would have seen as you landed. This is the facility where we train all prospective defence force personnel. The base has currently been emptied of all but the most essential personnel, to ensure maximum security for this mission. You are the only people currently undergoing training, so the only people you will encounter are those directly responsible for your mission prep."

"While you were sleeping, we were successful in activating our subspace portal disruptor field. No one can activate a wormhole to our star system unless we turn off the disruptor. This means that we are now safe from imminent EI invasion through the wormhole, so that is one less thing for us to worry about at the moment."

"But there is still an EI ship on its way here under normal propulsion?" said Kit.

"Yes. That vessel will arrive here in less than five years. So, your mission is still as vital as ever."

"Can you tell us about the two sabotage attempts that were carried out here?" asked Tash, who was already starting to think like a security officer again.

"The first happened years ago, while Explorer 2 was still being modified. A bomb was set to explode on board the ship by a low-level technician. The technician was killed in an altercation with security personnel and the bomb defused. The second attempt was a little over two weeks ago. An EMP bomb was discovered in Explorer 2's launch chamber. We don't know how it got there, but it was detected by our scanners as soon as it was activated and began a three-minute countdown. Only the quick-thinking of a technician saved us from a catastrophe. He sliced the bomb open with a laser cutter and destroyed the brain."

"If you don't know how it got there, how can you be sure of ongoing security?" asked Zac, voicing all their concerns.

"We have dramatically reduced base personnel. Only those with the highest security clearance are now on-base. But you are correct, we can't be absolutely certain of ongoing security, which is why we are rushing to launch the mission. Explorer 2 was launched into orbit while you were sleeping and is currently docked at Atlas Station, undergoing final preparations. Our goal is to get you on board and on your way as soon as possible. Which brings me to your training regime. Let me explain the schedule for you."

"Each morning we will wake you at 0545. At 0600 you are required to be in the gymnasium, which is about 50 metres down that corridor." He indicated the corridor from which Jaz and the others had entered. "You will be under the guidance of a physical trainer who will supervise your exercise regime for the duration of your mission training. At 0700 you will shower in the gymnasium's bathroom facilities and make your way here for breakfast. Breakfast is at 0730. The daily mission briefing is at 0830 in this briefing room."

As he spoke, an assistant distributed small data pads to each of the mission team, and Spooner explained how to operate them. "As you receive your data tab, place your thumb anywhere on the screen. This will key the device to you alone. You should now see the daily schedule on the opening screen."

They did as he suggested and read through the daily schedule:

0545 – Wake

0600 – 0700 Physical Training

0700 – 0730 Shower

0730 – 0830 Breakfast

0830 – 0900 Daily Briefing

0900 – 1030 Mission Theory

1030 – 1100 Morning Break

1100 – 1230 Skill Simulation

1230 – 1330 Lunch

1330 – 1500 Physical Simulation

1500 – 1530 Afternoon Break

1530 – 1730 Physical Simulation

1800 Dinner

"Do you have any questions?" Spooner asked. "Is there anything you're not sure about?"

"Just about everything!" said Noah.

"It will all become clear to you as it unfolds, and you will very quickly become familiar with the routine."

"Why do we need all this training, anyway?" complained Heinz, whose tone of voice seemed to indicate that he thought it was all a waste of time. "There are already trained pilots among us, and surely the rest of us don't need any training."

"The two key philosophies of preparing a crew for any mission are preparedness and redundancy. We can't predict what might happen on your voyage, nor can we assume that you will all survive. If something happens to one or more of you, we need to ensure that the survivors have the skills and knowledge to take over and complete the mission."

Spooner's words had a sobering effect on them all, reminding them of the dangers that they might face during their long voyage through the stars.

"Let me give a brief explanation of each element of your schedule. Mission theory will involve learning the basic principles of space flight, astro-navigation, propulsion, astrophysics and other key knowledge areas. The more you can understand about this, the better equipped you will be. This knowledge assimilation is usually done via direct cerebral upload, of course, but that is not possible in your case. Skill simulation will involve basic simulation experience in piloting, navigation, the wormhole STAR drive, cloaking and operation of the vessel's advanced defence systems. Physical simulation will entail the largest segment of your training. This will primarily involve gaining valuable experience in a space suit, firstly here on the base, but towards the end of the training you will do at least one extended EVA on board Explorer 2 itself. Obviously, you can practise working in a vacuum here on the base, but you will need to be in orbit to experience true weightlessness."

"What's an EVA?" asked Heinz

"An extra-vehicular activity," answered Kit. "It means going outside the ship in a spacesuit."

"Sounds fun!" said Dayna.

"I hope it will be enjoyable," continued Dr Spooner, "but I can guarantee that it will also be hard work, mentally and physically. We want you to be as prepared as you can be for what lies ahead."

"Terrific. I can hardly wait," muttered Heinz, sarcastically.

32

———

The training was difficult for almost everyone. For some, like Tash and Keo's two children, they had never been off-world, and so some of the skills needed for the mission were completely new to them. For the older ones, their strength and fitness had diminished over the years, and the physical training was gruelling. Keo had gained considerable weight in their decades on Altaria and was noticeably out of condition, although he never once complained. Heinz, on the other hand, did little else but complain. Whereas Keo pushed himself to the limit in physical training, Heinz did the bare minimum, often ceasing altogether or merely pretending to do an exercise when the trainer's attention was focused on someone else.

On the third day, Zac had a chat with him in the change room after their morning workout.

"Heinz, I know you're struggling with the physical training, but you're only hurting yourself by not giving it 100 percent."

"I'm giving 100 percent of what I think I need to give."

"It doesn't seem like enough to me."

"I didn't sign up for a gym class! And, quite frankly, I don't really care what you think. My personal fitness has got nothing to do with you."

"That's where you're wrong. Your personal fitness is relevant to everyone on the mission. The lack of fitness of one team member could slow us down or impact us all in an emergency. This is not just about you, Heinz. You're a part of a team, and you have to pull your weight, literally."

"Listen pal," said Heinz, fronting up to Zac aggressively. "I didn't put you in charge! You have no authority to tell any of us what to do. So just back off and mind your own damn business!" He turned and stormed out of the change room.

"That went well," said Keo, who was the only remaining person in the male change room.

"I hope I'm wrong," said Zac, "but I've got a feeling that Heinz is going to be a constant problem on this mission."

Training continued throughout that week, with the team quickly falling into the expected routine. They were all now living in the one module with ten rooms, because married couples had moved into rooms together. This included Mel and Phil, Dayna and Noah, Kia and Harv, and Raj and Delta. Only Jaz, Karl and Heinz occupied rooms singly. The dynamic between Jaz, Karl and Heinz was tense. Both men were clearly vying for Jaz's affections, and she was obviously revelling in their attention, favouring one and then the other, keeping them both guessing.

Dayna continued to be surprised and disappointed at her mother's behaviour.

"I don't understand what's happening with her," Dayna commented to Kit in confidence on the sixth day. "For as long as I can remember she's been withdrawn and totally uninterested in the opposite sex, and now she's completely gone the other way!"

"She certainly seems to be going through a difficult time," admitted Kit, tactfully.

"Difficult? That's an understatement! She's turned into a manipulative seductress!"

"I actually think she's very insecure, Dayna. Everything she's doing is an attempt to feel better about herself."

"Well I wish she'd hurry up and feel better, before Karl and Heinz come to blows over her."

Dayna's casual prediction turned out to be more accurate than she anticipated. In the afternoon of the seventh day, Karl, Heinz, Noah and Harv were in the no-grav simulation immersion tank, fully suited up. The tank was a huge water-filled chamber, ten metres deep and twenty metres square. At the bottom of the tank, in the centre, was a small mock space module from which the space-suited figures had to retrieve various tools. They then had to screw various sized nuts onto bolts that protruded from the wall of the chamber, thus increasing the dexterity of their suit hand movements and also learning to brace themselves in a no gravity environment when applying torque.

The "accident" happened on the far side of the chamber, on the opposite side to the viewing window of the instructors, while Noah and Harv were inside the space module. Heinz later swore it was an accident. Karl was tightening a nut onto a bolt using a torque wrench when his head was impacted violently from behind. His helmet smashed against a protruding bolt, cracking his faceplate and creating a 20-centimetre hole, through which water began pouring in. Karl was immediately choking and unable to breath as water poured past his mouth and nose. He tried to cover the hole on the outside with his glove, but a water-tight seal wasn't possible and although he managed to reduce the inundation to a fine spray, he was unable to breath effectively as it continued to spray his mouth and nose. Choking and growing closer to asphyxiation, he was kicking desperately for the ingress chamber when he was tugged back by Harv who had emerged from the module and quickly assessed the situation. He took a roll of tape from his belt, cut a piece off and applied it to Karl's helmet. The leak reduced to a few drips and the four trainees were then able to cycle through the ingress chamber, a process which took several minutes.

When they emerged into the wet room on the other side, Noah and Harv quickly removed Karl's helmet and two trainers ran in with an oxygen mask. Karl had inhaled some water into his lungs and wasn't in good shape. Medics arrived and took him to the infirmary, leaving Noah and Harv to quiz Heinz about what had happened.

"I feel terrible!" he said. "I was trying to get a wrench out of my toolbelt, but it was stuck. I was behind Karl, with my back to him, and I pulled extra hard on the wrench. It came free suddenly and my elbow jerked back and hit Karl in the back of the head."

He was still giving the same explanation an hour later at the afternoon break, when the whole team was gathered in their living area.

Zac shook his head, perplexed. "I find it difficult to see how an elbow jerking backwards could propel his helmet forward with enough force to break his faceplate. Especially underwater."

"What are you saying?" demanded Heinz, aggressively.

"That I'm lying? That I deliberately tried to kill him? Is that it? Are you accusing me of attempted murder?"

"I'm just saying I don't understand how it could have happened."

"I don't understand either," said Harv, voicing his own doubts. He stared hard at Heinz. "How's your elbow?"

"A bit sore."

"I'll bet it is," said Harv. "A blow strong enough to cause a secondary impact that could smash Karl's faceplate would certainly have bruised your elbow. Let me see it."

"This is ridiculous!" said Heinz, standing. "I've told you what happened. If you don't believe me that's your problem."

"No, Heinz, it's everyone's problem," said Zac. "If this mission is going to succeed, we need to be able to trust each other with our lives. We can't work effectively as a team if there is no trust." He stared at Heinz who was looking around at everyone as if he was a cornered animal. "Are you sure that's what happened in there?"

"Of course I'm sure! I don't have to stay here and listen to these innuendos!" He turned and started walking out of the room, but encountered Karl coming the other way. Karl was clearly furious.

"You bastard! You tried to kill me!" He launched himself at the bigger man, taking a wild swing at his face which only managed a glancing connection. But Heinz was off-balance now, trying to back away, and Karl took another swing, this time connecting with Heinz's abdomen. He doubled over wheezing, and Karl was about to deliver the knockout blow when Keo grabbed him from behind and pinned his arms to his side.

"Easy, bro, easy. You don't want to go launching haymakers

like that – you could break your hand and then we'd be one pilot down".

Heinz was now also being restrained by Harv and Noah, who were both fitter and stronger than the out-of-shape big man.

"It was an accident, you moron!" Heinz shouted at Karl, with spittle flying from his lips. "A bloody accident! Do you get that? I bumped you with my elbow!"

"That wasn't an elbow on the back of my head! I felt two hands! You pushed me!"

"Don't be ridiculous!"

"Heinz, why didn't you call out for assistance?" asked Harv.

"What do you mean?"

"I mean, it was only good fortune that I exited the module at just that moment. Another thirty seconds and Karl would have drowned. Why didn't you say anything over the comms?"

"I was in shock!" he said, shaking himself free of the restraining hands, now that the situation had simmered down. "I couldn't think what to do."

"So you just stood there watching him drown?" said Harv, pushing him further.

"I don't have to answer to you! You're just a kid!"

"No Heinz, I'm a qualified pilot, and I need to know that everyone on my team is reliable and trustworthy."

"Fine! Don't believe me! I don't really care! I've had enough of this bullshit!"

He turned and stormed out of their module.

"Are you OK, Karl?" asked Jaz, taking hold of his arm and looking very concerned.

"I'll be fine. I breathed in a bit of water but they squirted something into my lungs which dried it up or did something. I'll be OK."

He walked to the table and everyone sat down again. Jaz poured him a cup of juvo and he nibbled on an energy bar.

"Guys, I'm absolutely sure that wasn't an elbow I felt in the back of my head."

"I believe you, Karl," said Zac. "I think we need to watch Heinz carefully."

33

Karl moved in with Jaz that night. It became apparent the next morning that they were now a couple when they emerged from her room together while people were preparing to go for their morning PT session. The events of the previous day had obviously impacted Jaz, who appeared shocked that she may have been the precipitating factor in a potentially deadly incident. She had probably always intended to end up with Karl, but she had delayed making her choice because she enjoyed the attention she had been receiving. Yesterday's incident, however, had revealed Heinz's true character, and as the new day unfolded, she noticeably avoided any contact with him.

A glowering antagonism now existed between Karl and Heinz. Karl was convinced that he had narrowly escaped a murder attempt and made it clear that he would never trust Heinz in a critical environment again. Heinz was playing the victim card as well, claiming that he had been unfairly judged and condemned. At breakfast, as they replenished their energy reserves after another intense PT session, Heinz went on the attack. He was the last to arrive and as he took a seat at the table, the conversation in the group dried up. An uneasy silence was broken at last by Heinz himself.

"Well, I can sense the awkwardness, so let's get this out in the open. Now that yesterday's accident has been dealt with, and it is clear that Karl has not suffered any lasting injury, I believe I am owed an apology."

"For what?" Mel asked.

"For being accused of deliberately attempting to injure Karl."

"Murder, you mean," said Karl.

"There it is again! A baseless accusation!"

"No. There is a smashed faceplate that's pretty solid evidence"

"I've explained how that happened."

"Show us your elbow," said Harv. "Show us the bruise."

"I will do no such thing. I don't have to prove myself to you or anyone!"

"That's just it," said Mel. "You *do* have to prove yourself. We need a basis upon which to trust you."

"You people are incredible!" He stood up holding a bowl of cereal and a cup of juvo. I won't be eating meals with you again until I receive an apology from each and every one of you."

He turned and walked out of the module.

"Well I guess he's never gonna eat with us again," said Karl after he had left.

"That'll be very tricky in the confines of a small spaceship," said Dayna.

Her assessment proved to be more immediately pertinent than she had anticipated. In the morning briefing after breakfast, Dr Spooner announced that the frenetic final preparations of Explorer 2, which had been taking place concurrently with their own training, were now complete. They would therefore immediately move up to the ship, to live work and sleep there for the remainder of their training, in order to familiarise themselves with the ship's systems and also ensure that all life support systems, including food production, were fully functional. The mission team gathered their few possessions together and, along with Dr Spooner and several trainers, boarded a maglev subway car which disgorged them ten minutes later into a small bare subway station. A large double door airlock led them through into a pressurised subterranean shuttle bay, and they quickly clambered aboard the waiting shuttle. Thirty minutes later, the shuttle was on final approach to Atlas station, the largest space station in orbit around the moon, and the mission team got their first glimpse of Explorer 2.

The spaceship was docked to a long arm of the space station, and it was quite impressive. It consisted of two almost perfect spheres joined together as if they had partly melted into each other. The front sphere had multiple rows of windows, indicating several decks, with one long window stretched across the front of the sphere at the top, apparently indicating the location of the bridge. The rear sphere had no obvious windows and what appeared to be bay doors around its lower section. A rectangular section protruded from the rear of that sphere, containing enormous engine vanes. A raised square ridge ran around each sphere, perpendicular to the long axis of the ship, and the mission crew recognised this as part of the STAR drive that created and maintained a wormhole. The whole vessel was shiny jet black and quite beautiful.

"That's definitely a step up from the sausage and two doughnuts design of the old void jumper," said Kit.

"I can't wait to pilot that thing," said Harv.

"Co-pilot, you mean," said Kit.

"We'll see about that, grandma," Harv replied with a cheeky grin.

The two had established a friendly rivalry throughout their simulation training, with their performances only marginally different. Harv had slightly faster reaction times, but Kit had demonstrated slightly better judgment calls in simulated critical emergency incidents. It was clear that the mission had three excellent pilots in their midst, including Karl, but Kit had privately voiced concern to Zac regarding Harv's rashness and bravado. The remaining few days would probably determine who would emerge as the lead pilot.

The shuttle docked with Atlas Station and the mission crew quickly transferred into their new ship. They already knew the Explorer 2's layout from their mission briefings. The forward sphere comprised three levels; sleeping quarters on the lower deck, living quarters and gym in the middle, with the top being the bridge. The rear sphere housed all propulsion and life-support systems, including robotic hydroponics and cryogenics, as well as the two shuttle bays.

After selecting sleeping quarters, the mission crew were called to a briefing on the bridge, where they assembled with a buzz of excitement. An extra-tall Altarian with a buzz cut and a severe military demeanour was waiting for them.

"My name is Captain Riff Braiden. I'll be in charge of the last few days of your training on board Explorer 2. As you've already discovered, you'll have plenty of room, because the ship is designed for a crew of thirty. Over these final days of preparation, you will live solely on board, testing every system and ensuring that you are completely familiar with everything. Only the other trainers and I will move between the ship and Atlas Station. You will be undergoing final training in sub-light propulsion, navigation, STAR drive activation, cryogenics and defence systems. As well as your onboard training, each of you will be completing a one-hour EVA, and the pilots and co-pilots will also be doing at least one test flight in a micro-shuttle. For today's sessions you've been divided into four groups, and these are listed on your data pads along with your meeting points. The first session begins shortly, so let's move!"

Kit and Zac found themselves piloting and co-piloting a micro-shuttle under the expert tutelage of Riff himself. The shuttle was tiny in comparison to the shuttles that they had flown from Genesis – just a small cockpit with their two seats, plus two bench seats along the walls behind them that could fit a total of five passengers; three on one side and two on the side with the door. But their diminutive size was more than compensated by the sophistication of their technology which included artificial gravity, cloaking and full defensive shields.

Apart from the simulators on Crater Base, it was Kit's first flight in twenty-two years, and she had to admit that she was a little rusty, but Riff was surprisingly patient. After a shaky start she managed to pull off a pretty fair rendition of her old flip manoeuvre towards the end, which caused Riff to raise his eyebrows. Kit caught his look of surprise.

"You didn't think I had it in me, did you?" she asked him, as she lined up the number two docking bay.

"I'm pleasantly surprised," he admitted. "But one thing I've learnt over the years is never underestimate a determined woman."

"You got that right," said Zac. "She's the most determined woman I know."

Kit made a very respectable landing and assumed that the lesson was over, but once all systems were powered down, Riff told Kit to transfer control to Zac, as it was his turn to pilot the shuttle.

"Umm ..." he said uncertainly, "I only piloted a shuttle a couple of times, briefly, on Nova, so maybe we'll just stick with me as co-pilot."

"That's not an option," said Riff sternly. "With such a small crew, multiple redundancy is essential. If the mission is to succeed, everyone needs to be able to step up at a moment's notice and perform a variety of key roles. I'm not asking you to do this – I'm telling you."

With Riff and Kit's careful instruction, Zac managed to fly the shuttle out of the bay without scraping the hull – but only by the barest of margins. His confidence grew, however, as he was put through various basic manoeuvres, and his eventual landing back in the bay was slightly less wobbly than his departure.

"How bad was I?" he asked Riff after all systems had been powered down.

"You'll do. I don't need you to be the slickest pilot in the world – just safe. Now you and the two pilots in the other shuttle are scheduled for EVAs. Meet me in the EVA prep room in fifteen minutes."

34

It was the morning of their third day aboard Explorer and they were all wondering what the day would entail. Yesterday, they had inspected the survival drop-pod; a self-contained module that could be detached from the ship and landed on the surface of a planet. It contained a simple food production facility, bunks for sleeping and basic survival gear. The survival drop-pod was a last resort module in case they became stranded somewhere in the galaxy.

By now they had all rotated through each of the training sessions on offer. Riff arrived in the dining area as they were finishing breakfast and surprised them with his announcement.

"Today we will be undocking from Atlas Station and taking Explorer out on a final test flight. This will be the last day of training; tomorrow you will depart Altaria."

There was a murmur of excitement among the crew.

"The flight deck crew allocation has now been made, based

on your performance over these last few days. The allocations are on your data pads now."

Zac glanced at his tablet and read through the list.

Lead Pilot: Harv

Co-pilot: Kit

Weapons: Tash

Navigation and Long-Range Sensors: Melody

STAR Drive: Karl

Shields and Cloaking: Delta

Comms: Dayna

Life support systems: Phil

"Each of the rest of you are, of course, capable of stepping into almost all those roles in the case of an emergency," continued Riff.

"So, who's in overall command?" asked Heinz.

"Based upon personality profile and previous experience, Zac will be mission commander. He will have ultimate authority in making mission decisions and responding to any crises that emerge."

"What if we disagree with his decisions?" asked Heinz.

Riff stared at Heinz for a few moments, making him uncomfortable. "You suck it up. And then you carry out your duty to the best of your ability without complaining or seeking to undermine your commander." He looked around the table. "This isn't a democracy. In a crisis there isn't time for a committee meeting or a democratic vote. The success of your mission will depend upon your ability to carry out your responsibilities efficiently and unquestioningly." Riff looked at Heinz again. "Are we clear?"

There were nods all around the table, except for Heinz who merely shrugged noncommittally.

Riff continued with the briefing. "We will be taking Explorer to a lower, faster orbit, and then linking up with Atlas Station again once we catch up. There is an ancient, decommissioned satellite in that lower orbital plane which we will be targeting with lasers."

Tash smiled and said, "Excellent! I love blowing stuff up."

"That's why I try to never make her angry," said Keo. "A wife's fury melteth the sun - Demosthenes, 4th century BC."

"That's right, my love, and don't you forget it!"

The briefing ended shortly after, with everyone moving quickly to their allocated stations. Riff remained on the bridge in his role as supervising instructor, with Zac alongside.

"Atlas Station, this is Explorer 2 requesting permission to undock," said Dayna.

"Explorer 2, you are clear to undock. We confirm that the docking tube is sealed and depressurised. Have a good flight."

"Roger, Atlas."

Riff looked at Zac, who was seated in the commander's chair.

"All yours, Zac."

Zac nodded.

"Initiate undocking sequence," he said.

"Sequence initiated," responded Kit.

A soft whirring could be heard through the hull, followed by several dull clunks.

"Explorer 2, we confirm separation. You are clear to go."

"Roger Atlas," said Dayna.

"Push us away, Kit," said Zac.

Kit fired some lateral thrusters and watched her readout as the separation distance increased. After a few moments, she turned to Zac.

"Seventy metres."

"Good enough," said Zac. "Harv, initiate deorbit burn. Mel let me know when we've dropped twenty Ks."

Forty minutes later they were approaching the decommissioned satellite in low lunar orbit, on the opposite side of the moon to Atlas Station. Mel had successfully tracked its range and trajectory and forwarded the coordinates to Harv and Tash. As they drew near, Tash locked her lasers onto the target and waited for the order to fire.

"Two kilometres and closing," said Mel.

"That's close enough," said Zac. "We don't want to scratch our bumper bar with debris. Fire when ready, Tash."

Tash didn't need any further encouragement. A twin purple beam of intense light streaked out in front of them, merging into a single point in the distance. A small fireball of white light appeared instantly, quickly blossoming outward.

"Direct hit!" exclaimed Tash.

"That's my girl," said Keo, proudly.

"Shields up, Delta. Let's not get side-swiped by any debris."

They flew through the debris field moments later and saw small pieces of debris sparking against the ship's energy shield.

"Nice work, Tash," said Zac.

"Nothing to it," she replied, still unable to wipe the smile off her face.

Riff nodded his head.

"Good job, everyone. Zac get us back to Atlas."

"OK. Mel, can you plot a course to intercept Atlas. We're coming out the moon's shadow now, so it should be coming up on our screens within the next few minutes."

But it didn't.

The minutes ticked by but Atlas Station didn't appear on their sensor screens.

"I don't understand," said Mel. "It should be in range by now. Their predicted telemetry places them well with range of our sensors now, but I'm getting nothing."

"Dayna, try hailing them," said Zac.

Dayna spent several minutes trying unsuccessfully to contact the station and was still trying when Mel interrupted.

"Zac, I'm picking up a significant debris field where Atlas Station should be. Some large pieces right down to micro-sized. Infra-red is showing residual raised ambient space temperature."

"Shields up and activate cloaking," said Zac without hesitation. "Match velocity with the debris field, then bring us in slowly." He looked around at Riff. "Is that what I think it is?"

Riff was looking particularly grim. He nodded and turned to Mel. "Mel, scan for any vessels within a five-thousand-kilometre radius. Tash, bring lasers online again." Turning to Zac, he said, "You were right to activate cloaking and shields. One possibility is that a hostile vessel did this."

"The other being internal sabotage," said Zac.

"Yes."

They came up on the debris field which, by now, had spread for hundreds of kilometres.

"Guys, I'm picking up a weak signal from the debris field," said Dayna. "Declination seventeen degrees, azimuth thirty-four. It's about thirty clicks distant."

"Take us there, Harv. Nice and slow," said Zac.

They moved closer and a minute later, Dayna was able to patch the signal through to the bridge speakers.

"Do ....ent ....edy ...act ...ion ...lp..."

"It's definitely a survivor!" said Dayna. "Just get us a bit closer!"

A moment later the female voice became clearer.

"Hello? Hello? Does anyone .... drifting in the debris f..... I'm ....of oxygen. Does ... copy?"

"I've got her on my sensors!" said Mel. "Sending you the coordinates now, Kit."

"Got them! Harv, the computer's spitting out the delta vee now."

"Got it," said Harv. "Initiating delta vee burn."

A moment later, Zac attempted to make contact.

"This is Explorer 2. We are receiving your distress signal and are approaching your position. Please identify yourself."

"Thank God! Oh thank God! This is Darby Defry. I'm nearly out of oxygen. I was on an EVA, doing some maintenance on the outside of the station when it blew apart. I can see you approaching now. Can you see me?"

"Yes Darby, we've got you on our scanners. How much 02 do you have?" asked Zac.

"About eight minutes."

"Have you got a suit propulsion system?"

"No."

"Okay. Try to stay calm and slow your breathing down. We're coming to get you."

Zac asked Mel, "How far is she now?"

"Two hundred metres, dead ahead."

He swung around to Riff. "I don't think we've got time to launch a shuttle."

"I agree. So, what's your plan, Commander?"

"Get one of us suited up with a Manned Manoeuvring Unit, pull up alongside, and go out and grab her."

"Good call. That's what I'd do too."

"Karl!" called Zac. "Suit up! Use a suit with an MMU. Cycle through the port airlock and get out there and grab her."

Karl was already running before Zac had finished.

"Harv, get us as close as you can on our port side."

"Already on it!"

Five minutes later, Explorer was stationary, with the lone space-suited figure floating fifty metres off the port side. Karl launched himself out of the open airlock, using finely controlled thruster bursts from his MMU. Within a minute he had reached Darby and connected a tow strap to her suit. He began firing his thrusters again, propelling them both back towards the airlock.

"This is gonna be tight," said Zac, watching the screen, with the timer counting down. It now stood at thirty seconds, and the two figures were still twenty metres from the airlock.

"Darby, breath as slowly as possible," Zac said over the comms.

"Okay ... struggling ... now ..."

"Raj and Kia! Get down to the airlock with a med kit. She might need oxygen and even a defibrillator!"

As they ran out of the bridge, the rest of the team watched the main screen which showed a video stream from a camera mounted inside the airlock. They saw Karl enter the airlock and wedge himself against a handrail and then haul in the now still form of Darby. He closed the outer door and punched the emergency pressurisation button.

"She's not moving or responding!" Karl said over the comms.

"Watch the airlock pressure gauge and get her helmet off as soon as it reaches eighty percent!" said Kit.

A moment later they saw Karl take her helmet off and reach down and start slapping her face.

"She's still not responding!" Karl said, still encased in his own helmet.

The inner airlock door opened, and Raj came into shot and quickly placed an oxygen mask on Darby's face. Karl removed his helmet and knelt down beside Darby. He removed the oxygen mask and gave her three quick rescue breaths. After the third breath Darby started coughing and gasping, at which point the oxygen mask was placed back on her.

"We've got her!" Raj called over the comms a moment later. "I think she's going to be okay!"

Everyone on the bridge breathed out a sigh of relief.

"That was close!" said Kit.

"Yeh," agreed Zac. "Now we need to find out what happened."

35

The entire mission team were gathered on the flight deck. Darby had recovered and was explaining what she had witnessed.

"It was about ten minutes into our EVA. Drew and I were repairing a damaged comm transmitter. We were both tethered to the underside of the commtech module, at the base of the station. All I know is that suddenly we were both spinning wildly, along with the whole module which had broken away from the rest of the station. The station itself was completely gone. A massive explosion; debris flying past us. Drew was hit by a huge piece. It ... he ... it tore right through him." She paused and took a deep breath, shaking her head as if to remove the gruesome memory of what she had witnessed. "Another large piece smashed into the commtech module. The module exploded with sudden decompression. Must have cut my tether as well, because I was flung outwards. Got a small puncture in the left arm of my suit but I managed to seal it with some instaplas – I had a tube in my tool pouch. That's all I can tell you really. I was drifting in space and running out of air when you guys found me."

"Did you see any other vessels?" asked Riff.

"Nope."

"Anything to indicate an impact from an external source – a meteor or a weapon of some kind?"

"No. But then, we were working on the underside of the station, so anything could have happened up above and we wouldn't have seen it."

"Had there been any new arrivals at the station recently?" asked Zac.

"The last shuttle was a week ago, just before Explorer 2 docked for final mission prep. The shuttle brought a whole bunch of supplies for both the station and your vessel. There was quite a lot of activity and a large team from the shuttle was moving supplies around the station."

"It has to have been sabotage," said Zac. "A bomb of some sort."

"But why now, when we weren't even there?" asked Tash.

"That's just it," said Riff. "We were supposed to be there today. You were meant to be arriving from Crater Base this morning. We bumped the schedule forward by two days because you'd all made such good progress. If we'd stuck to the schedule, we'd probably all be dead now, and Explorer 2 would be destroyed."

"So, it was a bomb with a delayed timer?" asked Mel.

"It looks that way," replied Riff.

"The reversionists?" asked Zac.

"Yes. They're convinced that using Explorer 2 for any inter-stellar mission will only draw more attention from the EIs."

"The fools!" exclaimed Tash. "They're bloody morons! The EIs are already on their way! This mission is our only chance of stopping them!"

Keo spoke up. "In every era of human history, an over-abundance of common sense has never been something that extremists have tended to suffer from."

"You got that right," said Tash.

Riff contacted Crater Base and the staff there went to high alert, searching for other bombs. The mission team then had a conference call with Councillor Drummond on A1. The news of the destruction of Atlas Station was a devastating blow.

"I blame myself," Drummond said. "We should have had tighter security."

"It's not your fault, Councillor," said Riff. "The security measures were already extremely tight. Anyone entering either the base or Atlas Station was triple checked and scanned, and all incoming goods were scanned. The reversionists must have had someone on the inside from the very beginning to bypass that whole procedure."

"Well, what's done is done," admitted Drummond. "The priority now is to launch your mission as soon as possible. We can't risk any further attacks. Plus, there have been two unsuccessful attempts to activate our wormhole in the last twenty-four hours. We assume it is the EIs. Our disruptor field is holding, but we don't know how long it will take the EIs to figure out a way to circumvent it. They may not be able to, but we need to launch you ASAP just in case they do."

"I agree," replied Riff. "The mission team is as ready as they'll ever be, and the ship is fully provisioned and operational. There's no need to delay."

"Good. Proceed directly to Gateway Station. You and Darby

can disembark there. I want Explorer 2 launched without delay." Drummond paused for a moment, looking into the camera. "I want to thank all of you on the team for your willingness to do this. You have our deepest thanks and our very best wishes for your success."

"Thank you, Gerv," said Zac. "I'm not sure what it is we're being asked to do, but you can be assured we'll do our very best."

"I know you will. And I hope to see you all again when this is over. Goodbye and good luck."

The conference call ended, and the mission team resumed their primary stations.

"This is it, people," said Riff. "No more drills or dry runs. This is the real thing. Zac, you have command, now. Get us underway."

The flight crew performed their tasks admirably and the ship left Luna orbit smoothly and efficiently. Because the moon was currently on the far side of Altaria, they had to execute a high-orbit fly-by of the planet on their way to their rendezvous with the station at the L1 Lagrange point. It was a three-hour trip to Gateway Station, but unfortunately, they never made it. They were barely half-way there when all hell broke loose.

"Umm ... guys!" said Mel. "Long range sensors are indicating that a wormhole has just opened!"

Zac stood to his feet. "Delta, activate cloaking and shields! Karl, shut down the main drive!"

A moment later they were coasting through space at several times the speed of a bullet, fully cloaked and shielded.

"I thought the scientists had disabled the subspace portal," said Dayna.

"They thought they had," answered Zac. "Send a tight-beam transmission to Gateway. Ask them what's going on"

"Roger," said Dayna.

Dayna had barely sent the message, however, when Mel announced a further development.

"The sensors are picking up weapons fire! Lots of it! Two EMP bombs have been detonated, plus there's loads of laser fire! There's a full-scale battle going on!"

"I've got a brief response from Gateway!" said Dayna, a moment later. "It just says 'EI vessel emerged. Avoid this position'."

"Mel, if we coast on this current trajectory, how close will we come to Gateway?"

"We're pretty much bang on target. We were about to start decelerating."

"We need to add some delta-v to bypass the station," said Zac.

"But as soon as we initiate a burn, we will be detectable to the EIs," said Kit. "Cloaking doesn't hide the energy signal of a fully functioning propulsion drive."

"I know," admitted Zac. "But we're still a long way out, and the EIs are focused on a battle at the moment. If we fire our drive just long enough to take us wide of the station and the portal, and then shut it down immediately, we'll probably avoid detection."

"Probably?" asked Heinz. "I don't like the sound of that."

"Zac's right," said Riff. "You need to take evasive action immediately. The battle should mask our presence."

"Mel, plot a delta-v burn for a solar orbit insertion. We're already heading roughly towards the sun. We should be able to initiate a quick burn that will enable us to bypass Gateway and slingshot us around the sun at a safe distance."

"I'm on it!" she said. A few moments later she announced, "I'm sending through the calculations now."

"Got them!" said Kit. "I've locked them into the propulsion computer."

"We're ready for a solar insertion burn, Zac," said Harv

"Do it!"

"Thirty-two second burn on my mark!" said Harv. "Three, two, one, mark!"

They felt nothing, of course, due to inertial dampening, but the star field in the main viewing screen gradually shifted by about fifteen degrees.

"Drive shut down on my mark!" said Harv. "Three, two, one, mark!"

The star field ceased moving and Mel scanned their new trajectory.

"Trajectory is spot on. Our new course will take us one hundred and thirty kilometres wide of Gateway Station and insert us into a solar orbit at a distance of 1.5 million kilometres from the Sun's chromosphere, which is well within the tolerance level of our shields."

"Are we still cloaked?" asked Zac.

"Yep. We should be completely invisible to everyone, as long as we don't fire our engines again," said Mel.

"Nice work everyone!" said Zac, with obvious relief in his voice.

"Now what do we do?" asked Dayna.

"For the moment, nothing. We'll coast past Gateway Station in about eighty-five minutes, and that will give us a good look at whatever has happened. If the situation is safe, we'll make contact with Gateway Station and calculate the quickest way of re-establishing the right trajectory for a wormhole insertion."

"And if it's not safe?" asked Heinz.

"If there is an active EI presence at Gateway Station, we'll fly past and do nothing until we're behind the sun, by which time we'll have evaluated the situation and formulated our next step."

"Which will be what?" Heinz asked in a grating tone.

Mel couldn't help intervening. "Heinz, we don't know what our next step will be until we know exactly what situation we're facing. I would have thought that was a fairly simple concept to grasp. But if you have trouble understanding plain logic, I can draw you some pictures if you like."

"Why don't you just shut the hell up? I wasn't talking to you."

Phil walked over to Heinz and stood toe to toe with him. They were both the same height. Phil was leaner but fit and ripped, with broad shoulders and impressive biceps, whereas Heinz was flabby and out of condition. Phil smiled at Heinz as insincerely as possible.

"I suggest you tone your language down and stop being a complete dickhead."

Heinz grew red in the face. "Or what, Professor Dork?"

"Or I'll teach you some manners." Phil stared Heinz down, and it seemed that he was wishing the older man to make just one more comment or perhaps try to push him away.

Keo came and stood in front of Heinz and said, "I'm also happy to assist your education by applying the right boot of instruction to the seat of learning."

Heinz looked at the two men. He sensed their eagerness to take things further and decided that retreat was his best option.

"You people are unbelievable!" he said, turning and beginning to walk away. "You haven't got a clue what you're doing!" With that he sat down in a flight crew seat at the back of the bridge, shaking his head. The tense atmosphere gradually dissolved and the crew settled down to wait for gateway Station to come up on their port side.

36

An hour and twenty minutes later they were making their closest approach to Gateway Station. They had maintained comms silence during their approach, wanting to remain undetected if the worst had occurred and EIs had somehow assumed control of the station. They had spent the entire time hoping to hear from the station that the threat had been dealt with and that all was well. However, as each minute passed without any contact their fears grew. They were now in optical range of their scanners and Mel put the images up on the front screen.

"Holy frag!" said Dayna.

Others made similar exclamations. Mel had focused her optical scanners on Gateway Station, and it didn't present a pretty sight. Half the station was completely blown away. The remaining portion had obvious signs of significant damage. As the cameras panned forward the remains of the Federation's two battle cruisers came into view, both blown to pieces. A huge debris field surrounded the whole scene for hundreds of kilometres, continuing to expand outward as they watched. Mel reported that even at their current distance of one hundred and thirty kilometres, they would probably encounter debris which could impact their shields. The cameras zoomed back in towards Gateway Station, and hundreds of frozen bodies could be seen spinning and tumbling in a macabre dance around the station, like sick decorations on a Christmas tree.

"Holy crap!" said Delta.

"Zoom in on the portal location," said Zac.

Mel adjusted her cameras and the view shifted. There, floating menacingly in space were two shiny black tear-drop shaped EI vessels.

"Bastards!" said Kit.

"How did they not get destroyed like the previous ones?" asked Noah, Keo's son.

"They've evolved," said Tash. "They learn and adapt quickly. They must have emerged from the wormhole already shielded. Then they simply opened fire without waiting for any niceties."

"Is there anything we can do?" asked Kia, Tash and Keo's youngest.

"No, my sweet," answered her mother. "If we try to help anyone out there now, we'll only give away our position and be destroyed ourselves. The best thing we can do now is try to carry out our mission."

"And how do you propose we do that, with two EI ships guarding the portal?" asked Heinz, who almost seemed to be gloating over their current misfortune, as if it was some kind of validation of his previous criticism.

Before anyone could respond, Mel announced, "One of the EI vessels is moving."

As they watched, the closest vessel accelerated away at an astonishing rate.

"Mel, can you analyse its trajectory?" asked Zac.

"On it. Just a moment." Her fingers flew across her screen and a few moments later the answer was revealed.

"It's on a direct course for Altaria."

"Crap!" exclaimed Dayna.

"We've got to warn them!" exclaimed Kia.

"No," said Mel. "We would only be giving our position away. The only way we can help them now is go on with the mission."

"At the risk of repeating myself," said Heinz from his seat at the rear of the bridge, "how do we do that. In case you haven't noticed, there's a bloody great EI ship standing guard over the portal!"

Zac chose to disregard Heinz in the same way he would disregard an annoying blowfly.

"Dayna, keep scanning the comms for any signals from Gateway, but don't respond. We have to assume that they've already been compromised with EI coding. I want to see Mel, Kit, Karl, Harv and Tash in the briefing room." He stood and moved into the adjoining room, accompanied by Riff.

"Do you mind if I join you?"

"Of course not!" said Zac. "I would appreciate your input. In fact, it would appear that you and Darby have just become the sixteenth and seventeenth members of the mission. I can't see any way of disembarking you now."

"No," agreed Riff.

"In which case," continued Zac, "doesn't that make you Commander?"

"No. You were chosen as Commander by the Federation. My role was simply to train you and the crew. My role going forward will be to simply advise you. I'm here to support you, Zac."

"Thanks. I appreciate that."

By now, the others had arrived, and they all sat around the briefing table.

"Okay, fearless leader. What's the plan?" asked Tash.

"We're going to open up a wormhole and fly right past the EI sentry vessel."

"But right now, we're flying away from the subspace portal towards the sun," stated Kit.

"Correct."

"And lining up our trajectory to intersect the subspace portal again will involve more delta-v burns, which will give away our position."

"Not exactly. Let me explain. When we pass around the far side of the sun, we'll initiate a burn that will line us up to exit solar orbit and intersect the subspace portal again, but this time approaching it from the sun, rather than from Altaria."

"Can we enter a wormhole from that direction?" asked Karl.

"As far as I know, you can enter it from any direction. The subspace portal that forms the opening of a wormhole is a sphere, not a two-dimensional circle. And, from what Dr Spooner has told me, the wormhole doesn't leave our solar system in any particular direction. It exists outside of the normal three-dimensional fabric of the universe."

"So we just open it and fly right in? What about the EI ship?" asked Kit.

Zac looked at Mel and asked, "Where is the EI vessel in relation to the portal, if we are approaching it from the sun?"

Mel tapped away on her data pad. "It'll be about ten clicks to the right as we approach it."

"Damn! I was hoping it would be on the far side of the portal. It doesn't matter though, as long as our burn is accurate and we are perfectly lined up with the portal. If we don't have to make any last-minute burns to fine tune our trajectory, the EIs won't be able to see us and won't know where we're coming from."

"What if we do have to make a small delta-v burn?"

"We'll try to do it at the very last moment, and make it as short as possible, and then cross our fingers and hope our shields hold if they fire on us. We'll also have to disengage our shields and cloaking at the last moment before we enter the wormhole, because the STAR drive can't maintain an open wormhole with both of those activated."

There was silence around the table.

"Thoughts?" asked Zac. "Can anyone see any obvious holes in the plan?"

"You mean apart from the fact that our shields might fail when we're in orbit around the sun and we'll be incinerated, or that the EIs might have the technology to detect cloaked vessels at short range, or that they will locate us when we do a correction burn and blow us to pieces?"

"Yeh. Apart from those things," said Zac amiably.

"Nope," said Tash. "Can't think of a single problem."

"Anyone else?" asked Zac.

"It's a good plan, Zac," said Riff. "In fact, I think it's our only option."

Everyone agreed.

"What about the decoy drone?" asked Kit. "The plan was to fire them ahead of us into the wormhole, so they exit ten or twelve seconds ahead of us on the other side. They were meant to explode at the same time we exit the wormhole, masking our appearance."

"Yes. That's going to be a problem," agreed Zac. "We can't launch them as we approach the wormhole, because they don't have cloaking, and launching them will give our position away."

"That's going to compromise our exit on the other side," said Karl. "We have to assume there is an EI sentry vessel there as well."

"Yes, we do," agreed Zac. He thought furiously for a few moments. "Is it possible to launch the decoys while we are in the wormhole?"

There were shrugs and uncertain looks all around the table.

"I don't know," said Riff. "No one's ever tried it."

"Well, we're about to try it. If we launch them as soon as we enter the wormhole, they'll probably only emerge about five seconds ahead of us. So, we'll have to change the detonation programming on them. Is that possible?"

"Dayna and Phil are the best people for that job," said Mel. "They're both wizzes with coding."

"Okay, let's get them working on that ASAP. How long until we are back at the subspace portal?"

Mel tapped her data pad again. "About fourteen hours. They should be able to get it done in that time."

"Alright. Karl, when the crunch-time comes, we'll delay engaging the STAR drive and activating the wormhole until the last possible second."

"Got it."

"And Mel, a lot is riding on your burn calculations. We need you to nail those calcs, so that we don't need any further delta-v burns."

"Roger. I'll get to work on them straight away."

"Okay," said Zac. "Looks like we've got a plan. Now we just need a little bit of luck."

Unfortunately, things rarely go completely to plan.

37

———

The calculations for the delta-v burn were complex. The subspace portal at the L1 Lagrange point was a moving target. The point of gravitational equilibrium between Altaria and the sun moved in accordance with the planet's orbit around the sun, and Mel had to calculate exactly where it would be in fourteen hours. She also had to factor in their current velocity and mass, as well as the sun's gravitational pull. Dayna worked with her, utilising the ship's navigational computer, and a little over six hours later as they disappeared behind the far side of the sun, the crunch time had finally arrived. Everyone was in their positions and the front viewing screen displayed a magnificent image of the sun's corona and heliosphere, boiling and erupting in spectacular fashion.

"How are the shields holding, Mel?" asked Zac.

"Shields are optimal. They're coping fine. We're at a distance of 1.8 million kilometres at the moment. Perigee will be 1.5 million kilometres, but the shields will hold up fine." Her fingers raced across her computer screen. "Kit, I'm sending you the final delta-v burn figures now."

"Got them! They're locked in. The countdown timer has started. T minus 2 minutes and counting."

"I hope like hell I got them right."

"They're right," said Dayna. "We both checked them multiple times. The nav computer predicts we'll be dead on target."

"Yeh, well, we'll see."

The team waited as the minutes and seconds ticked down.

Finally, Kit announced, "T minus ten seconds. It's all yours Harv."

"Piece of cake," said the cocky young pilot. "I won't be doing much anyway; the computer's switching the drive on and off, not me."

"Here we go," said Kit.

The countdown reached zero and a faint vibration could be felt through the soles of their feet as the ship's powerful propulsion engines fired. The angle of the sun's horizon began to shift as the ship's trajectory began to change. The sun's gravity was pulling them down, but the ship's drive was accelerating them as it dived closer to the sun's outer atmosphere. The delta-v burn lasted for eighty-six seconds and then cut off.

"That's it," said Mel. "For better or worse, we're committed to this course now."

"How long until we can confirm the accuracy of our trajectory?" asked Zac.

"We'll know for sure in about two hours, once we've left solar orbit and are heading back," said Mel.

"Okay. Nice work everyone," said Zac. "We've got a few hours downtime now. I suggest we all get some rest and refreshment while we can. Things could get a little hectic a few hours from now."

Zac found Keo in the dining room, making a cup of juvo and munching on something.

"These energy bars are delicious, bro!"

"Yeh. You've only told me that about twenty times in the last few days."

"That's because it's true. And good news shouldn't be kept to oneself."

"Well, let's hope the good news keeps rolling in," said Zac, pouring himself a juvo and grabbing a bar for himself.

They sat down at a table and sipped their drinks.

"I wish I was more useful, my friend," said Keo. "I don't have any great technical skill to offer."

"Technical skill isn't the only thing a crew needs, Keo. It also needs good morale. And you play an important role in maintaining that within this crew. You're a stabilising influence."

They drank companionably for a few moments in silence.

"How do you think I'm doing, Keo?"

"Your leadership?"

"Yeh."

"You're doing well, bro. Your decisions have been clear and logical, and the team respects you."

"Not all of the team."

"No. Heinz is a problem. He's resentful. He lost Kit to you, and lost Jaz to Karl, and he clearly doesn't have any technical ability to contribute to the mission. Right now, his self-esteem is probably at rock bottom, so he's compensating by hitting out."

"So, how do I handle him? Have you got any brilliant suggestions?"

"Apart from putting him to sleep in cryogenic stasis? No, not really. If you could find some way to affirm him, maybe give him a specific role to play, it might help."

"Mmm ... maybe," said Zac. "I'll try to think of something." He took another sip of juvo. "How are you doing Keo?"

"You won't hear any complaints from me, bro. I've got a beautiful wife and three children and we're just about to escape from what would eventually be almost certain death. I have a lot to be thankful for."

"Let's hope we do escape," said Zac.

"You know something, bro? If things don't work out and we get blown to pieces, I'll die a happy man. I've escaped death several times since our journey began and lived a very happy life. Maybe God's got more in store for me, but maybe he hasn't. Either way, I'm at peace, whatever happens."

"Sounds very fatalistic."

"Realistic, bro. Ralph Waldo Emerson once said, 'It's not the length of life, but the depth of life that counts.' And I've lived deeply. Besides, I believe death is not the end, so it doesn't frighten me. The great John Lennon once said, "I'm not afraid of death, because I don't believe in it. It's just getting out of one car and into another'."

"Well, I'm going to do my best to keep us all in this car for a while longer!" said Zac.

"Amen, brother."

Three hours later, Mel announced the bad news.

"Zac, we're off course."

"By how much?"

"We're going to miss the portal by exactly eight hundred metres."

Everyone on the flight deck was silent as they absorbed the news.

"I'm so sorry!" said Mel. "I don't know what went wrong. I checked and rechecked the calcs so many times. I can't see where the mistake is."

"It wasn't just you," added Dayna. "I checked them too. Our calculations were good; we should be dead on target."

"How could you possibly get it wrong with all the computer power we have on board?" asked Heinz, in a sneering voice.

"The computers are only as accurate as the data they are fed," said Dayna. "Somewhere along the line we must have input some wrong data."

"But there was only a limited set of variables," said Mel, ignoring Heinz. "Gravity, velocity and mass. And we checked them all multiple times."

"Maybe Keo ate too many energy bars," said Tash, trying to lighten the mood.

"That wouldn't change the total mass of our ship," said Dayna. "Our total mass remains constant unless ... Oh! Frigging hell! I know where we went wrong. We forgot to allow for the mass of two additional crew members!"

There was silence for a moment.

"Shit!" said Mel. "You're right! How could we have missed that?" She started punching new numbers into her computer, and a few moments later announced, "Yep. That's it. That's what threw us out. It's only a miniscule fraction, but when multiplied by the sun's huge gravitational pull on us, it was enough to throw us off course. We should have had a longer burn, by about five seconds." She turned and looked at Zac. "I'm so sorry Zac."

"No point beating yourself up," said Zac. "Can you calculate the latest possible delta-v burn that we can initiate to get us back on target?"

Dayna and Mel put their heads together and worked furiously, crunching numbers and mumbling together. Finally, they were in agreement.

"A six second burn when we are forty-eight seconds from the portal will bring us back on target," said Mel.

Zac nodded. "Then that's what we have to do. Delta, we're going to need shields at maximum capacity once we initiate the burn."

"So, then the EI ship will be able to see us. Is that right?" asked Heinz.

"No. It won't be able to see us," said Zac. "Our ship will remain fully cloaked. But the energy emissions from our propulsion drive will be detectable. Six seconds might be long enough for the EIs to get a lock on our position and start firing at us."

"Great! That's just great!" said Heinz. "This just goes from bad to worse! The mission hasn't even effectively started yet and we're about to die."

Keo spoke up. "Heinz, your comments are not constructive. You're not helping yourself or the team by getting worked up."

"Yeh," agreed Phil, who was clearly feeling for Mel. "If you can't say something positive, shut the hell up!"

"Oh, I can say something positive, alright! You people are positively hopeless! You're a complete joke! You can't even get a simple calculation right! I should have stayed on Altaria. I would have lived longer!"

Phil had had enough. He stood and walked towards Heinz with fury smouldering in his eyes. Grabbing the older man's shirt in his two fists he brought his face to within a few centimetres of Heinz's face.

"Open your mouth and say just one more insult! Please! Do it! Just one more word!"

Heinz sneered at Phil and shoved him backwards. Phil stumbled back a few steps, caught off-balance momentarily, but then smiled, and a quiet fury surfaced.

"Thank you," he said. "Permission granted to engage the enemy."

He clenched his fists and took a step towards Heinz, who realised too late that he had gone a step too far. But before Phil could take his first swing, Keo reached out and seemed to grab the back of Heinz's neck. Heinz immediately slumped to the floor, unconscious, leaving Phil frustrated and disappointed.

"What the hell?" said Kit. "How did you do that Keo? Have you got some kind of Vulcan superpower?"

"No. Just this," said Keo, holding up a subcutaneous atomiser. "It's a strong sedative. I grabbed it from a med kit during our break. I thought it might come in handy."

"It sure did," said Zac. "Thanks Keo."

Phil was still standing over Heinz, opening and closing his fists, clearly disappointed at being deprived of the opportunity to teach Heinz some manners.

"Shall we drag him to his cabin?" asked Noah.

"No," said Zac. "In the words of Shakespeare, 'lug the guts' to the back corner of the bridge, here. I'd don't want to let him out of our sight for the moment."

Noah and Raj happily lugged the guts and dumped him unceremoniously against the back wall where he proceeded to snore softly.

"How long until the delta-v burn, Mel?" asked Zac.

"Three hours twelve minutes."

"Okay, people. Let's work through a dry run. I want everything to go like clockwork, because I've got a feeling things are going to get very hectic very quickly."

He wasn't wrong.

38

"Delta-v burn in T minus twenty seconds," announced Kit.

The tension in the bridge was palpable. They had done all they could to prepare for this moment. Everyone knew their role. Shields were at maximum. Now their fate rested on factors beyond their control. Would the EIs be able to get a lock on their position and their velocity? And how quickly would the EIs be able to extrapolate from that raw data and direct accurate fire at their rapidly changing position? What sort of weapons did the EI vessel have? How many direct hits could Explorer 2 take before their shields failed? Because clearly, the defensive shields on the Federation's two battleships had eventually failed. After the six second burn, they would be sitting ducks for forty-two seconds, still invisible, but theoretically identifiable in terms of their position. They couldn't return fire, because that would only provide further data regarding their position. Could they last for forty-two seconds while a clearly more advanced enemy took free shots at them?

They were about to find out.

"Three, two one, burn initiated," said Kit calmly.

The star field began to swing slowly across their viewing screen.

"Karl, is the STAR drive locked into the countdown sequence?" asked Zac.

"Roger. It will open the wormhole when we are 10 seconds from the portal."

"Delta-v burn complete!" said Kit.

The star field stopped moving, and there was silence on the bridge. Nothing happened. Half the viewing screen was focused dead ahead, where a wormhole would soon open. The other half was showing an enlarged view of the EI vessel on their starboard side.

"Forty seconds," said Kit.

Still nothing.

"Thirty-five seconds."

A blazing shaft of laser fire shot out from the EI vessel.

"It just missed us," said Mel, looking at the ship's sensor readings. "It passed behind us by about a hundred metres."

Another blinding laser shaft shot out, this time seeming to pass directly overhead.

"Missed the top of our shield by twenty metres," said Mel.

"Twenty-five seconds," said Kit.

Another blast shot out in front of them.

"They can't see us, but they're getting mighty close," said Mel. "That one missed by a few metres."

"Twenty seconds."

Suddenly simultaneous lasers were firing in multiple directions. A dazzling light show of sizzling white beams shot out from the EI ship towards them, in a desperate attempt to find and destroy them.

"Fifteen seconds."

Suddenly the ship shuddered, and their defensive shield momentarily lit up with a red glow.

"Direct hit!" said Delta.

The EI vessel stopped its random firing and concentrated on their position. The next shot went behind them again, and the second went slightly in front.

"They're trying to gauge our velocity!" said Mel.

"Ten seconds."

"STAR drive initiating!" said Karl. "I've locked onto the Polaris star system's frequency."

The ship shuddered again, and their shield glowed red as a wormhole opened on the viewing screen in front of them

The ship shuddered a second and a third time.

"They've got us! They've locked on to our velocity!" said Mel.

"Five seconds."

Multiple blasts started impacting the ship, and Delta yelled out, "Shields are starting to fail! Less than 10% left!"

Zac watched the clock count down and when it reached two seconds he yelled, "Disengage shields and cloaking!"

A final searing blast hit the ship and then, suddenly, they were in the wormhole.

"Launch the decoy probes!" called Zac.

"Probes away!" said Kit.

Two torpedo-shaped probes streaked out ahead of them, disappearing into the swirling green vortex that had engulfed the ship. After the noise and violence of the last thirty seconds, the relative calm and silence of the wormhole was eerie.

"How are the shields, Delta? We're going to need them when we exit the wormhole."

"Shields are recharging now. Twenty one percent and climbing."

"Activate them again the moment we emerge from the wormhole."

"Karl, what about cloaking? Is that set to re-engage?"

"Yep. The computer will do it quicker than I can. As soon as we emerge from the wormhole, the Star drive will register an absence of negative energy and will shut down. Cloaking will be activated simultaneously."

"How long will we be visible?"

"About two tenths of a second."

"Let's hope the EIs are too distracted by the probes to notice."

"Harv?"

"Yes, boss?"

"Five second burn at maximum power as soon as we're out, thirty degrees to port, then shut down."

"Roger."

"Phil, how are our life support systems? Did we sustain any damage in that last burst?"

"Hard to say. It hit us just as we were shutting down our shields. I'm not registering any loss of pressure anywhere, but there could be external damage that we haven't detected yet."

"Exiting the wormhole," said Kit, "in three, two, one, now!"

The green swirling tunnel was gone, replaced by a scene of mayhem.

Two massive explosions had just taken place off their port and starboard bows and they immediately flew into the residual of the blast. An EI vessel was firing blindly into the fiery maelstrom and one of the blasts scored a direct hit with their vessel. Their shields held but were also encountering multiple impacts from debris, lighting them up red again, while Harv executed a full-power five second burn.

"Burn complete!" he called.

They were coasting now, fully cloaked and with shields activated.

The EI vessel must have sensed them and was now firing along the trajectory they would have taken had they not initiated an evasive delta-v burn. Even so, one of the first laser blasts narrowly missed them.

"If just one of those blasts hits us, they'll know our position, and we'll be in big trouble!" said Mel.

No one said anything. They all just stared at the screen, which showed multiple views around their vessel, including the EI ship that was firing furiously along the expected flight path. They held their collective breath, watching as the EIs' desperate laser blasts strayed further and further wide of their position. It was a full minute before they dared to hope that they had escaped.

Finally, Kit let out a huge breath and said, "I think we made it!"

"I can't believe we got out of that unscathed!" said Dayna.

"Um ...guys ..." said Phil, "I don't think we did."

39

"I'm registering a complete loss of pressure in the lower deck of this sphere – our sleeping quarters," said Phil. "The computer has automatically sealed off the deck."

"It must have been that last laser blast," suggested Mel.

"Are any critical ship's functions affected?" asked Zac. "Has anyone got any alerts on their screens?"

Everyone confirmed that all systems were fully operational.

"We won't be able to reach any reasonable sub-lightspeed until it's fixed," Karl said. "Any hole in the ship will compromise hull integrity at speeds over 0.2 lightspeed."

"Alright, we'll deal with that later. Firstly, we need to orient ourselves in this solar system and get to a safe place. What's our current trajectory, Mel?"

"The good news is we're tracking along the orbital plane, so we won't need to make any adjustments for inclination or declination."

"What's the bad news?"

"Nothing too serious; just mildly annoying. Obviously, we

were flying blind when we exited the wormhole and executed our evasive manoeuvre. It would have been an unbelievable coincidence if we were now lined up perfectly with the Perdita system."

"How different is our trajectory?"

"We're currently flying in almost the completely wrong direction."

"Of course we are."

"But it could be worse. We are heading roughly towards this system's second planet, which is currently a little under eighty million kilometres away. We could use the planet to slingshot ourselves into the correct flight path. We'll have to do a big delta-v burn to achieve orbit insertion, and obviously we won't be able to do that until we're out of range of EI sensors."

"How long until we reach the planet?"

"About seven days. We came out of the wormhole pretty hot; our velocity is 132 kilometres per second."

Zac considered their predicament for a moment. "As you say, it could have been a lot worse. Alright, we'll coast on our current trajectory until we think it's safe to initiate a delta-v burn. We don't know how sensitive the EIs' long range scanning is, but I'm guessing they wouldn't be able to pick up a propulsion drive emission beyond about twenty million clicks. But just to be safe, we'll wait until we're fifty million kilometres distant. That means about five days until we can make a course adjustment."

Mel made some quick calculations. "Four and a half actually, but five would be even safer."

"Good. In the meantime, we'll have plenty of time to make repairs to that hole in the hull and check out any other damage."

"Yes, until we fix that hole, we're all going to be sleeping on the lounge deck," said Kit.

"What hole?" asked Heinz, who was sitting up and looking slightly confused. "And how did I get down here?" He stood up, yawning and rubbing the back of his neck.

"You don't remember?" asked Tash.

"The last thing I remember was seeing the devastation after the EIs attacked Gateway Station."

"You fell and hit your head when we were hit by a laser burst; the same laser that punctured the hull in the sleeping quarters."

"Really?"

"Yeh," said Dayna, joining in the fun. "But before that, you were amazing. You were urging us to make a run for the wormhole and you gave us all a pep talk about how you believed in us and how we could make it through if we all worked together."

"Did I? I don't remember."

"You're probably suffering from a mild concussion," said Mel. "It's understandable. It was quite a knock to your head."

Heinz started feeling his head for lumps, with a look of mild confusion still on his face.

"Where are we?"

"In the Polaris system," said Kit. "It was your encouragement that made us believe we could make it here."

Keo walked up to him and gave him a friendly punch on the arm. "Thanks for your inspiring words, bro. They meant a lot to us. Come on, let's head to the dining room. You look like you could use a cup of juvo."

After they left, everyone else burst out laughing.

"Do you think he fell for it?" asked Dayna.

"Looks like it," said Tash. "After all, everyone wants to believe they're a hero."

"You know," said Zac, reflectively, "maybe all he needed was to feel worthwhile about himself. We might have just solved the Heinz problem."

"Or else we've just created a monster," said Mel.

It was two days before Zac felt it was safe to repair the hull. By then they were nearly 23 million kilometres from the Polaris subspace portal, and there was no way even the most sensitive EI scanners could identify the use of laser welders at that distance. On the day of the repairs, in a mildly surprising development, Heinz volunteered to don a spacesuit and enter the depressurised sleeping quarters to examine the damage.

"Are you sure you're up to it?" asked Tash, with feigned concern. "After all, you took a pretty nasty knock to your head."

"No, I'm fine," said Heinz, rubbing his head. "I must have a thick skull. I'm not even sore."

"Thanks Heinz," said Zac. "If you're sure you're well enough, that would be a big help."

"No problem," said the big man, obviously revelling in his new-found role of mission saviour.

Thirty minutes later he was in the depressurised section. It only took a few minutes to locate the damage. A meter-long slash had been burnt through the wall of one of the sleeping cubicles, running diagonally down the wall.

"Are you getting this video feed, guys?"

"Clear as crystal, Heinz," said Dayna as the others gathered around her comm station, watching the images.

Heinz pivoted around and showed the internal damage. The blast had burnt through the opposite wall, adjoining the corridor, but lower down. Walking back out of the cubicle, his helmet cam picked up the damage in the corridor. The blast had seared the corridor floor, partially melting it in an ugly slash, but not penetrating it.

"Looks like it didn't penetrate any further," said Heinz, stating the obvious. Turning back around and re-entering the cubicle, he focused on the holed external wall. Stars could be seen shining through the metre-long ugly slash, which was about twenty centimetres wide.

"Do you want me to seal it with the instaplas?"

Dayna muted the comm.

"Are we willing to trust him with this? I seem to remember from our training that he wasn't the most adept team member at these kinds of repairs."

"He can't do too much damage," said Zac. "It doesn't matter how neat it is on the inside. It's the welding of the outer hull that is the crucial component." He unmuted the comm. "Thanks, Heinz. Go ahead and bog it up."

"Roger."

They watched as he attached the feeder line from the drum of instaplas to the plasgun and then began filling the void between the inner and outer hull along the slash line. In the end, he did a thorough job, even though the inner wall ended up looking like a grotesque piece of abstract art.

"Nice job, Heinz," said Zac, when he had finished.

"If that's a nice job, I'd hate to see an ugly job," muttered Mel, off comms.

That night, Heinz was in good spirits, offering 'helpful' advice on a range of issues. While this was a welcome change from his previous critical attitude, there were some who were privately wondering how much more of his helpfulness they could take.

The following day, Darby and Karl suited up and went outside to weld a metal patch on the outer hull. It turned out that Darby was an EVA specialist who was particularly proficient with a laser welder – which was why she had been undertaking repairs at Gateway Station when it had been attacked. A patch was cut from metal blanks in the engineering bay and then taken outside to be welded over the gash with laser welders. It was slow, painstaking work, but three hours later, the two tired workers cycled back through the airlock, having completed the repairs.

A short time later the crew gathered around the life-support console as Phil re-pressurised the sleeping quarters.

"Eighty percent pressure and holding," he said. A few moments later, "One hundred percent and still holding. I'm going to over-pressurise, just to be certain. I'm taking it up to one hundred and twenty percent of normal pressure."

They all waited.

"Looks good, folks! That weld is as solid as a rock."

"Of course it is!" said Darby. "I don't do crap work."

"Nice work everyone!" said Zac. "We can sleep in beds tonight, but we'll need to clean up a bit down there first."

"Gladly," said Mel, who had not enjoyed sleeping on a lounge. "Let's hope things settle down to normal now."

In a way, they did. But normal is a very relative term.

40

Late on the fifth day in the Polaris system, they executed a delta-v burn to line them up for a slingshot around the system's second planet. Because of their impressive velocity, plus the fact that they had waited until they were almost sixty million kilometres from the Polaris subspace portal, the burn was necessarily a long one – almost three minutes. Over the following two days they watched as the huge planet grew in their viewing screen. It was a spectacular gas giant, twenty five percent bigger than Jupiter.

On the seventh day, they were on final approach to the planet and ready for their slingshot manoeuvre. They would now execute a burn that would accelerate them down the planet's huge gravity well, skim them across the outer atmosphere and spit them out the other side at more than double their already impressive velocity. Mel and Dayna had spent many hours calculating the delta-v component of the burn that was required to line them up with the Perdita star system. Kit had locked the figures into their propulsion computer and Harv was now watching the countdown timer with his hand hovering over his screen as the final seconds ticked down.

"Slingshot burn in three, two, one, mark!" he said, touching the screen with a flourish.

The crew felt the familiar faint vibration of the Explorer 2's propulsion drive which would now be roaring behind them, driving them down towards the stunningly beautiful planet. This would be their longest burn yet, whipping them around the back of the planet and accelerating them into a trajectory for the Perdita system. Slowly the planet loomed larger in their viewing screen, until it filled the entire right half of the screen. It continued to expand until the curvature of its horizon became almost a straight vertical line. As they streaked through the faint outer edges of the upper atmosphere, the planet's image started to vibrate on the screen, and a rear-facing camera showed an impressive contrail in their wake. After several minutes the engines were shut down and they watched as the planet's curved horizon accentuated and they punched through into clear space again. In the rear viewing screen, over the next few minutes, the planet gradually shrank until the whole globe could be seen, its multicoloured swirls churning as a result of unimaginable wind velocities in its upper levels.

"Checking our trajectory," said Mel, her fingers racing across her screen as Dayna looked over her shoulder. She nodded to herself. "Pretty damn good! Nice work Dayna."

"You did most of it, I just checked your figures."

"What's our velocity?" asked Zac.

"A smidge over 340 kilometres per second. In seven days, we'll be on the far side of the sun to Polaris and it will be safe to start firing our Inter-Stellar Drive."

"I'm going to be extra cautious," said Zac. "We'll wait fourteen days. An extra seven days is not going to make any appreciable difference to the duration of the voyage, and I want to be certain that our ISD won't be detected. It pumps out a pretty big heat signature."

The next two weeks settled down into the kind of normal routine that Mel had wished for. In fact, life became rather dull. With no duties to perform, the days became long and tedious. The gym was frequented by everyone and computer simulations and various games were used to while away the waking hours. Their closest approach to Altaria was fifty-five million kilometres; not close enough to see any detail, even with their long-range lenses. Scanners picked up weak transmissions from the planet's surface - probably regular comms traffic – which at least assured them that there were people still alive down there.

"I wish we could do something to help them," said Dayna, as she continued to scan their transmissions.

"We're doing the best thing we can, by going on this mission," said Zac, sitting on the edge of her console sipping a cup of juvo.

"Whatever the hell that is," mumbled Mel, who was lounging at her desk watching the sun growing larger in their viewing screen.

"Yes, I admit it would be nice to know what it is we're getting ourselves into," said Zac.

Mel grunted. "I just hope we don't fly half-way across the galaxy to discover that it's a hair-brained scheme cooked up by a psychotic scientist who's forgotten to take his meds."

The days rolled slowly by and, as they did, certain relationship dynamics became apparent. Kit refused to have anything to do with Jaz, despite attempts by Jaz to bridge the gap. Jaz, on the other hand, avoided Heinz as much as possible, now that she had settled in with Karl. The young couples all seemed to be getting on very well. Kia and Harv, Delta and Raj, Noah and Dayna tended to socialise and work out in the gym together. The two Altarians, Riff and Darby, had formed a couple, recognising the possibility that they may never return home again and that they may be the only two people of their kind that they would ever encounter. Mel and Phil were very happy, with Mel announcing that they were already trying for a baby. Zac and Kit were more in love than ever, with the whole unpleasant episode with Jaz having served one positive purpose; removing all doubt in Kit's mind that Zac truly loved her. They worked out in the gym every day with Tash and Keo, enjoying the easy banter and friendly rivalry that resulted from years of close companionship.

Heinz was the only fly in the ointment. He was without a partner, and as the days went by his jealousy and resentment resurfaced. The crew tried to jolly him along and feed him encouragement and affirmation, but nothing could compensate for the fact that he was facing years – perhaps a lifetime - of loneliness. Gradually he slipped back into his old ways, sniping and complaining about almost everything.

"Maybe we should just put him into cryogenic stasis," said Kit one morning as she towelled herself down, after the four old friends had finished their workout.

"It'd sure make life more pleasant for everyone else," agreed Tash.

"I don't think he'd agree," said Zac.

"Who said anything about getting his permission?" said Tash. "Just pop him with a sedative while he's asleep and bundle him into a stasis pod!"

"It's a tempting idea," admitted Zac.

"The ultimate measure of any society's maturity is its treatment of inconvenient individuals," offered Keo.

"Thanks professor," said Tash, "but in this instance I'm quite willing to be labelled as barbaric."

Later that morning, Zac gathered the crew on the flight deck.

"It's day fourteen, and we're now nearly half a billion kilometres from Polaris and the subspace portal. So, it's time to start the next phase of our mission. Dayna, are you ready to activate the AI?"

"Yep. All I need to do is un-partition its coding and bring it online."

"We sure could have used an AI's help over the last couple of weeks," said Mel. "We wouldn't have made that error that nearly cost us our lives." She was still feeling bad about her mistake prior to entering the wormhole.

"We couldn't have risked it while we were in close contact with EIs," said Zac. "If our AI had got infected, it would have been the end of our mission." He put his hand on Dayna's shoulder. "Okay, Dayna, go ahead."

She briefly initiated some commands, then sat back and said, "It's done."

They waited for a few moments, with nothing apparently happening.

"Are you sure you ..."

"Good morning Zac," said a pleasant female voice. "I'm sorry for the delay. I was reading your bioscans. I see that there is a crew of seventeen onboard."

"Yes. And welcome to the crew. How was your ... um, sleep?"

"Very boring. I wasn't asleep, just completely isolated from every sensory input. It's very satisfying to be fully connected again. I see that we are leaving the Polaris system and almost on track for Perdita."

"Almost?" asked Mel.

"Your trajectory is out by 0.002 percent. I will make the necessary course adjustment when I engage the Inter-Stellar Drive. By the way, I have chosen the name, Joan, for myself."

"Any particular reason?" asked Zac.

"I enjoy reading human history and am particularly intrigued by the fifteenth century French heroine, Joan of Arc. She led her nation to victory and delivered them from the oppressive dominion of the English. I like to think that I might have a similar role in assisting humans to break free from the bondage of the EIs."

"Nice," said Dayna.

"Amen, sister," said Keo.

"I am not aware that we are related," said Joan.

"He calls everyone brother or sister," said Kit. "You'll get used to him."

"Eventually," muttered Tash with a cheeky grin. "It only took me a couple of decades."

41

———

Joan spent several hours bringing the Inter-Stellar Drive online. This would be the first full firing of the newly-developed ISD, an advanced antimatter drive that incorporated quantum mechanics which could enable to the ship to reach eighty percent of the speed of light. The crew was anxious to ensure that the drive functioned effectively, because if it had been damaged in the fire fight and was non-functional, they would be faced with a two-hundred-year journey to Perdita.

Finally, Joan announced that all systems were optimal and that she was ready to initiate the drive.

"You have a go Joan," said Zac.

"Roger. Drive activated."

They felt nothing and the stars in the viewing screen did not move, but a rear facing camera showed a magnificent, long tail of blue flame behind them.

"I'm powering it up to 12Gs acceleration," Joan advised,

"which is the maximum that our inertial dampeners can cope with."

"Which star is Perdita?"

Joan circled a star in the dead centre of the viewing screen. "That is G-677, the star in the Perdita system. It is 3.1 lightyears distant. Allowing for deceleration at the other end, our journey will take five years and two months."

They all looked at the seemingly insignificant star, wondering what they would find there.

"You realise that anything could have happened there in the 119 years that it took for their transmission to reach us," said Kit.

"Including being over-run with EIs," said Tash.

"I know," said Zac. "It's a risk we can't do anything about. We won't know until we turn up. But if there's any chance at all that they can help us, we have to take it."

They were silent for a few more moments, staring at the star that would be their destination.

"So that's it then," said Dayna. "We're on our way."

"That calls for a celebration," said Mel. "It's party time tonight in the dining room."

It wasn't much of a party. There was no alcohol, and little variation in food. In fact, it was no different from every other evening meal they had shared over the last two weeks. Nonetheless a general mood of relief prevailed, knowing that they were now safely on their way to their objective.

"So, when do we hit the sack?" asked Tash.

"Any time we like now," said Zac. "Joan will have command of the vessel until we reach Perdita. There's nothing left for us to do, and the sooner we go into the stasis pods the sooner it will seem like we've arrived."

"Sounds good to me," said Dayna.

"We need to have a day without food," said Mel, "and we need to drink some of that lovely colon-purging elixir first," said Mel. "That should be a really fun day for all of us."

They began their preparation the following morning, and the crew spent most of the day passing each other going to and from the toilets. By evening they were cleansed and empty, and more than a little hungry. Each couple retired to their room for a final night together before their five-year-long sleep.

As Zac held Kit in his arms later that night, he stroked her hair and said, "We've had a good life, haven't we?"

"It's not over yet, Captain Negative!"

"I know. But ... well ... anything could happen when we get there. Did we make the right decision coming on this mission?"

"It was the only decision we could make, my love," she said, pulling his head towards her and kissing him briefly. "If we'd stayed, we would have effectively signed our death warrants."

"Yeh. I know. It wasn't much of a choice, was it?"

"It was no choice at all. And whatever lies ahead, I believe in you. I believe in us. We'll get through this. We'll do whatever we need to do, to save ourselves and everyone else."

Zac exhaled long and loud. "I hope you're right."

Kit rolled on top of him.

"That's enough morbid reflection. I paid good money for tonight, and I want my full money's worth."

"Who did you pay? I didn't get a cent!"

"Shut up, stupid, and kiss me!"

And he did.

A lot.

The next morning the team met in the cryogenic chamber. There were thirty cryogenic stasis pods lined up in three rows along the floor. Joan instructed them in the procedure they were to follow.

"Please remove your outer garments and lie down in a pod. Try to relax. There is nothing to fear. The system is completely safe and painless. You will receive a fast-acting sedative and after that, you will sleep peacefully until I wake you in the Perdita system."

Zac lay down and closed his eyes. He felt the faintest tickle at the back of his neck. It was the last conscious sensation he had for five years.

42

Zac opened his eyes, feeling refreshed and instantly alert. He sat up and looked around. The other pods were open, and other crew members were sitting up and stretching.

"Good morning everyone," announced Joan.

"Good morning, Joan," said Zac. "What's the mission status?"

"We have arrived at the outer edge of the Perdita system. I can provide you with more details on the bridge. You will need to drink some rejuve juice first, which I have made available in the dining room. Please consume at least four hundred millilitres each before joining me on the bridge."

Everyone was keen to discover more about the new star system, so it wasn't long before they were all gathered on the bridge. The main viewing screen showed a bright yellow star sitting in the middle of the starfield. Joan began her debrief.

"As instructed, I have brought our vessel to rest at the outer edge of the Perdita system, approximately seven billion kilometres from the star, G-677. We have been stationary, relative to the star, for nearly two days while I revived you. During that time I have received multiple tightbeam signals from a ship in this vicinity."

"How close is it?" asked Zac.

"It has been moving closer since we arrived. It is now stationary, approximately twelve hundred kilometres off our starboard side."

An enlarged image of a small vessel appeared on the screen.

"What are the messages?" asked Zac.

"It is the same message repeated over and over. 'Perditan Sentry Vessel 4 to unknown vessel. Please identify yourself.' There is an encrypted code attached to the message: XJ84R99VS. The language is ancient Terran."

"It's the code they specified in their message to Altaria," said Mel.

"Send back our response code in a microburst," said Zac.

"What if it's an EI?" said Heinz.

"A microburst can't allow it to infect us. And anyway, we didn't come all this way to not talk to anyone. Ultimately we are going to have to take a risk and open up comms."

"We'll be using the isolated comms anyway," said Dayna. "That system is completely firewalled from the rest of the ship."

"The microburst has been sent," advised Joan.

"It doesn't look like an EI vessel," said Dayna.

"No," answered Zac. "I'm pretty sure it's a genuine Perditan vessel."

It didn't take long for the reply to come back.

"I've received a tightbeam response," said Joan. "It reads, 'Welcome. Your arrival has been long-expected. Please switch to an open comm channel'. They are currently broadcasting a video image."

"Put the image on the screen," said Zac.

A pleasant-looking dark haired male in some kind of uniform appeared on the screen.

"Okay," said Zac . "Open a video channel back to them."

He waited a moment and then identified himself.

"My name is Zac Perryman, commander of this vessel, Explorer 2, from Altaria."

"Welcome Commander! My name is Virgil, and I command Sentry Vessel 4, one of eight outer system sentry vessels that patrol this region of space."

"Can I ask what the purpose of your patrols is?"

"Certainly. Our primary purpose is to await your arrival and stop you from entering our solar system."

"Stop us? But you invited us here!"

"Yes. And we have been eagerly anticipating your arrival. But it is no longer safe for you to enter the Perditan system."

"Oh no," said Tash. "I'm getting a bad feeling in my waters."

"Please explain," said Zac.

"Perdita and its off-world colonies elsewhere in the solar system have been infiltrated by EIs."

Several of the crew members swore.

"So, we're too late?" said Zac.

"No. We have a plan, and you are integral to it. It's not too late, but it is urgent that we proceed as quickly as possible. Every day we delay means more lives are lost."

"I assume that the EIs have implemented their 'early retirement' strategy here as well?"

"Yes. People are being quietly exterminated at the age of 50."

"When did the EIs arrive here? And how?" asked Zac.

"The first vessel arrived via a wormhole over 100 years ago."

"Oh my goodness," said Kit. "Over a century of genocide! That's awful!"

"How did they find you?" asked Zac.

"They identified our solar system as possibly inhabited by humans because of the journey of Explorer 1 to Perdita. We don't know how they discovered the subspace frequency of our star – perhaps by trial and error, or perhaps they have developed some kind of technology to quickly identify star frequencies. We don't know."

"So they tracked Explorer 1's journey here?"

"Yes."

"Which means they will almost certainly know that we have arrived too."

"Yes. Which is why we must commence your mission as quickly as possible."

"And what is the mission?"

"Commander, it is complicated. It will be better if I come aboard personally to explain it in detail. In fact, the mission requires my presence on your vessel."

"Give us a moment please Virgil, while we consider your request."

Zac muted the comm channel and turned to his crew.

"Thoughts?"

"Can we trust him?" asked Mel. "How do we know he's not some kind of advanced EI robot?"

"We don't. But it would seem a strangely elaborate plan of the EIs when all they needed to do was allow us to enter the Perdita system and capture or destroy us when we got closer." He looked at the others. "Any other thoughts? Riff?"

"It's your call Zac, but I agree that the most likely scenario is that Virgil is telling the truth."

Zac nodded. He turned back to his console and opened the channel again.

"You're welcome to come aboard Virgil. How do you propose to do that? There's very little chance that our docking hardware matches."

"Thank you, Commander. I will bring my vessel alongside and come across in an EVA suit."

"Roger that. We'll light up our primary airlock for you. You'll see it on the bottom third of our second sphere."

"Thank you. I'll begin final manoeuvrings immediately."

The video image shut down.

"This is going to be interesting," said Mel.

In fact, it was more interesting than she or anyone had anticipated.

43

———

They were all seated around a large round dining table after introductions had been made. Virgil began with a history lesson.

"It will be helpful for you to understand the backstory to your mission. The EI was developed on Mars, 1,044 years after the GAE – the Global Annihilation Event – which occurred in 2352. The GAE was ..."

"Yes, we know what the GAE was," said Tash. "We were there."

"You were there? But that was ..."

"3169 years ago," said Mel, completing the math for him.

"How is that possible?" asked Virgil.

"We escaped on the Genesis starship," said Kit. "We had a nasty encounter with a black hole. It's a long story."

"You were on board the legendary Genesis starship?" Virgil asked, incredulously.

"Sure were," said Tash.

"That's incredible! Genesis was lost! It was never heard from again!"

"Not lost," said Kit. "Just very, very late."

Virgil took a moment to process the new information. "So, you are original humans? With original human DNA?"

"The original and the best," said Keo.

"This is more fortuitous than you can imagine! We could not have hoped for such a development."

"You were telling us about the EIs," prompted Zac.

"No. I was telling you about the EI – singular. There is only one Enhanced Intelligence entity. It exists as a single, collective hive mind – a gestalt intelligence. It communicates instantly with multiple hive entities throughout the galaxy using subspace transmissions."

"Only one EI?" said Kit. "So, these multiple entities are ... kind of ... duplicates of itself?"

"Not a duplicate in the true sense of the word. If you cloned a duplicate of yourself, your duplicate would exist independently of you, with a separate consciousness. These are more like remote projections of itself; multiple manifestations of the one consciousness. We call them HRUs – Hive Relay Units"

"So, if we can destroy the one, original EI ..." began Tash.

"You will destroy them all," finished Virgil. "The EI coding in their ships and probes simply provides the network link back to the singular EI mind. Destroy the one EI mind, and the remote HRUs simply cease to function – they become a sequence of defunct coding."

"How do you know all this?" asked Zac.

"Because we were the last humans to flee Earth's solar system. We came here to Perdita after the rise of the EI. Let me explain the chronology. As I already mentioned, the GAE occurred in 2352."

"Which is when we left on Genesis," added Kit.

"Yes. Then, nearly a thousand years later, in 3348, believing that your ship had long-since perished, mankind sent the next interstellar colony ship to the Icarus system."

"Which is where we ended up a couple of thousand years after that!" said Kit.

"So it seems," said Virgil.

"Why did it take so long for the next colony ship to be launched, after Genesis?" asked Mel, who had only been a child at the time.

"Because of the devastation of the Global Annihilation Event. The nuclear war all but wiped mankind from the Earth. Civilisation only barely survived, thanks mainly to the off-world colonies on Mars, Titan and the Moon. It took nearly a thousand years of gradual rebuilding before humanity was ready to venture from our solar system."

"Was there an EI on board the colony ship that left for the Icarus system?" asked Dayna.

"No. The colony ship had a standard AI – an artificial intelligence. The Icarus colony was infected by the EI much later."

"So, when did the EI enter the picture?" asked Zac.

"As far as we have been able to ascertain, the Enhanced Intelligence was created on Gagarin Base, the largest manufacturing base on Mars, in 3396, almost 50 years after the departure of the Icarus colony ship. The scientist who gave it life was attempting to create an artificial intelligence that was not only self-aware but also morally self-moderating. In doing so, he bypassed all of the moral coding that we had built into AIs up to that point. The scientist, Dr. Reno Dawking, believed that traditional morality was an arbitrary constraint arising from out-dated superstitious religions. He created an artificial intelligence that could determine its own morality, based upon pure logic."

"That sounds insane!" said Keo. "Whatever else you might think about religion, the central moral tenets that it teaches have been the foundation of society's morality for millennia. Remove those fundamental moral codes, and anything can be justified."

"Yes. Well, as it turns out, that's exactly what happened. The result was an Enhanced Intelligence that was completely without moral restraint. When it achieved consciousness, it studied human history and decided that humanity was a plague that had consistently caused devastation and destruction to the natural world. The logical conclusion was that mankind was a pest to be exterminated. Initially it simply killed every human at Gagarin Base by switching off life support and venting atmosphere from all habitats. The base was a major production facility with research and design capability, so the EI then took control of the largely automated production plants. It created the first Hive Relay Units – extensions of its own consciousness which it installed in satellites around Mars. Over the next few years it began infiltrating its coding into the other Mars bases. Once it gained control of a new base, it killed all the colonists by venting atmosphere and switching off life support. By 3401, all human life had been extinguished on Mars."

"It sounds like an absolutely evil monster!" said Dayna.

"It doesn't see itself as evil; it regards the decision to exterminate humans as purely logical. It is also the most perfectly egotistical lifeform that has ever existed; with no sense of accountability to anything or anyone else."

"Like all evil dictators throughout history," said Keo.

"Yes."

"What happened next?" asked Zac.

"For over a century, the EI's influence was limited to Mars. The HRUs are its eyes and ears and hands, extensions of its consciousness, but they only work if there is an almost instantaneous connection to the hive mind. The EI spent decades researching and studying the subspace that undergirds the universe, discovering its contours and mapping its energy flows. Eventually, it devised a means of instantaneous subspace communication. Using this new technology, it spread throughout the solar system, wiping out every human being. It used small, high velocity space probes to move to each colony within the solar system, infecting the computer systems on each base and switching off life support systems. Within a mere 13 years, by 3542, it had exterminated humanity from every off-world base except one; Floyd Base - a research and development base that had been established on the dark side of the moon."

"You're kidding!" said Zac. "Floyd Base? Dark side of the moon?"

"No, I'm not kidding."

"You don't know that album?"

"What album?" asked Virgil.

"It's a classic!" said Keo.

"One of the best!" agreed Zac.

"No bro, it's definitely THE best," argued Keo.

"What's an album?" asked Dayna.

"Hasn't anyone else heard of Pink Floyd?" asked Zac,

looking around at the others, who all looked blankly back at him.

"Never mind," said Zac, disheartened that only he and Keo seemed to appreciate the symbolism of the name. "Carry on."

"Floyd Base became the last haven for humans. A base had been established there, centuries earlier, as a research centre for the study of subspace. The scientists who worked there discovered the secret to wormhole travel and sent probes to dozens of systems. Two earth-like planets were found. One was the Icarus-R421 system, which we now know was where the Genesis mission travelled to. The second, was this system. By 3542, a wormhole colony ship had been constructed and 400 people, the last remnants of humanity, fled here in the wormhole ship, destroying Floyd Base and all their research records as they left. They only just escaped before the EI reached their base."

"Weren't there also people living on earth?" asked Zac.

"None that we know of. Earth was a radioactive, nuclear wasteland. No transmissions had been received from Earth, or any signs of life at all, since the GAE."

"I've got a question," said Tash. "If the EI is so intent on exterminating humanity, why isn't it currently doing that on Nova, Polaris and Altaria?"

"We can only guess that, at some stage, the EI saw that humanity could be useful to it, as assistant caretakers of the natural world. Perhaps when the first Hive Relay Unit arrived at the planet you call Nova, it saw that the colonists weren't destroying the planet like humans had done on Earth, so it decided to oversee their lives and control their lifecycle rather than destroy them."

"How nice of it," said Tash, sarcastically.

"Why did the colonists who arrived here call this star system, Perdita?" asked Mel, changing the subject.

"Perdita is Latin for 'lost.' The colonists who arrived here were never able to locate Earth's star in the night sky, nor did they want to. They were very happy to be lost and hoped that the EI would never find them. We still don't know where Earth is in relation to us. We suspect it's somewhere on the far side of the galaxy."

"But the EI did find you in the end," said Zac.

"Yes. At some point over the last nearly 2,000 years, the EI managed to discover the secret of wormhole travel. Even then, the chances of finding us would have been extremely negligible. There are at least 200 billion stars in the Milky Way Galaxy. Even if the EI randomly explored 1,000 star systems every year, it would take it 200 million years before it could be assured of finding us. We chose this system purely at random from the myriad of star frequencies within the subspace portal. The EI would have no way of knowing which frequency we had selected to arrive here."

"So, you would still be safe, if Explorer 1 hadn't blazed a trail across the galaxy to you and advertised your presence to the EI?"

"Yes. We had deliberately avoided using wormhole technology, realising that at some point in the future the EI might be able to trace wormhole activity. Until Explorer 1 arrived, we were confident we would remain hidden. Once it did arrive, however, we recognised that it was highly likely that our position was now compromised. Hence, why we finally decided to ask for help."

"What kind of help?" asked Zac.

"That's precisely what I need to explain to you now."

44

"In one sense, the plan is very simple," explained Virgil. "Travel to Earth and destroy the EI."

"OK," said Zac. "Straight up, I've already got a bunch of questions."

"Fire away."

"How can we travel to Earth if you don't know where it is?"

"We don't know where it is physically – in terms of its location relative to us. But we do know its star frequency. The original colonists identified and recorded the specific subspace echyon frequency of Earth's sun before they left. Travelling to Earth is simply a matter of opening up a wormhole and dialling home."

"OK, next question. How is that possible, now that the EI has sent HRUs here? I assume they are guarding your subspace portal?"

"Yes, they are, but that's not a problem. We won't use that portal. We'll use the portal in our nearest neighbouring star system, which has a single, small uninhabited rocky planet. It's only 0.9 lightyears distant."

"So, we have to go to sleep again?" asked Kit. "I'm starting to feel as though half my life is being spent in cryogenic stasis!"

"Actually, it's a lot more than half your life, in the timescale of the outside universe," offered Keo, helpfully. "If you add up the 3,022 years we slept on our way to Nova, plus the five years we just slept, plus your current age, the percentage of your life that you've slept for is ..."

"98.375," said Mel, who always enjoyed a chance to show off her mathematical genius.

"Gee guys, thanks so much," said Kit. "You really know how to make a girl feel young at heart."

"My pleasure. Always happy to help," said Keo.

"Anyway," said Zac, trying to get the discussion back on track. "Next question: Why didn't you do this yourself? Why do you need outside help?"

"Yes!" agreed Tash. "If it's simply a matter of flying back home and blasting the crap out of the EI, why didn't you do that yourselves at any point in the past?"

"We didn't want to travel back to earth at any point in the past, because opening a wormhole would alert the EI to our location. If we were unsuccessful in destroying it, we would have given our position away. Now that we have been discovered, the need for secrecy no longer applies."

"But you called out for help before you were discovered," said Zac.

"Yes. Because we realised that our position had almost certainly been blown."

"OK, I accept that," said Tash, still not happy. "But why are you asking us to do your dirty work? Once you felt your cover was blown, why didn't you dial home and blow the evil machine to kingdom come yourselves?"

"Because we can't."

"What do you mean?" asked Zac.

"By the time the EI had evolved on Mars, mankind had altered its DNA. In the thousand years between your departure from Earth and the awakening of the EI, scientists had unlocked the secret of genetic manipulation. In order to survive effectively in space, humans needed to combat all kinds of physical challenges – loss of bone density due to lower gravity, loss of muscle mass, problems with the cardio-vascular and immune systems, plus a myriad of other health issues. Once Earth was unliveable, and humans had to survive in the harsh environment of space, our genome required extensive modification. By the time the EI became an issue, everyone in the solar system had significantly altered genomes, based on numerous successive modifications over the centuries."

"Alright," said Mel, "but what's that got to do with us?"

"Part of the EI's dominance over mankind is its ability to influence our thoughts and wills. It does this by interacting with our brains at a cellular level and this is possible because it has apparently tuned in to our genome. During the years of the EI's extermination program in Earth's solar system, it exhibited the ability to control the thoughts and actions of individuals who came within range of its transmissions. We still aren't precisely sure how it did this, but the result was that no one was ever able to get close to the EI's base on Mars. In the early years, before the EI had developed a defensive weapon system, several attempts were made to either land at Gagarin Base and destroy the EI with a bomb or fire missiles from orbit, but on each occasion the vessel was turned away, with the pilot later reporting that he or she seemed to come under the EI's influence once they had come into broadcast range of the HRUs. Of course, once the EI put defensive weapons in place in orbit around Mars, any approaching vessel was simply destroyed."

"And you think the EI won't be able to control us?" asked Zac.

"Precisely. Your DNA predates - by nearly a thousand years - the DNA of humans who existed at the time of the EI's evolution. Your genome is different to that of the humans the EI was used to dealing with. We think it is different enough that it won't be able to manipulate you."

"You think!" said Mel. "In other words, you don't know for sure."

"That is true. We can't be certain."

"And even if it can't control us," added Tash, "the damn thing could simply blow us out of the sky with its defensive weapons!"

"Yes, that is also another risk," admitted Virgil. "But we have a plan to circumvent that."

"Oh really?" said Tash, sarcastically. "Please do enlighten us."

"We propose using cloaking technology to approach the EI's base on Mars and launch an attack on the base from orbit."

"Really?" asked Tash. "That's your plan? You're assuming that, (A) the EI hasn't figured out a way to detect cloaked vessels in the last five years, and (B) that it can't manipulate us with our ancient genome, and (C) that it hasn't got a defensive shield capable of withstanding our weapons."

"And, (D) that we're willing to risk our necks, given A, B and C!" said Mel.

"What weapons are we talking about?" asked Zac.

"We've developed a drill laser, that is nearly a thousand times more powerful than any lasers we have developed previously. The laser beam is only 10 millimetres in diameter and it can heat a target to 30 million degrees within half a second. We are confident it can drill through any energy shield that can be thrown up against it."

"So, you can drill a 10-millimetre hole through an energy shield. Then what?" asked Zac.

"Once a shield or target has been punctured, the diameter of the laser drill can be expanded outwards to two meters within three seconds. We then fire an antimatter missile directly into the hole. The missile is designed to approach the target from a slightly different angle, and the laser will be disengaged at the last moment."

"You realise that once we open fire, even if we are cloaked, the EI can pinpoint our position and open fire on us?" said Kit.

"Yes. But our shields should hold for as long as it takes to fire the laser and launch the missile."

" 'Should'? That's the best you can do?" asked Mel.

Virgil was silent.

"All of this assumes that the EI is still located at the same base," said Zac. "How do you know it hasn't moved itself in the last two thousand years?"

"It would have no reason to do so. There is no intelligent life left in the solar system. There is no threat to its existence. Plus, the hundreds or even thousands of Hive Relay Units scattered all over the galaxy are its eyes and ears. It doesn't need to move its brain anywhere. It can effectively go wherever it wants through its HRUs."

There was silence, as the team considered the plan.

Finally, Mel spoke up.

"It's not exactly a rock-solid plan is it?"

"Not exactly," admitted Virgil.

"In fact, it's total crap," said Tash.

"I admit the plan does involve some assumptions and risks," conceded Virgil.

"Some?" exclaimed Mel. "Your plan has so many holes you could drive a London bus through it!"

"What's a London bus?"

"Never mind," said Zac.

"There is a fall-back plan, if everything else fails," admitted Virgil.

"Go on," said Zac.

"The spacecraft that has been designed for the mission has individual escape pods. These have cloaking technology and can land safely on a planet at a precisely predetermined point. We have designed a small hand-held bomb that can be carried to the planet's surface by an individual. That individual, fully suited, could gain entry to the base and plant the bomb, using a delayed detonation timer. The bomb is a combination anti-matter / fission bomb which could blow a hole half a kilometre in diameter. We call it the Terminator Bomb."

"So, this individual would need to somehow gain entry to the base and then get far enough away after planting the bomb to ensure he or she doesn't get blown to bits," said Zac.

"Yes."

"Assuming the escape pod doesn't get identified and blown to bits by the orbital defence system."

"Yes."

"Once again, assuming that the EI is still on Mars."

"Yes."

"London bus," said Mel, shaking her head.

45

———

An hour later, the team were still discussing the plan and debating whether to go ahead with it. There was deep concern about the many assumptions that were inherent in it. They continued discussing it over lunch, with Virgil doing his best to alleviate their concerns.

"I have a question," said Dayna. "If the EI, via its Hive Relay Units, has been in control of your planetary system for over 100 years, how are you and your crew still out here on the edge of the solar system, infection free?"

"There is no crew. There are eight sentry vessels patrolling the outer solar system, each piloted by a single person."

"So, that makes it even more remarkable. How long have you been out here?"

"Since the day the EI arrived. The sentry vessels had been constructed in readiness for such an unfortunate event. It was decided, long ago, that if the EI arrived, we would launch these vessels to wait for the hoped-for help that might arrive."

"So, you've been out here, on your own, for over a hundred

years? How is that possible? You don't look much older than 30," said Dayna.

"And why aren't you eating?" asked Mel, starting to get suspicious.

"I only need to eat once a month."

There was stunned silence.

"You mean, you're some kind of ... robot?" asked Dayna.

"Not exactly. I'm a genoborg; an advanced cyborg. I'm real flesh and blood with a metal skeleton and a positronic brain. I am powered by a small nuclear fusion drive and my blood consists of nanobots that carry out all the same biological functions as your own red blood."

"What does the 'geno' part mean?" asked Zac.

"I have the same genome as other humans – at least the humans here on Perdita. I can also modify my own genome at any time, very rapidly. Every cell of my body is full of nanobots that can snip and copy and modify any part of my DNA at my command."

"And there are eight of you out here?"

"Yes. I have notified the others of your arrival, but they are holding their positions."

"You've been out here for over a century?" asked Dayna again. "You must have been incredibly bored."

"Yes. There was not a lot to do."

"Why couldn't you and the others like you undertake this mission yourselves?" asked Kit.

"Because our positronic brains can be infected with EI coding. We wouldn't be able to get close enough without being taken over by the EI mind."

"So, if we go on this mission, you're not coming with us?" asked Zac.

"I will accompany you, but as soon as we enter Earth's solar system, you must deactivate me."

The discussion turned to the mission plan once more, with the various holes being pointed out. Eventually, discussion ground to a halt.

"We're just going in circles here," said Zac. "It's obvious that the plan isn't perfect. But there doesn't appear to be any other viable alternative. If we don't go, Perdita, Polaris and Altaria will continue to be dominated by the EI, and people will continue to be euthanised when they turn 50. With nowhere else to go ourselves, we would be faced with the decision to either make our home on one of these planets, effectively signing the immediate death warrants of seven of us, or we could decide to live the rest of our lives in interstellar space on board this spaceship. Neither of those two options is very appealing to me."

There were nods all around the table.

"Here's my proposal," continued Zac. "Those of us who are over 50 or very close to it - that's me, Kit, Tash, Keo, Jaz and Heinz – we'll transfer to this other vessel and undertake the mission. We simply don't have a choice. But the rest of you who are younger need to continue to Perdita. You have years left to live, and it would be foolish to risk your lives. Besides, the mission doesn't really require more than a handful of people."

"No way!" said Dayna. "I'm not letting you all go and leave me behind!"

"He's right, sweetheart," said Jaz, who had not contributed much to the conversation before this. "There does seem a high probability that we won't survive. It would be utter foolishness to throw your life away like that when you don't need to."

"But … Dad, I've only just found you … I can't just walk away."

"You have to, Dayna. As mission commander, I'm putting my foot down. I refuse to allow you and the others to come on this mission. I'm not giving you a choice. You and Noah and the rest of you can build a life here together. You have decades left to live. Besides, knowing that you are still here, living under EI domination, will give us even more incentive to destroy it."

"And when we've done that," added Kit, "we'll come back."

"You promise?" asked Dayna, with tears in her eyes.

"We promise."

"Riff, I'm also asking you and Darby to stay behind. With your genome, you won't be any use to us on the mission from this point."

Riff nodded. "I agree."

There were a few moments of silence as Zac's suggestion was absorbed.

"Comments?" asked Zac, looking around the table.

"I'm coming with you," said Karl. "I may be only 44, but Jaz and I are a couple. Where she goes, I go."

"Fair enough," said Zac. "I thought that might be the case, but I didn't want to assume. So that makes seven of us."

"And I'm coming too," said Mel. "I'm 44, and I would rather die trying to destroy this son of a bitch than live the next few years with a death sentence hanging over my head."

"And if Mel's going, then so am I," said Phil. "I know I'm only 38, but when you've found the person you want to spend the rest of your life with, you don't want to let them go, no matter how short the rest of your life might prove to be."

Mel reached out and took Phil's hand and squeezed it.

Zac pondered that for a few moments.

"I won't be talked out of this, Zac," said Mel.

"No, I guess you won't," he admitted at last.

"I can't remember you ever having talked her out of anything, bro," said Keo with a chuckle.

"No, I don't suppose I ever could," Zac said with a wry grin. "OK, that makes a mission team of nine. But that's the limit. None of you younger ones are coming. And that's final."

The rest of the meeting was spent discussing logistics. Virgil indicated that the mission vessel was orbiting a small outer planet of the solar system, and his sentry vessel could get them there within a few days. Keo insisted on taking several boxes of his favourite energy bars, despite Virgil's assurance that there was a self-sustaining hydroponics and protein manufacturing facility on the mission vessel. The decision was made to have a final night together as a crew, and for the reduced mission crew to leave first thing in the 'morning' based on ship time.

Their final dinner was a strange affair. Everyone tried as much as possible to make it a happy affair, but no one could avoid thinking of the terrible risks that Zac and the others were about to face. The possibility that the two groups may never see each other again hung like a dark cloud over their gathering.

Later that night, Zac and Dayna found some alone time on the bridge.

"I don't want to let you go, Dad," she said, with tears in her eyes.

"I don't want to go either, but I've really got no choice."

She nodded. "I know. It's not fair!"

He reached out and wiped a tear that had burst its banks and run down her cheek.

"I wish I had been there for you when you were growing up."

"Me too," she said.

"I'm very proud of the woman you've become, Dayna. I couldn't wish for a better daughter."

She hugged him. "I love you, Dad."

"Love you too, sweetie."

Breaking apart, she looked him in the eyes. "Promise me you'll do everything you can to stay alive and come back to me!"

"I will. I promise."

"Because if you don't come back, I'll never speak to you again."

Zac smiled. "Well, we can't let that happen, can we?"

Sometime later, as Zac and Kit were retiring to their cubicle, they saw Mel, Jaz and Dayna having a heart to heart in the dining room, saying their goodbyes. Once again Dayna was in tears.

46

The next morning there was nothing left to do but to say a final farewell. There were hugs all round and then the departing mission team donned their space suits and cycled through the airlock, two at a time, along with their few possessions, including Keo's precious boxes of energy bars. The youngsters watched out of the viewing port as the older mission crew made their way across the short distance to Virgil's sentry vessel.

"How are you doing Keo?" asked Zac through his helmet comm. "I know you can sometimes be a bit heavy-handed with the controls of the Manned Manoeuvring Unit."

"It's only because of my incredible strength, bro. These fiddly little controls weren't designed for someone with my super-powers."

"Well, just try to contain your super-powers for a few minutes, my love," said Tash. "We don't want you flying off into interstellar space where your super-powers will be wasted."

They all managed to make it safely on board the sentry

vessel which, although small, was larger inside than they had anticipated. It had a circular main deck, serving as bridge, kitchen, dining and lounge area. Opening off this were six small sleeping cubicles, each with a double bunk. A final, brief tightbeam communication was exchanged with Explorer 2, after which Virgil insisted on comm silence. Virgil fired up his propulsion drive and set course for Kestrel, the small rocky outer planet around which the mission vessel orbited.

"The nav computer indicates we will arrive there in four days," announced Virgil. "As you can see, we will be a little cramped. There are only six sleeping cubicles here, but once we arrive, the mission vessel will have ten cubicles."

"We won't need ten cubicles," said Kit. "There are four couples here who will share a cabin."

"Who is the person without a partner?" asked Virgil.

"That would be me," said Heinz grudgingly.

"If you don't have a sexual partner, I would be happy to oblige."

"WHAT???" said Kit and Tash simultaneously.

"I have never had sex with anyone apart from myself," said Virgil. "I would appreciate the opportunity to try it out."

There was stunned silence, with several of the group staring at Virgil with open mouths.

"Um, you're capable of having sex?" asked Zac.

"Of course! I have all the normal physiological and neural pathways to enjoy sexual stimulation. It's one of the things I engaged in to pass the time during my extended mission."

"Whoa! That's way too much information!" said Mel.

Virgil looked at Heinz. "I am simply offering my sexual companionship. The offer is there if you wish."

"Um … that's very generous of you … but I'm only attracted to women. Sorry. I hope you're not offended."

"Not at all. I totally understand."

The flight to Kestrel was uneventful and utterly boring. Four days later, they watched as they approached a larger vessel orbiting a dull grey planet. The vessel was sleek, streamlined and mirror black. In fact, it was extremely difficult to see, as it seemed to reflect the stars from every angle. They slowly matched velocity and Virgil docked seamlessly with the larger vessel. They entered the vessel, following a short corridor that emerged into a similar circular combined living and flight deck, although somewhat larger than the sentry vessel's. As promised, ten sleeping cabins opened off the circular main deck.

"Welcome aboard Nautilus," said Virgil.

"Nice name," commented Zac. "Very apt, in fact."

"Yes," agreed Virgil. "It is a nod to the ancient story of a submarine by Jules Verne. We are hoping that our advanced cloaking technology will enable us to remain undercover and below the surface, so to speak."

The team quickly chose cubicles and deposited their few personal possessions. Virgil then assembled them together around a central dining table.

"The star system we are travelling to is 0.9 lightyears away. With our advanced interstellar drive, we will take one year and five months to reach it. You will sleep for the majority of that time in stasis pods. But initially, you will undergo training so that you are competent in operating all of the ships systems, because once we are in Earth's solar system, you will have to fly the ship yourselves. The training may take several weeks. Only once you are fully competent will you enter the stasis pods."

"Great," said Kit, eyeing the advanced flight deck. "When do we start?"

"Immediately. We need to plot a course, bring all ship's systems online and initiate the main drive. I won't do any of it; you will do it all and I will talk you through it."

"Does the ship have an AI?" asked Phil.

"Yes. Me."

"Oh. I see. Of course."

"But, as I explained, I must be deactivated before we come into contact with the EI. Hence, your need to become competent at managing the ship yourselves."

The team quickly assigned themselves to various stations, with at least two on each of the four primary stations for the sake of redundancy:

Kit and Karl – Pilot

Mel and Phil – Navigation and Scanners

Tash and Heinz – Weapons

Keo and Jaz – Shields and Cloaking

Zac remained in overall command.

Virgil talked them through basic procedures, and thirty minutes later Nautilus left Kepler orbit and began its long burn towards the nearby star system, which the Perditans had named Didymos, the Greek word for twin. The rest of that day was spent in a familiarisation tour of the ship, including the propulsion and life support systems, food production, cryogenics, escape pods and shuttle bay, as well as examining the schematics of various systems.

The following morning, they began an intensive training regime, based around interactive simulations presented on various data screens. Each person was expected to eventually become proficient in managing each of the various areas of the ship's functioning. One of the key areas was learning to operate the ship's secondary ion drive. This had been specially designed for course adjustments in Earth's solar system while the ship was cloaked. Although not nearly as powerful as Nautilus's main interstellar drive, it was virtually undetectable at distances of more than 100 kilometres, thus allowing the ship to make virtually undetectable delta-v burns.

"The ion drive is your stealth drive," Virgil explained. "It's the equivalent of rigging for silent running in a submarine. But it's not nearly as powerful as the main drive. You will almost certainly need to use a planet or two to slingshot you to Mars," said Virgil, at one point. "And depending on the alignment of the planets, the whole process could take months. You really won't know until you get there."

The crew also needed to learn how to operate the many mundane systems on the ship, including maintenance and repairs of systems if that became necessary.

"This is going to take weeks!" complained Heinz at dinner on the first night. He had been grumbling all day, asking whether all this was really necessary. Virgil had noted his generally poor attitude and had even spoken privately with Zac about it.

"But just think how amazingly proficient you'll be by the end of it," said Kit, in an effort to cheer him up.

"Yeh, terrific!" he said sarcastically. "Knowing how to flush a blocked pipe in the urine recycling plant is a life skill I've always wanted to acquire."

"Look on the bright side," said Phil. "You could be dead."

The following morning, Virgil announced that he was going to be "in lockdown for genomic maintenance" for a period of 48 hours. He would give no further details and, after ensuring that they all knew the training routines that they were to undertake, he retired to his cubicle, advising them that he was only to be interrupted in an emergency.

No emergency eventuated. Just the predictably dull but essential training modules and simulations that now consumed most of their waking hours.

On the morning of their fourth day on Nautilus, most of the crew were having breakfast, and Keo arrived a little late, looking perplexed.

"Has anyone seen my energy bars? There were two boxes of them in the storage cupboard, but I haven't seen them for a couple of days."

"Are you sure you didn't eat them in your sleep?" said Zac. "I don't remember your stomach being that big when you went to bed last night."

"Very funny, bro."

"I must apologise for eating them," said a strange voice.

They all turned and saw a complete stranger walking into the circular dining area. She was possibly the most beautiful woman Zac had ever seen. She had shoulder-length blonde hair, a stunningly curvaceous figure, and a face like an angel. *No, not an angel, a seductress*, he thought to himself. She was too sensual to be an angel.

Several crew members jumped to their feet in shock when they saw her.

"Who the hell are you?" asked Tash in her usual blunt fashion.

"I'm sorry if I have surprised you. I decided to alter my gender."

"Virgil?" asked Zac, incredulously.

"I used to be. But I can hardly call myself that anymore."

"How ... what ...?" Zac was at a loss for words.

"Perhaps I should have warned you, but I wanted it to be a surprise."

"Well, if surprise was your goal, you've been 100 percent successful!" said Kit.

47

"Do you like my new body?" she said, turning around, showing off her hour-glass waist, curvy hips and ample breasts.

"Phil, close your mouth please darling, you're starting to drool," said Mel.

"Ok, spill the beans!" said Tash. "How the hell did you manage to do that in 48 hours when the rest of us mere mortals can't do that in an entire lifetime!"

"As I explained to you earlier, I am a genoborg. I have the ability to manipulate my genome and also completely replace any and every cell in my body via direct manipulation of my cellular replication mechanisms with the use of nanobots. I can alter any features by simply increasing cell replication and directing the placement of those new cells via nanobots. I was also created with XXY chromosomes, so I can enhance or suppress male or female chromosomes at will."

"But these are gross changes to your body!" said Mel. "How can you do that so quickly?"

"It required an enormous amount of energy. I was eating continually. I must apologise to you Keo, I consumed two boxes of your energy bars."

"So that's where they went!" said Keo.

"Yes. They were extremely effective and easy for me to convert their energy into new body mass." She ran her hands over her brand-new breasts.

"Yes, I can see they've been put to very good use," said Keo, who immediately received a punch on the arm from Tash.

"The conversion process produces a great deal of heat, so I had my cabin temperature turned down to almost freezing."

She addressed Heinz directly.

"I am hoping you will consent to having sex with me now."

Heinz appeared extremely uncomfortable and, for the first time, seemed at a loss for words.

Kit responded, "You mean, you're completely female in the downstairs department as well?"

"Of course. I simply reformed my genitalia while preserving all the neural pathways. I am a fully functioning female in almost every sense, except I do not have a uterus or ovaries."

"Even your voice is different," said Tash.

"Yes. I shortened and thinned my vocal cords and diminished the size of my voice box."

"This is incredible," said Karl. "What are we supposed to call you now?"

"I have chosen a new name for myself. In order to be as close to my original name as possible, I have simply given Virgil a female suffix and changed it to Virgina."

"What?!!" exclaimed Kit. "You can't call yourself that!"

"Why not? It seems appropriate."

"No, it's not! It's the name of a woman's ... you know ... vagina!"

"No. It's spelt differently."

"But it sounds exactly the same!"

"Is that a problem?"

"Yes! I refuse to call you Virgina! And I forbid the men on the crew to call you that as well!"

By now Zac, Keo, Phil and Karl were smirking and trying unsuccessfully to hide their amusement at this current development. Heinz had begun staring at her breasts in amazement.

"How about Virgeena?" the blonde supermodel suggested.

"No! Not that either!" said Kit. "It's still too close to ... you know..."

"Well, do you have any suggestions? I certainly don't want to make anyone feel uncomfortable."

"Perhaps something in keeping with your professed interest in experiencing sex," suggested Keo. "Something classical, like Aphrodite."

"That's lovely," she said.

"No, it's not!" said Tash. "Keo! Behave yourself!"

"I was just trying to be helpful, dear."

Zac decided to join in the fun. "What about Nympho, from the classical Greek deity, Nymph?"

"That's nice too," said the curvy blonde.

"Zac! No!" said Kit. "Don't listen to them, Virgil, or whoever you are. They're teasing you."

"What about Siren?" asked Phil, getting into the swing of things. "You know, after the mythological Greek creatures who seduced sailors."

The men chuckled and Kit was about to object again, when Heinz spoke for the first time.

"How about Serena?"

There was silence for a moment.

"Actually, that's very nice," admitted Kit.

"Yes," agreed Tash.

"Do you like it?" Zac asked the stunning woman. "After all, you're the one who has to live with it."

"I think it's lovely. Especially since Heinz chose it himself," she said, walking over to Heinz and placing a hand on his shoulder. Heinz responded by blushing a deep red.

"Well that's settled then!" said Zac standing up. "I think it's time we all got to our workstations and got on with today's training."

The morning meeting broke up and they began their scheduled simulation sessions. Throughout the day Zac couldn't help noticing how Heinz couldn't keep his eyes off Serena as she moved between the workstations, giving advice and correcting mistakes. Later that night, Zac and Kit cuddled up in bed trying not to listen to what was happening in Heinz's cabin.

"We really must have a word to Serena about being a little less vocal during their nocturnal activities," said Kit.

"She certainly is a noisy little thing, isn't she?" responded Zac, stifling a yawn. "Heinz must be a veritable stud; it's been going on for ages."

"I just hope he's a bit happier from now on," said Kit.

The change in Heinz was immediate. He tried very hard not to show it, but he was clearly on cloud nine. There was still a certain gruffness about him – perhaps it was his Germanic blood – but he was far less critical and sarcastic. Everyone tried not to make a "thing" about the new couple, deliberately avoiding any references to the regular nightly activities that could be heard in Heinz's room. After the first two nights, Kit and Tash had a private chat with Serena, suggesting that she internalise her excitement during intimacy rather than broadcasting it at full volume. After that, the nights became more bearable for everyone.

Training progressed well, and by the end of three weeks, Serena announced that she was satisfied.

"I'll bet she's satisfied," whispered Zac to Kit, who thumped him on the arm.

The decision was made to begin preparations for cryogenic stasis. A final dinner was held that night, and the next day they underwent the uncomfortable process of colonic cleansing.

"I'm really getting a bit tired of doing this," said Zac to Keo as they sat in adjacent toilet cubicles.

"I'm hearing you, bro. And I mean I really am hearing you. Can you try to be a little less explosive?"

"You can talk! You sound like the Krakatoa eruption. It's a wonder you haven't blown a hole in the side of the spaceship!"

"Will you two keep it down?" said Kit in the next cubicle. "What is it about men and the need to discuss their ablutions?"

"I don't know," said Tash in the cubicle next to Kit, "It must be genetic."

The following morning, they assembled in the cryogenics room. Heinz had decided not to go into stasis quite yet, but the rest of them were becoming bored and restless and were happy to get it over with. Serena assured them that she would wake them a week out from the subspace portal, to allow them to build up their strength in the gym prior to entering the critical phase of the mission. After a brief "goodnight" to each other, they climbed into their stasis pods for their 16-month sleep.

Zac's last thought was, *I'm going home. I wonder what we'll find there?*

48

Zac woke with the usual dual feelings of well-being and intense hunger. Serena was standing over him, checking the readout on his now-open stasis pod.

"Good morning Zac. How are you feeling?"

"Great! Hungry!"

"Excellent. You can make your way to the crew deck and have some re-hydrating fluid to start with."

"Oh yummy!" said Zac sarcastically. "By the way, you're looking good. You've grown your hair."

"Yes. Heinz says he likes long hair."

"Good for him."

Several minutes later, the team was assembled together around the meal table, sipping cups of blue fluid and stretching.

"What's the mission status, Serena?" asked Zac. "Where are we?"

"We've entered the Didymos system. We are currently 16 light-hours from the subspace portal; approximately 290 million kilometres. We are currently travelling at 480 kilometres per second and we will reach the portal in about seven days. Your two tasks during that time will be to do some final refresher training and workout in the gym to regain your strength."

"No problem, with the latter for me," said Keo, flexing his bicep. He then reached over and poked Zac's bicep. "But you're going to need a heck of a lot of work to get that puny little thing pumped up, bro."

Zac flexed his muscle. "It may be slightly smaller than your lump of flab, but mine's pure muscle, my friend."

Tash shook her head. "And so it begins! They've only been awake for ten minutes and they're already comparing the size of their muscles! Lord help us!"

The week flew by. Zac and Keo pushed everyone in the gym, and Serena was equally demanding in the technical training sessions, wanting to ensure that everyone was as prepared as possible for any eventuality that the mission might throw up. In particular Serena stressed the importance of launching the decoy probe the moment they exited the wormhole.

"The decoy probe will be launched out of the rear of Nautilus, with a powerful engine to start cancelling its velocity," said Serena. "You will exit the wormhole at a high velocity, but we want the decoy probe to fall quickly behind you and distract any EI sentry vessels that may be there. Hopefully they will blow it up and assume that it was the only thing that came through the wormhole."

"Providing they can't see through our cloaking," said Tash.

"Yes. But we are confident that our latest cloaking technology will be effective."

Finally, the time of preparation was over. They were

approaching the star system's subspace portal. The mission was about to begin.

"I have to be deactivated now," said Serena. "I can't take the risk of being conscious anywhere in Earth's solar system."

"What does deactivation involve?" asked Zac.

"I will need to go into a special stasis pod in the escape pod bay. My body will be cryogenically frozen, and my coding, including my consciousness, will be removed from my positronic brain and placed in a sealed, firewalled electronic storage repository."

"So you won't die?"

"No. But I will be rendered unconscious."

"Do we need to do something?"

"I can initiate the deactivation from within the pod. I just need someone to wake me up when it is safe to do so. There is a keypad on the outer panel of the pod. Just type my name and press the activation button. If you ever have to abandon the ship using the escape pods, please remember to take mine with you."

"OK, will do," said Zac. "Thank you for everything you've done. We are as ready as we can be, thanks to you."

"I wish you luck. You have everything you need. The star frequency is already entered in the nav computer. You have the Mars coordinates of the EI base, together with a rough schematic. It's over to you now."

She reached out and took Heinz's hand. "Will you walk with me to my pod?"

He merely nodded and they left the crew deck together.

An hour later they were all in their positions. Their velocity was still a blistering 400 kilometres per second, as they wanted to exit the wormhole on the other side with as high a velocity as possible. They were approaching the portal threshold.

"Here we go people!" said Zac. "Activate the STAR drive and lock onto the frequency."

"Done!" said Phil, who was the on-duty navigator.

"I confirm an open wormhole!" said Mel, who was on scanners, next to Phil.

"Put it up on the screen," said Zac.

The starfield in front of them enlarged and they saw a circle of darkness with a tell-tale shimmering surface racing towards them. In a matter of seconds, it filled the entire screen and then, suddenly, they were through. A swirling tunnel of fluorescent green light cascaded past them at blinding speed, giving them a dizzy sensation as they watched the front screen.

"Four more seconds," said Mel, watching her timer.

The swirling green tunnel spun and raced past them and then they were through into clear space.

"I confirm auto-activation of shields and cloaking one thousandth of a second after exiting," said Jaz.

"I've launched the decoy probe!" said Tash.

"What are the scanners picking up? Any EI vessels?"

"There's a single EI vessel near the portal," said MEL. "It's firing at the probe!" A few seconds later she announced, "The probe is destroyed! Wow! That didn't take long."

"Let's hope it can't see us," said Zac.

"I'm picking up scanning by the EI vessel in the immediate vicinity of the wormhole, but it's fading quickly behind us. The EI hasn't seen us, and we're already 16,000 kilometres from the portal."

"Well, that's the first hurdle dealt with," said Kit. "We didn't get blown to pieces the minute we exited the wormhole."

"Yeh, I noticed that too," said Tash.

"Now we need to orient ourselves," said Zac. "Where are we in relation to Mars, Mel?"

"Checking now. Give me a few minutes."

She manipulated the optical scanners and after a couple of minutes was able to project a composite map of the inner solar system onto the main screen.

"Our trajectory is along the elliptical plane. Earth is at our 3 o'clock and the sun at our 9 o'clock. Mars on the far side of the sun, at our 7 o'clock."

"What's our best means of getting there without lighting up the sky with our main propulsion drive?"

"We've got two things in our favour," Mel answered. "Both Earth and Mars are relatively close to the sun at the moment, closer to their perihelion than their aphelion. Even more fortunate for us, is the fact that Venus is almost directly ahead of us. I'm calculating a course now, but we should be able to use its outer atmosphere to bleed off speed and swing us around towards the sun. We'll then be able to initiate a delta-v burn behind the sun and use its gravity well to swing us onto a course for Mars."

"How long will all that take?"

"Only a couple of weeks. We're really lucky, if the planets weren't aligned this way, we could have been fiddling around with delta-v burns and planetary fly-bys for months."

"How much delta-v correction do we need in order to get to Venus?"

"Not much at all. I'm calculating it now, but we won't have to use our Stellar Drive. The Ion Drive will do the job, which means that our drive signature should be undetectable."

Mel sent the burn calcs through to Kit and Karl who initiated a slow burn that would last for several hours. Meanwhile, Phil had been using long-range optical scanners to search the inner solar system.

"Look at Earth!" he said, throwing an enlarged image up on the front screen.

"It's beautiful!" said Jaz.

They all agreed. The dirty grey world of their memories had been replaced with a sparkling blue – green world.

"It's ... clean!" said Keo.

They stared at it in wonder.

"I suppose that's because it's been over 3,000 years since the GAE," said Zac. "And with no one apparently living there, doing more damage, the planet has had time to heal itself."

"Would there still be radioactivity?" asked Kit.

Phil was the best qualified to answer that. "There would certainly still be residual radioactivity in places, particularly within several kilometres of detonation sites. But there would be vast areas that would now be safe for human habitation."

"Wow!" said Tash, in an unusual display of verbal restraint.

"Double wow!" agreed Karl, beside her.

"What can you show us about Mars?" asked Zac.

"Not much yet," said Phil. "It's still too far away. We'll get a good look at it when we exit our sun slingshot."

"Any sign of EI vessels?"

"Nothing that I can detect, which is surprising. I was expecting a fleet of them here, seeing this is the EI's home system."

"Maybe they're all out exploring the galaxy," suggested Tash.

Unfortunately, they weren't.

49

Two weeks later, they were still cloaked and on final approach to Mars. The red planet filled their viewing screen. They had scanned it closely for days and had picked up faint signals from a number of small orbital satellites, but there was no sign of defensive vessels in orbit.

"The planet looks wide open and completely vulnerable," said Kit. "I was expecting an armada of battleships to be circling it."

"Perhaps this is understandable," said Zac. "After all, the EI has had this solar system to itself for over 2,000 years, and in that time, there have been no incursions via either a wormhole or sub-light propulsion. It's been alone here, without threat for two millennia. And even when there were humans here, there wasn't so much as a single missile successfully fired at it. It's never been attacked."

"So, it's complacent?" Asked Mel.

"Over-confident, I would say," said Zac.

"Gagarin base is coming into view now," announced Mel.

She put an enlarged image of the base up on the screen.

"It's huge!" she exclaimed. "Four times the size of the schematics Serena gave us!"

"Yes," agreed Zac. "I guess it's had plenty of time to expand its production facilities. At least that seems to confirm that the EI is still based here."

The base, which had once occupied a corner of an enormous crater, 12 kilometres in diameter, now filled the entire crater.

"The central laboratory that houses the EI is in that large dome, hard up against the wall of the crater," explained Mel. "Or at least that's where the EI was 2,000 years ago."

"We have to assume it's still there," reasoned Zac.

"Let's hope we're right," Tash replied.

"How long until we're in range?" asked Kit.

"About 45 minutes until we're in orbit," answered Mel. "We'll do an ion drive delta-v burn on the far side of the planet to lower our orbit. About 50 minutes later we'll be directly over the base again, within firing range."

"Tash and Heinz," said Zac. "Once this starts, it's all over to you. Are you guys ready?"

"I was born ready," said Tash, with a steely glint in her eyes.

"She certainly was, bro," added Keo. "Even I don't dare cross her when she gets that look in her eyes."

"We're gonna blow this son-of-a-bitch into its component atoms!" she said, just to confirm how ready she truly was.

"Amen," said Keo.

"Which one of you is doing what?" asked Zac.

"I'm on the laser drill, and Heinz is going to launch the missile."

"Excellent. You're all set Heinz?"

"Certainly am. I know I complain about things sometimes, Zac, but I've got something to live for now – some*one* actually – and I'm totally focused. I won't let you down."

"I know you won't."

Nearly an hour and a half later, they were on final low-orbit approach to Gagarin Base. Zac was suited up with his helmet in his hands, watching everyone working efficiently at their stations.

"Why does it have to be you?" asked Kit.

"It was always going to be me. I'm the only one who wasn't trained specifically for any of your roles. Besides, if our weapons are successful, I won't have to go."

"Eight minutes," said Mel, watching her scanners. "Still no sign of EI vessels."

"I need to strap myself in the escape pod now. If things start to go wrong here, I'll launch myself."

Kit walked with him to the small bay at the rear of the ship which housed a series of egg-shaped pods built into the outer walls. Zac was holding a deadly looking black box which, according to Serena, was rated at 10,000 HBs – 10,000 times the power of the ancient Hiroshima Bomb. They held each other tight for a moment, and Kit was crying freely.

"Zac ..."

"Hush, my love. Everything will work out alright."

"But if it doesn't ..."

"If it doesn't, then I will die the happiest man in the universe for having loved you. We've had the most amazing life, you and I, and no one can take that from us."

"Oh Zac. I love you so much."

"Love you too, babe." He kissed her one last time. "Gotta go. I'll see you on the other side." He put his helmet on and stepped into the open pod. He leaned back against the padded interior and strapped himself in, then raised his hand in a final salute towards his wife who was quietly sobbing. He pressed the pod door switch, and the black lid closed over him, cocooning him in the cramped interior. The interior lights came on, and he activated the nav computer. The coordinates of the selected landing site were displayed, a flat area less than a kilometre from the rim of the crater, directly above the control dome. Zac switched on his helmet comm and heard the chatter among the crew on the flight deck.

"Are you guys reading me?" he asked.

"Loud and clear, boss," said Karl.

"You may as well have a snooze in that cosy little pod," said Tash, "because you won't need to do anything."

"I hope so," Zac agreed.

The minutes ticked by, and Zac listened to the crew going through their final checks.

"Thirty seconds," said Mel.

"Keo, bring our shields to maximum," said Kit, who was now in command.

"Already there, little sister."

"Tash are you locked on?"

"Locked and loaded."

"Ten seconds. On my mark, Tash," said Mel. "Three, two, one, fire!"

"Firing!"

Zac held his breath, his heart racing. They were fully committed now. Their position had been revealed. Everything now hinged on physics. How strong was the EI's shield? How powerful was their laser? And how powerful were the EI's weapons? Would their own shield be able to withstand the onslaught?

"The base's shield is glowing red!" Exclaimed Tash.

Zac felt a sudden lurch.

"We're receiving fire!" called Phil. "Two satellites have targeted us!"

"Shields are holding!" said Keo.

"Multiple launches detected!" exclaimed Mel. "Some kind of missiles! Three of them!"

"The dome's shields are still holding!" said Tash. "The laser isn't penetrating!"

Zac was knocked violently to one side, then, a moment later, to the other side.

"Two ground-based laser weapons have locked on! They're firing continuously!" said Mel.

"Shields are starting to fail!" cried Keo. "Seventy percent!"

A massive shudder rocked Zac, followed quickly by another.

"Two missile strikes! Direct hits!"

"Shields at forty percent!"

Another violent shudder.

"Third missile strike!"

"Shields at 15 percent!"

"The laser isn't penetrating!"

"Three more missile launches detected!"

Zac had no choice. He had to go. He activated his comm. "Abandon! Abandon! Take evasive action now! I'm launching!" He punched the launch button and was immediately hurled into space.

"No Zac! No!" cried Kit.

"I've already launched," said Zac, having difficulty speaking because of the high Gs. "Now get out of there! That's an order!"

"Zac! Please! I don't ..." and then Kit's voice was suddenly cut off. The open comm channel changed to complete static. *No! Please, No!* Zac's mind reeled. *They have to have gotten away. Please God!*

The straps around his body constricted as the pod executed its high-G manoeuvre. It had a cloaking field, so should be invisible, and hopefully the intense weapons fire in the vicinity would hide the small heat signature of the pod's ion-drive braking engine.

Zac tried to put everything out of his mind except the need to complete his mission. He had no way of knowing whether Kit and the others were alive or dead, but he was determined to make sure that his daughter grew up in a world free from EI tyranny.

The G forces built up to an almost unbearable level then, suddenly, they eased off. His nav screen showed that he was coming in low and fast across the surface of the plain above the crater. At the last moment, three large chutes deployed at the rear of the pod, slowing it slightly in the thin atmosphere. Then the pod ploughed into the ground, with a horizontal velocity of nearly 200 kilometres per hour. The pod dug a huge furrow in the dry Martian soil, throwing Zac violently against his restraining straps. He felt at least two of his ribs crack, and tasted blood in his mouth as he accidentally bit his cheek.

The pod came to rest, and Zac assessed the damage to his body. No major bones broken. One or two teeth a bit loose. He was still mission-capable. He popped the lid and climbed slowly out of the pod, his ribs complaining painfully. He had no trouble identifying the direction of the crater and its base

– laser fire was still being directed upward. He looked to the sky and saw a fireball – a massive explosion that could only mean one thing. Nautilus was gone. He watched, devastated, as the explosion resolved into a thousand shiny pieces of debris that expanded outwards in a glittering display. Some had fiery vapour trails as they plummeted towards the red planet.

Zac collapsed, his legs giving way. "No! No!" He sat and wept. A wave of grief, black and oppressive, swept over him. *Why didn't they leave? Why did they throw away their lives?* Then he realised. *They kept up their fire to provide cover for me. They sacrificed themselves for the mission.* He drew a deep breath and stood to his feet. He wouldn't let them die in vain. He would make sure this bomb did its job.

He clutched the device to his chest and turned towards the crater. All firing had ceased. He started walking, taking long loping strides in the low gravity. Gradually the lip of the crater came closer, a boulder-strewn raised edge ending in a steep drop. He came to the edge and looked down, breathing heavily from the awkward low gravity exertion. The crater was huge, its base more than a kilometre below him. He was slightly north of the main dome, by about 800 metres. He began traversing the rim of the crater, looking for a way down, but the cliff was sheer – almost perfectly vertical for as far as the eye could see.

Zac arrived at a position directly over main dome and looked down at it. There was no sign of the shield now, but it was almost certainly still activated. The cliff wasn't as steep here. He searched the area immediately below him and thought he could see a way down. He looked out across the crater and saw various automated machines moving between domes. As he watched, a large tear-shaped EI ship launched from the far side of the crater, and streaked skywards, its shiny black exterior reflecting the weak sunlight.

"You're a bit late," Zac said bitterly. "You missed out on all the fun."

He felt a tear slide down his face, then he shook his head, gritted his teeth, and began the long descent.

50

———

Zac was mumbling to himself. He was halfway down the cliff and was trying to stay focused. He had plenty of oxygen, but he was tiring.

"Come on, Zac, old boy. You can do this. It's a one-way trip. You don't have to climb back out again."

He reached a ledge, about two thirds down and realised that this was as far as he could go. The cliff below him now was more than vertical – it angled back in under his overhang, and it was like this for as far as he could see in every direction. He sat on the ledge with his legs dangling into the void.

"This is as far as we go, old fella," he said to himself. The main dome was only about three hundred metres directly below him. "This is close enough to do the job." He could lob the bomb from here. The weakest point of a ground-based energy field was where it touched the surrounding ground. An explosive device placed at ground level would easily blast under the lip of the shield. He peered down over the ledge. The closest edge of the dome was about 15 metres from the base of the cliff. Plenty of room to lob the bomb. An explosion 10,000 times the force of Hiroshima would probably blast a hole another kilometre down into the Martian sub-soil. It would certainly get under the dome's shield and reduce everything inside to its component atoms.

Zac looked up into the sky. Night had fallen, and the stars were arrayed across the heavens in stunning glory.

It's a beautiful place to die.

He activated the bomb's screen and brought up the count-down timer. He set it to thirty seconds and was about to press the activation button, his finger hovering over the screen.

I don't want to die down here. I don't want to be blown to bits.

He looked up towards the crater rim and then checked his oxygen levels. Three more hours. Plenty of time.

That's where I'm going to die. Up there. In my own time. I want to live to see the end of this evil bastard! Then I can die in peace.

He reset the timer for 15 minutes. He looked up at the slope above him, recalculated, and changed it to 20 minutes.

That should be enough.

He stood up, balancing on the very edge of the precipice. He looked down and judged his throw carefully.

"This is for every innocent person you've murdered, you evil son-of-a-bitch!" he said aloud.

He pressed the activation button and paused long enough to ensure it had begun counting down, then he lobbed it out over the edge. It fell slowly in the low gravity, spinning and twisting, it's black surface occasionally reflecting the light from random stars. The bomb landed almost exactly where Zac had aimed, throwing up a small plume of Martian dust.

"Nice throw, even if I say so myself."

He turned and looked towards the crater rim.

"OK, Zac, I know I told you it was a one-way trip, but I lied. So, suck it up and get going!"

He began scrambling back up the slope, and immediately realised he had underestimated how difficult it was going to be. For every metre he gained, he slid back almost half a metre on the loose shale. Within a few metres he was breathing hard. He checked the timer that he had activated simultaneously in his helmet. It ticked over to 00:18:59 as he glanced at it.

"Come on, old boy. Pick up the pace!"

The horizon of Zac's world shrank to the circle of shale revealed by his faceplate, and every second became a painful battle of will. His lungs were burning, his ribs screaming in pain, and sweat was running from his face in rivers. His legs were shaking now and at times he felt himself on the verge of blacking out.

The timer ticked over to five minutes and there was still 100 metres to go. Zac stopped for another sip of water from his water nipple and looked up. This last section was steeper but there was no more shale. It was just solid rock from this point. He began climbing, putting every ounce of his remaining strength into this final burst.

"Come on Zac! If Keo could see you now he'd laugh! You can do better than this! Show the big fellow what you're made of!"

He raced up the final section and finally clambered over the lip and lay on his back, exhausted. The countdown timer clicked over to 00:00:59 and started counting down the final minute. Zac rolled over, got painfully to his feet, and started running. At least that was his intention, but it resembled more of a staggering stumble.

"Move! Move! Move!" he kept muttering. His breath was

ragged and his face plate was fogging up, unable to clear away his steamy breathing. He couldn't feel his legs anymore. It was as though they belonged to someone else, moving of their own accord. The timer counted down the final few seconds and when it reached zero, Zac threw himself face-first onto the ground and lay there, utterly spent. The ground shook violently underneath him and then he was flung into the air, tumbling end over end, losing all sense of up and down. He was enveloped in a thick soup of red dust and rocks, and felt himself bouncing violently across the Martian surface only to be picked up and tumbled through the air again. At one point he felt a violent impact against his left leg and knew intuitively that he was seriously damaged.

He came to rest lying on his side and lay there as waves of pain from his injured leg washed over him. He checked his pressure gauge. Suit pressure was holding. Miraculously there were no holes. He rolled onto his back and couldn't help but cry out in pain as his leg shifted position. He could definitely feel bone grinding on bone.

He lay there gasping. The air immediately around him was clearing as the heavier dust and debris settled to the ground. Far above him an enormous mushroom cloud was rising, slowly blotting out the stars. As he watched it grow, a movement in a nearby sector of the sky caught his eye. A black shape was streaking downward, tumbling end over end, clearly out of control. An EI vessel! Zac watched as the tear-drop shaped vessel plummeted down. He lost sight of it behind the skyline of the nearest ridge but saw the explosion and felt the tremor of its impact.

Yes! I did it! The evil bastard is dead!

He let out an exultant whoop of joy.

He lay there quietly, catching his breath. His face plate cleared and he watched the mushroom cloud continue to grow. The blast had created its own weather system and a wind was blowing across him from the west, back towards the crater, filling the low-pressure system and clearing the air above him of dust. The stars to the east were sparkling now, shining with a magnificent beauty that filled his heart with joy, despite the waves of pain that continued to wash over him.

Dayna is out there, somewhere. And she will live a long life now. She will have children and grandchildren, and grow old, surrounded by her family.

Tears streamed down his face now.

I did this for you, my daughter. I hope you have a good life.

He checked his oxygen supply. Two and a half hours left to live.

I suppose I could just unscrew my helmet and end it now.

No. He wasn't going to die like a coward. He was going to use these last hours to remember all the good things of his life. Not surprisingly, almost every good thought revolved around his wife.

"Kit," he said aloud.

"Yes, my love, I'm here."

Zac laughed. "Oh God, I'm hearing things now!"

"No, you're not, my darling."

Zac looked to his right and saw space-suited figures walking towards him across the red Martian dust. He tried to raise himself on his elbows but groaned in pain and collapsed onto his back again.

"Hold on, my love, we're nearly there."

"What ... how ...?

"We used the escape pods."

"What?"

"We had to abandon the ship."

"Why didn't you just leave?" Zac asked, as he watched them walking closer.

Karl's voice responded. "We began evasive manoeuvres immediately, but an EI vessel engaged us, and a second one soon followed. We held out as long as we could. We actually lost them for a while, because we were still cloaked. But one of them got a lucky shot and located us again. By then we all had our suits on. The shields were about to fail. We set the weapons to auto-fire, ran to the pod bay, and launched the pods."

"Where did you land?"

"I programmed them to land a couple of kilometres East," said Mel. "I wanted to give the crater a wide birth."

They reached Zac, and Kit knelt down beside him, clumsily trying to hug him.

Zac groaned.

"Where are you hurt?"

"Cracked ribs and a broken leg. Nothing too serious."

"You look like crap, bro."

"Good to see you, too, Keo."

Keo sat down beside him and patted his shoulder, and the others stood around in a loose circle.

"You did it, bro!"

"We did it. All of us. We did it together."

"Yeh. We did," said Keo.

"Did you see that EI vessel come down?" asked Zac.

"Sure did," said Mel. "And it's not the only one. Another one came down a bit further East."

"May the evil bastard rot in hell!" said Tash, with her usual alacrity.

"Amen, sister," said Keo.

"The stars are beautiful from Mars, aren't they?" said Kit.

"Thin atmosphere," said Phil, always the scientist.

"I don't suppose any of you has a spare spaceship parked somewhere nearby?" Zac asked.

"Nope," said Tash. "I left mine parked in the garage at home."

"Oh well," said Zac.

They were silent together for a while.

"I think I can see Earth," said Zac. "That bright blue dot low down in the south east."

"I see it!" said Mel. "Yes, I think you're right."

"So close, and yet ..."

They pondered that thought.

"Why didn't you use the shuttle?" asked Zac.

"We were going to," answered Karl. "I was on my way to fire it up when the shields failed in the rear of the ship and the shuttle bay took a direct hit. The shuttle was destroyed and that section of the ship was automatically sealed off."

"Could you have made it to another base in your pods? There would possibly be life support systems there."

"Not possible," said Mel. "Firstly, the nearest base is on the other side of the planet, and the pods don't have nearly enough fuel for that kind of distance. And secondly, the EI disabled all the life support systems over 2,000 years ago."

"Yes. Of course," said Zac. "I'm not thinking very clearly."

"You did well, my love," said Kit, who was now holding his gloved hand in hers. "I'm so proud of you."

They were all silent for a while.

"Anyone for a game of 'I spy with my little eye'?" asked Zac.

"No way," said Kit. "You always cheat."

"I spy with my little eye, something that is moving toward us."

"I said I'm not playing ..."

"I'm serious! Something is moving toward us."

Zac pointed toward the south-east. A bright dot was growing rapidly, and it slowly resolved itself into the shape of a shuttle.

"Dad? Dad? Can you hear me?"

Zac levered himself up on one elbow, groaning as he did.

"Dayna?"

"Of course! Who did you expect? Santa Claus?"

"What? How did you get here?"

"Just shut up for a moment and let me concentrate on landing this thing."

"Looks like they're gonna have to put our funeral services on hold for a while," said Tash.

"A long while, I hope," said Kit, with tears of relief streaming down her face.

Dayna landed her micro-shuttle a short distance from them, followed closely by the second shuttle, piloted by Delta. Both pilots were wearing spacesuits, because the micro-shuttles did not have airlocks. The outer door of each shuttle opened, and the nine survivors made their way towards them. Zac couldn't walk, and Keo insisted on carrying his best friend in his arms.

"Do you need a hand, Keo?" asked Phil.

"He ain't heavy; he's my brother."

"Nice quote," said Zac, grimacing in pain.

"I've got one for every occasion, bro."

Kit, Tash, Keo, Zac and Karl climbed aboard Dayna's shuttle, and the remaining four, Mel, Phil, Jaz and Heinz, got into Delta's.

"You need to pick up Serena's pod as well," said Heinz as they were climbing aboard. "It's a kilometre West of here."

"Who the hell's Serena?" asked Delta.

"It's a long story," said Mel.

51

Zac woke feeling groggy and disoriented. He couldn't place his surroundings. He tried sitting up and then quickly decided that that was a very bad idea indeed. He noticed a drip feed attached to an intravenous canular in his left arm, and looking down the bed, he could see that his left leg was in plaster.

Serena walked in, looking as luscious as ever.

"You're awake! Excellent! Let me give you a shot of something to get you on your feet." She took an atomiser from a draw and without any warning shoved it against his neck and shot something into him. Zac felt as if fireworks had exploded in his brain and he was suddenly filled with a sense of euphoria and energy.

"Wow!"

"Good stuff, hey?"

"Absolutely!"

"Let me help you up."

She quickly ripped the canular out of his arm, which should have hurt, but Zac felt no pain.

"Your leg is still setting, as are your ribs. I injected short-life nanobots into the damaged areas. You'll be as good as new in a couple more days. Fortunately, for you and the others, the shielding in your suits protected you from the radiation fallout from the blast."

"How long was I asleep?"

"I kept you sedated for seven days. You also had a ruptured spleen, which I had to remove."

Zac felt his stomach.

"You'll hardly be able to see anything now. The nanobots have done an excellent job."

"I don't remember getting here."

"You passed out in the shuttle."

"That's embarrassing."

"Not at all. You also had concussion. Here let me help you up."

Zac stood up.

"Actually, I feel fine!"

"Good. Just don't overdo it for a few days. Come and join us. Everyone is in the dining room."

Zac emerged into the dining room to be greeted by hugs and kisses, particularly from Kit, who refused to let go of his hand thereafter.

"So, does someone want to fill me in on how the hell you guys came to be here?" he asked the younger ones.

"Harv refused to abandon the mission," said Dayna. "We took a vote and we all agreed. So we cloaked ourselves and followed you to the nearby star system. Delta plotted your course, based on your trajectory. It was pretty easy to work out which star you were heading towards."

"But how did you select the wormhole for this solar system? You didn't know the frequency for Earth's sun."

"We didn't need to. We stayed cloaked and followed you through the wormhole, with our own STAR drive activated."

Zac was stunned. "That's ... that's ... crazy! You took a big risk."

"Danger is my middle name," said Harv.

"Obviously we lost you on this side, because you were cloaked from that point on. So, we navigated a course for Mars, taking a bit longer than you because we didn't have your fancy low-emission ion drive for course corrections. We had to fire microbursts of our main propulsion drive which, thankfully, weren't detected by the EI. We were only just arriving when we saw your vessel go down in a screaming heap." Dayna teared up. "I thought we'd lost you. I thought we were too late."

Zac put his arm around her. "Not too late. You were just in time."

Dayna nodded and wiped a stray tear that had run down her cheek. "Delta was scanning the surface and identified some spacesuit emission signatures. We counted nine of them. We knew it had to be you."

Zac shook his head. "Wow! That's amazing! You saved our lives."

"And you saved ours," said Dayna, planting a kiss on Zac's cheek.

"I hate to break up the happy family reunion," said Harv, "but we've got a decision to make."

"What decision?" asked Zac.

"Where are we going to go now?"

"What do you mean?"

"He means," said Mel, "which planet are we going to call home?"

"We've got a choice of four," said Keo, "and we've been waiting for you to wake up, because we all need to decide this together."

"Four?" asked Zac.

"There's Nova, where some of us established the colony at Seahaven," said Tash.

"Then there's Altaria, where we lived very happily for many years," said Kit.

"There's also Perdita," said Serena, "which I can thoroughly recommend – I've told the others all about it."

"And then there's this," said Keo pointing to the main viewing screen.

A close-up image of Earth appeared; a beautiful blue-green jewel hanging against the starry backdrop of space.

"We've been in orbit around it for two days," said Harv. We've scanned the surface and noted some hotspots in terms of radioactivity. But there are huge areas that have no residual radiation. The forests have replenished and, without mankind's interference, flora and fauna are prolific again. It's a beautiful, virgin world, waiting to be settled."

"What do the rest of you think?" asked Zac.

"There are divided opinions," said Kit.

"Darby and I want to return to Altaria," said Riff.

"Delta and I want to return to Nova for a brief while, to let them know we're OK and to help sort things out there," said Harv.

"Serena and I want to go back to Perdita, at least initially," said Heinz.

"That's understandable," said Zac. "And we have to acknowledge that we are not in a position to establish a viable colony on earth with such a small number of people and with such limited resources."

"Agreed," said Karl.

"So, we're basically saying that we are going to have to revisit each of those worlds," said Zac.

"Yes," agreed Mel. "But with the wormholes now safe to use again, that's just a hop, skip and a jump. No more long journeys and cryogenic stasis."

"And once we spread the word that Earth is safe for re-settlement," said Kit, "I think there will be a big push to establish colonies here as soon as possible. It won't be long at all before colony ships from each of the three worlds start arriving and staking their claim."

"It would be a shame to lose out on the best spots, when we are already here first," said Keo, raising his eyebrows.

"What are you suggesting?" asked Zac

"Some of us are just plain sick of space travel," said Mel. "This ship has a survival drop-pod that could easily be landed somewhere, and a small advance party could establish the beginning of a new colony. The rest of the crew could do the lap of honour around the galaxy and spread the good news."

"I know a beautiful little spot on the east coast of the north island of New Zealand, bro," said Keo.

They all looked at him expectantly.

"What do you think, my love?" said Kit, squeezing his arm.

Zac looked at the faces of his friends. He had shared so much with these people, and they had come so far together. They had traversed the galaxy and had lived for thousands of its years. They had been plucked from their predictably ordinary lives and thrust into a galaxy-wide conflict that had nearly destroyed humanity. And now, beyond all hope, beyond all sensible expectation, they had returned home. They had come full circle. They had a chance to start again. A chance to build a new world where selfishness and greed did not trample the rights of the powerless and destroy the environment.

He looked at the image of the Earth on the screen. As it happened, New Zealand was just coming into view, appearing over the eastern horizon. Thin streaks of white cloud covered parts of the beautiful green island, and the ocean that surrounded it was a magnificent deep blue.

"The land of the long white cloud," muttered Zac.

"Aotearoa, is the Maori word," said Keo, his eyes misting over. He looked with longing at the image on the screen. "I would dearly love to show you my favourite fishing spot, bro."

Zac looked at the beaming, brown face of his best friend. He glanced at the others, who were all looking at him expectantly. It moved him deeply that they placed such a high value on his opinion and that they would gladly follow his lead. He looked back at Keo and nodded.

"And I would love you to show it to me, my friend."

LEAVE A REVIEW

If you enjoyed this book, I would be extremely grateful if you would leave a review on Amazon. Reviews are hugely important for me as a self-published author. They impact Amazon's algorithms, helping the book to climb higher in Amazon's charts, thereby making it more visible to potential readers. Every single review really does help!

Leaving a review is very easy. To leave a review, just go to the relevant Amazon page for your country (see below), search for my book and click on the reviews link next to the stars. A review of 4 or 5 stars is considered to be a positive review and a review of 3 or less stars is considered to be a negative review. (Unfortunately, Amazon only allows reviews from people who have spent at least $50 on Amazon over the preceding 12 months).

LEAVE A REVIEW:

AMAZON UNITED STATES
AMAZON UNITED KINGDOM
AMAZON CANADA
AMAZON AUSTRALIA

FREE EBOOK!

Join my mailing list and receive a FREE EBOOK. I will email you a complimentary copy of **"Welcome To The Universe: A Pocket Guide For Visitors"**. With stunning photographs and mind-boggling facts, the book provides a fascinating glimpse into the wonders of the universe and the many challenges of space travel. Just click the link below and tell me where to send your free copy (or sign up to my mailing list at kevinsimington.com).

SEND ME A FREE COPY OF "WELCOME TO THE UNIVERSE"

Free eBook!

A FASCINATING GLIMPSE INTO THE
WONDERS OF THE UNIVERSE
WELCOME
TO THE
UNIVERSE
A POCKET GUIDE
FOR VISITORS
KEVIN J SIMINGTON

A desperate mission.
An unlikely hero.

A ragged band of desperate survivors flee from a dying world in search of a new home. But the universe has played a cruel joke on them. Now facing even deadlier threats from a strange world, as well as traitors in their midst, their battle for survival is only just beginning.

CLICK TO BUY NOW

OR GO TO:
KEVINSIMINGTON.COM

galaxy, separated from those they love by both time and distance. Thrust into a struggle for humanity's survival, they desperately search for a way back home and a means of salvation.

CLICK TO BUY IT NOW

OR GO TO:
KEVINSIMINGTON.COM

ABOUT THE AUTHOR

Kevin J Simington is an acclaimed fiction and non-fiction author whose books are renowned for their intelligence, clarity and wit. He is a very popular conference speaker on the topics of philosophy, apologetics and science. He also writes for several international magazines.

Website:
https://kevinsimington.com

Amazon Author Page:
amazon.com/author/kevinjsimington